The People in His Life

THE PEOPLE IN HIS LIFE

A Novel
by
Maia Rodman

STEIN AND DAY/*Publishers*/New York

First published in 1980
Copyright © 1980 by Maia Wojciechowska Rodman
All rights reserved
Designed by Louis Ditizio
Printed in the United States of America
Stein and Day/*Publishers*/Scarborough House
Briarcliff Manor, N.Y. 10510

Library of Congress Cataloging in Publication Data

Rodman, Maia, 1927-
  The people in his life.

  I. Title.
PZ4.R6917Pe   [PS3568.3486]   813'.54   79-9661
ISBN 0-8128-2717-1

The character of Hal Hubbard was suggested by the life of Ernest Hemingway, but all of the other characters in this novel are products of the author's imagination.

for Sol Stein,
or whoever made him a great editor

Contents

Clara Hubbard 15

Yolanda Hubbard 29

Larry Dort 55

Carole Scolfield Hubbard 87

Robert Hubbard 115

Carl Hubbard 141

Anne Hubbard 155

Benjamin and Maggie Horn 173

Sally Reynolds 207

Hal Hubbard 235

THEY had just brought him back to his room after another shock treatment. He meant to keep score. Was this his fifth? Or seventh? With each, details were being eliminated from his memory, but what was still left was the distilled essence. What if the essence should begin to go? It was then that the idea entered his head with the sharpness that was familiar. Sharp, clear, urgent ideas were the ones he trusted best.

Make a list of all the people who have lived off of me.

And then, just as clear, and even sharper and more urgent, the justification for that first idea.

Invite them all to see how I can die off of them.

The only good thing about not being able to write anymore was that he could be sloppy with the mother tongue. Off of. Offal. Offset. Offshoot. Offside. Offshore. The idea had to be kept on course.

He was not a list maker, hated lists, but this list was very important, probably the most important thing he would have to do. Once the list was made, he would send it to Sally. In a month's time he would be fifty-seven and the list would serve as his birthday guest list. Except it would be his deathday as well.

The thing to do was to be meticulous. He would invite only the ones who had nourished themselves well. He would be careful not to include the nibblers. He had to make the list as true as his memory of how they fed, from within, like hyenas. He had to keep the list short, only those who were made fat from his flesh, the ones who made the hole within.

He had been generous once; had he said to any, or all of them: "Help yourself?" Had he been whole once? Or had the hole been made from the start? He would make sure if he started at the beginning and worked toward the end. And at the end he would be whole again. The hole he would do himself.

It took him two days to make the list. It could have been twice as long, but the process of elimination had been like a good editing job. It was lean. Each name was vital. They numbered ten. Apostles. Aphorism. Apocalypse. Apostasy. His ten apostates. Was he theirs, or were they his appendages now? They had appropriated. And he would apprehend by apprising.

When the list was ready he spoke to Dr. Konski about getting a weekend pass. He explained about his birthday and how his wife had always celebrated it with friends. He showed him the letter he had written her, and the doctor added a note:

> He is looking forward to this and I highly recommend the party. Progress is being made each day.

He had composed the letter very carefully for he knew he had to be careful with her. He had to let her know that he would come back to the hospital without a fight. He would give her a last chance, on the outside, to lick the bones clean.

Dear Sally,

Would like to be out for celebration of own birthday. Hate to step on your territory, but this time would like to make own list and keep it small. Know you can get them all to come. Just the following: my mother, my sister, Larry Dort, Carole, Bobby, Bean and Shrimp, Benjamin and Maggie.

Important that they all come. We could have another party for the locals, but I just want the ten (counting you) nobody else. I know you'll use all your charms so they show up. Send Bobby a ticket, and if anyone else is broke, pay their fares.

Will take advantage of whole month to try to climb out of rotten rabbit hole. Promise to be good and kind to you and self when home again. If promise impossible to keep, will willingly come back here after birthday party for more treatments until everything fine.

Hugs,
Hal

He would wait out the month and waiting, he would remember how each had fed on him until there was nothing left that he could call his own.

Clara Hubbard

MAYBE it was not the first thing he remembered about his mother, but it was what he remembered best—her ability to shrink his father. He would come into the room, a tall, gaunt man, and by the time she spoke her first words to him, he would become smaller—and not gaunt—but as if rounded unto himself with none of the edges that were there before, blurred to the boy and limp. The shrinking would become noticeable even before he reached his chair and the boy always wondered how she could do that, and why. If his father remained standing, if he went directly from the door to the window, his surrender would be postponed for awhile.

It didn't make any difference whether his mother was standing or sitting or walking. She would become rounded when his father entered the room. It was as if she could fatten herself on his mere presence. There was something else she was doing to his father, but the boy was only dimly aware of it at first. When, at seven, he realized that she had two, not one, tricks up her sleeve, he thought that what she was doing was driving his father into an ever smaller space, a circular space which, like a corral, would isolate his father from everyone else. The shrinking would happen inside that circle. She used words to get him inside. Sometimes the words would stretch, allowing him more space, and sometimes the words came tight and he had no elbow room at all. The boy listened to her words carefully and would learn to measure their tight hold on his father.

"When are you going to have time for us?" she would ask, the lasso of her words a loose noose. The tightening would come with the second and third sentences. "We had planned a picnic for today. We waited for you." And then the circle closing and tightening. "You forgot again."

The boy liked to go to the courthouse to see his father in his judge's robes, sitting high above the courtroom. She was never there and the lack of her seemed to make all the difference. The boy's father, in his courthouse, was the size the boy wanted him to be. Sitting there, so alone, so black in his robes, his father would know how to fight the shrinking and the encircling that she did to him at home. Sometimes, the boy felt, he could remember times, when he was very young, that the father would fight her back. He was sure that he fought her with his silences. They were his weapons, but then she seemed to use those same weapons against him. At eight, the boy realized that his father would never win because she had the best of all weapons—hatred. And the father was a stranger to it. The father had indifference, but it was a blunt weapon in comparison to hers.

He was ten years old before he knew that she was using him against his father. There were accusations being made more and more often of what he didn't do for the boy, what he could no longer do for him.

"Other fathers take time to be with their sons. He might as well be an orphan. Why don't you take him fishing, or hunting?"

It was she who got the boy his first gun, a .22 for Christmas in 1910. And from the attic one day she brought down another, an older gun with a long muzzle, and thrust it at her husband when he was sitting inside the circle she had already made for him, reduced in size, limp in his chair.

The next day, Saturday, they went out into the woods together.

"Do you want to shoot?" the boy's father asked.

"Yes."

"What do you want to shoot?"

"A bird."

They walked through the crackling fall leaves of the oak forest. After awhile, when his father said nothing, he raised his gun and shot a woodpecker. And then, defiantly, he picked the dead bird up by the tail and thrust it at his father, as she had thrust the gun at him the day before. It was then—at that very instant—that he noticed that he had his mother's powers, for his father seemed to shrink and go limp. And in that instant he felt what she must have been feeling all along, a strange strength, and he was both afraid and pleased to possess it, and appalled. Appalled that he would use it.

His father turned back then, and again the boy shot. This time he brought down a dove and, picking it up by the wing, offered it to his father. But his father would not look at the offering. He walked faster toward the house now, while the boy ran after him, stumbled and fell on top of the two birds that were still warm. He watched from the ground as his father walked very straight, very fast, toward the big house and inside it. Then, the boy threw the birds away and climbed a tree that he liked to climb. It was near his father's study, which was an addition to the house above the kitchen and pantry.

The leaves had fallen off the tree and the boy was sure that he was not hidden from his father's view should his father go to the window and look out. He watched the door open to the study, and his father paused before closing it behind. The gun with the long muzzle was still in his hands. He looked toward the window, and the boy did not know if he had been seen. His father walked slowly, still holding the gun, to the desk and wrote something very fast on a piece of paper. The boy saw him bend down, and the chair turned toward the window. The right foot was bare. His father inserted his big toe in the trigger of the gun. Very gently, he placed his right temple to the barrel. His eyes were closed, but his face was to the window. Then he opened his eyes and winked at his son.

The sound of the shot was very loud. With the sound, the boy's father's head jerked back, but the wink seemed still to be there. Somehow, like a Cheshire cat's smile, it stayed there for a long time, until dusk wiped off the windowpane. By then there was a lot going on below. Screaming and shouting, a doctor's car then an ambulance, had come and gone. And Yolanda, alone, had wandered out of doors and found her brother up on the tree branch and called for him to come down.

"Mother isn't home," she said.

He came down then because she was only five and he had to take care of her.

"Daddy's dead," she said as he took her hand and led her inside into the living room that was dark and empty of them both now. He shouted for Martha, the housekeeper, and she came rushing downstairs, her apron stained with his father's blood and something else which he thought might be his brains.

He dreamt that night that his father was out in the woods behind the house with him again and that again he had shot the birds, but they were bigger and so heavy to carry that he never reached the house.

At twelve the boy began to think that his mother had been born to be a widow. She devoted herself almost exclusively to preserving her husband's "legacy" as she called it. She had all his letters bound in leather scrapbooks, and a much larger leather-bound book of clippings about him lay now on the coffee table. From these the boy learned much about his father, but nothing he read explained to him the shrinking process that used to happen when his father was alive. Possibly, he thought, now that he was dead his mother wished to germinate inside of her son an idea for his first short story. When he wrote it at fourteen, it was about a woman who goes shooting ducks with her husband. When he shoots none, and she has downed half a dozen, the man takes off one shoe and, while his wife thinks he's busy with a stone or sticker embedded in his foot, he puts his big toe in the trigger of his shotgun and blows his head off.

The story ended with:

> Somehow she must have known how well she would look in black, for she accepted the many compliments with the expression that they were her due. She remained a widow for the rest of her life and secretly enjoyed his absence from her house.

He sent the story to a New York magazine, but it never even came back. He kept a carbon of the story and reread it sometimes when he wanted to remember his childhood.

Clara Hubbard had definite ideas about what she wanted from her children when they grew up. Hal would become a lawyer and later a judge like his father. Yolanda would be a concert pianist. She started lessons at the age of three and by the time she was twelve showed no talent whatever for the piano, although she practiced faithfully each day and gave every indication that she wished to please her mother and become a concert pianist. Clara, after a concert her daughter gave together with other students, took her daughter home and, in the presence of her older brother, said, "I've wasted my time all these years. You never will play the piano decently enough even to entertain half-deaf friends."

Yolanda burst into tears and rushed out of the room. Hal turned to his mother with a look she had never seen before.

"You are an ugly woman!" He said this between his teeth, not raising his voice. And when Clara, not sure she had heard clearly, looked up at him, he continued, enunciating very distinctly. "You killed father with your hatred of his presence, and you are stifling us with your resentment of us." He was about to leave the room when she called to him.

"You are totally wrong, young man."

He turned and faced her.

She said calmly, "I worshipped the very ground your father walked on. Your father killed himself, like his father before him, and with the very same gun. They both suffered from melancholia. I understand it is a hereditary disease. And if I were you, I would be careful not to fall prey to it." The next day, taking his savings, he left for Chicago on a bus.

When he saw his mother again—he was twenty-one by then—several by-lined articles had appeared in the Trib. He found them all bound in a book. It was lying on the coffee table next to the larger one with clippings about his father. His book contained everything that had appeared about him or by him since babyhood and the notice, next to it, of his birth from *The Lakeland News.* There was a clipping about his winning an essay contest when he was in the eighth grade, stories about his boxing in high school and a tennis tournament he had won, and another about the record-breaking walleye he caught when they had gone to visit his grandmother in Minnesota the year after his father's suicide. She had also pasted, on a separate page, the prediction from his high school yearbook.

Hal Hubbard will become a famous writer and Lakeland, one day, will be famous because of him.

On another separate page was the only post card he had written to her. It bore a view of Venice, a post card he had picked up in a bookstore in Chicago. On it he had written: "I have been wounded, mother. But it's not a grave wound, not a fatal one. I shall recover. Your son, Hal." Next to that was a notice from *The Lakeland News* which simply said that no details were known about the wounds received in Italy by Mrs. Hubbard's son, Hal. She told him that she had written the note herself. Each one of the stories that he had written for *The Chicago Tribune* were also there, carefully pasted and hand dated. That album was to grow over the years, and five other similar books of clippings were to join it in time.

He came home because she was said to be dying and Yolanda thought he should be there. He was ready to forgive her for everything. During the week that he stayed, he tried to get close to her, but with great sadness realized that his mother, even on what was believed to be her deathbed, was unapproachable.

Polite concern was all the warmth that she was capable of. And as he sat, exchanging inconsequential conversations with her, he became very frightened, for the first time, not for her, but for himself. What else could he be than the reflected image of his parents? They were both very withdrawn, and everything in him was crying out to be outgoing. What was his true self? In his father, there was a melancholia that ultimately killed him. In his mother, there was a reserve of such proportions that even her bowel movements were part of it. She suffered, ever since he could remember, from chronic constipation, and he knew now that this was but a physical reflection of her emotional state. What gifts, if any, did he inherit from them? Perseverance, fortitude, calm authority, direction, and will were part of the heritage from his mother.

"What was father like?" he asked her on the evening of his return to Chicago. She had recovered enough for the doctor to predict that all danger was passed.

"He was an honorable man," she answered without hesitation. But no matter how much he wanted to hear more about what she thought of him, she would not say anything except, "If you're so interested, why don't you read the book about him?" She always referred to the bound volume of letters and clippings as "the book."

"I can't find his essence there," he answered.

"There is no need for essence," she had replied. And in saying that, she gave him another fear—that possibly there was no core to these people who were his parents. But honor, he knew, he had inherited from his father, and it cheered him to know that if, indeed, his father was an honorable man, his own legacy was not as poor as he had thought.

Upon his return, he continued to write the "Slim Taber" stories. They would appear eventually in *The Saturday Evening Post* and, when Hal Hubbard was twenty-five and living in Paris, were collected in the first of his published books. In Slim, Hal Hubbard created what was to be known as "the most masterful autobiographical fiction in American literature." The collection of twenty-four stories earned its author an almost instantaneous fame.

When writing the Slim Taber stories, Hal was interested in finding out if he could create the kind of boy he never was and wished he had been, the kind of man he would grow into. He conceived himself in sin, for he erased the truth of his childhood and counterfeited his Calvinistic parents into human beings they never were.

And yet, there must have been resemblance enough between him and Slim, for the kids who knew him in school assumed that Slim and Hal were interchangeable. "Of course I didn't know that . . ." would preface their reminiscences.

What both appalled and fascinated him was that his own mother accepted Slim as her son. Interviewed years later, when he received the Pulitzer Prize for *Goodbyes,* Mrs. Hubbard remembered incidents from Hal's boyhood that never happened in life, but did happen in the stories of Slim Taber. By then, Clara Hubbard was convinced that Dr. Taber was her husband and that she herself was Clarissa Taber, a courageous woman who gave up a brilliant future as a concert pianist to assist her country doctor husband. Judge Hubbard's book of letters and clippings was removed from the living room. The details of the house in which Slim grew up slowly became the details of her house. A lamp described in a story entitled "Cold Night, Warm Morning" was searched for and found by Clara Hubbard in an antique store in Cleveland and installed in what used to be Hal's room. Except the room had undergone a drastic change and now looked like Slim's room.

In the last Slim Taber story, "The End of Light," Dr. Taber meets his untimely death when he goes hunting in the woods with his son Slim. A stray bullet from the gun of a deer hunter penetrates the main artery, and Dr. Taber is carried by his son into the house. Mrs. Taber is described as

> standing in the door, her face frozen as all faces of women whose men are brought home dead have been frozen. Slim had never seen grief before although he would, in years to come, see it many times. It always looked and sounded the same. His mother inhaled air as if through punctured lungs and then, like a shadow, silently followed them to the living room.
>
> He still had a few moments to live, but his eyes were already empty of light. If only he could wink, the boy thought desperately. If only he could wink and tell us everything was going to be all right. When the eyes were lifeless, his widow closed the lids and then, with the hand that brushed them shut, she touched her lips. They were alone now, the two of them, each with a different loss.

When a reporter from *Time* magazine came to interview Clara Hubbard on the occasion of her son's winning the Nobel Prize, she asked her about her husband's death.

"It is all described in 'The End of Light'" she said. And taking out a leather-bound volume of Slim Taber stories, she read the last few pages to the woman.

"Is everything that he wrote in those stories pretty much as things were?" the reporter asked.

"Yes, except in living one misses the art of a writer," Mrs. Hubbard said. The same day she signed a check with the name Clarissa Taber and did not notice it until the check came back from the bank.

When he was giving birth to himself in those stories, he did not guess that his mother wished him to conceive her as well. The first time he noticed that she had accepted his fiction as truth, he felt a grave wave of compassion for her. Was she as unhappy being who she was as I am? he wondered. Did I give her a gift? Something her own parents did not, could not, give her? Something she could not give herself: an identity? What other needs did this woman, my mother, have? Needs that I could take care of?

He had come for a brief Christmas visit, and because for a change he had money, he arranged for much-needed repairs on the house. There was enough of that house in Slim Taber's stories to render it now interesting if not dear to him. It was all so different now. His sister was away visiting their grandparents. His mother wished to talk as much now as once she had avoided talking. But she did not want to find out about his life as a writer or about what he would be working on next. Her interest was completely limited to his boyhood.

"When you went fishing that time with Dad, the time you both saw the demented old woman...."

"But, mother, we never went fishing. It was just a story."

"What was the old woman's name?" his mother wanted to know.

"Mrs. Petsky."

"No, no. Mrs. Petsky was in your story, but the real crazy lady's name? Oh yes, Mrs. Watts, wasn't it? Now didn't you use Mrs. Watts in that story?"

"I don't remember any Mrs. Watts," he said.

"Of course you do, or else how could you have written about her?" She looked at him with a small, accusing smile. "I know how you writers must change names. Isn't it for some legal reason?"

During that week, whenever she had a chance she would bring up one or another incident described in the stories and would try to enlist his help in remembering more details. He kept trying to make her realize that all those things were imagined by him, all had been made up, but she would say, "... from whole cloth. You made them up from whole cloth." And he gave up trying then and let her confuse things. Yet, he didn't feel that she was confusing anything. She was taking. He wished she had asked his permission. But she did not. It was not until years later, when there was no vestige at all of his real father, that he screamed accusations at her.

He had asked her, that time, about the note his father had written before he shot himself.

"What note?"

"The note he was writing at his desk just before he shot himself. I saw him scribbling something. I was up inside that tree, and I saw him write something. What did he write before he killed himself?"

"Your father did not kill himself. He was shot by a deer hunter," she said firmly.

"Mother! That was a story. I'm talking about real life! I want to know if you read the note and what you did with it!"

She was spending her days doing crewel work, and whenever she did not wish to pursue a subject, she would lower her head and work faster on whatever she was doing.

"Don't you want to face any reality about him?" he asked then. She did not answer. He wanted desperately to hurt her, stab through the concrete that separated them, make her bleed. But he would bleed as well. Out of his wallet, he took the piece of paper on which his father had written his last message to the world. He had found it crumpled in the corner of his father's study, and he knew that it was she who had thrown it there. She did not want to face it then, but he would make her face it now. He spread the piece of paper on the table.

"Read it," he said.

She did not look up. Not controlling his hatred for her, he spun her around, pushed her head toward the table, then jerked it away so that she could see the paper.

"Read it," he repeated. "Aloud." But she would not do it. Perhaps her eyes were closed against the truth of it. He read it to her then.

Life is not worth living.

She went back to her crewel work as if nothing had happened. As if the words had not been shouted. As if no violence had been done to her body. He was trying to free himself from the message, that's all he was doing. But the message stayed. Maybe because she could not accept it. She left it for him to face alone what he now knew to be the truth of her husband's last words.

He would often think about that scene in the living room and the reasons why he wished her to read those words aloud. Did he think she would not survive the guilt of accepting the truth? Did he want his mother to take the dread away from those words by denying their truth? From the hopelessness of this last possibility he wrote his best short story.

Although he could never write about her as she was, he thought about her while writing *Teresa*. In *Teresa*, the female character that was said to be his most memorable one, he created the kind of woman she could have been if her strength had been used for something else rather than for self-protection alone. He did not give Teresa any of his mother's qualities. Nor did he give her anything that his mother might appropriate. When the book came out to great critical acclaim, he received a letter from his mother:

> I am sure your latest book will be greatly praised. I have never offered you any criticism as you well know. And I probably should not offer you any now, but in Teresa you have created a most un-Christian woman. You should bear in mind that middle-aged women differ greatly from middle-aged men. I think the novel would have been much more successful if Teresa was not in it. Or if she had been a man.

Again and again, during his life and in his writings, he would travel over that empty landscape that was his relationship with his mother. As he grew older, he realized that he had great difficulty accepting the fact that she had never loved him, that she had never wanted him. When things went bad, he would clutch at some half-remembered memory of how once she had smiled in the rose garden on a hot summer day, or how her hand reached to him when he was about to fall, how she brushed the hair away from his eyes, but he was never sure whether those were remembered things or part of dreams he had as a child.

By the time Hal was forty and she sixty-two, Clara Hubbard was asked by the editor of a woman's magazine to write an article about Hal's childhood. Using his Slim Taber stories, she gave him a boyhood, but did not attempt to give him a childhood. She ended the article with this sentence: "A mother of a famous son is probably the last to fully understand where his talent came from."

Two years later, Clara Hubbard began her career as a college lecturer. Her fee was $300 a lecture, and she would tell her audience about how it was with Hal when he was growing up in Lakeland, Illinois. A few times she called him Slim, and each time a student or teacher would ask if the mistake was a Freudian slip or whether she often thought of her son as Slim. She always gave the same reply to that question. "Names are unimportant. In his stories Hal retained the essence of things as they were."

Her son had not seen her for years, but she would always remember his birthday and send him a birthday card. At Christmas she would send her grandchildren presents. She lived alone with her daughter and her memories of Doctor Taber's household as it was during the first decade and a half of the twentieth century.

*

Hal Hubbard didn't trust anyone at the clinic, but Dr. Robinson he trusted least of all. He judged him to be in his fifties, and the danger he presented would have been hard to explain to anyone but a fellow writer like Fitzgerald. Zelda might have understood it too. Dr. Robinson was an aging frustrated writer, and frustrated writers when old were dangerous in ways that could only be understood by pros. He had smelled the danger coming from Robinson even before he knew that he was a frustratred writer.

On the third day of his stay at the clinic, Dr. Robinson had come into the room and begun to talk about writing. At first it was general, observations about the difficulties of finding agents and publishers, but soon Dr. Robinson was asking him specific questions. How did he write? Was he following a schedule? Was the schedule the same each day? Was he able to work on two things at once? Did he think characters were more important than the plot?

Hal answered his questions politely, but hoped the man would leave him alone. He didn't until Hal said that he was tired now and wished to nap.

Almost every day he would see Dr. Robinson, and each time there would be a question waiting, as if prepared beforehand, and all of them dealt with his craft. After several weeks, there was a shift in the questioning, and he knew for sure that the man had made a decision. He would write a book, and it would be about Hal Hubbard's stay at the Albuquerque clinic. What Dr. Robinson had failed to do all his life—have something published—he would now accomplish.

It was difficult to tell, as time went by, whether Dr. Robinson had already contacted an agent or a publisher. He might have decided to wait until he had something down, some interesting tidbits gathered perhaps during the sessions. Or during the time that passed, the time Hal was not aware of. He suspected that he was being hypnotized during the sessions with Dr. Walter Konski. They were clever at the clinic and could turn back the clocks. The patients were not allowed to have watches. But he was more clever than they. He noticed the sun's position through the window whenever he came to those sessions and the sun indicated the loss of at least an hour each time. How they managed to hypnotize him he did not know for sure. He was always given shots and pills, and it could be through them that his hypnotic trances were induced. They would extract information from him then.

The danger that came from Dr. Robinson was a definite feeling that he was learning as much as he wished from Hal without his consent. It was a danger that could not be discussed, of course, but a danger of such proportions that even his thoughts were unsafe from it.

Yolanda Hubbard

WHEN at the age of thirty, Yolanda Hubbard was told by Dr. Pacheco that she would shortly become irreversibly blind, she smiled at him and said that after all that she had seen she did not mind all that much.

She was born with minimal sight in her left eye and a weak right eye that grew progressively weaker. She had expected eventual blindness ever since her brother raised that possibility when she was ten.

"You know," Hal had said, "even if you were going to be blind one day, you'll be luckier than most."

"Why?" she had asked.

"Because blind people are gifted with inner vision, that's why."

She had always been shy with Hal and did not want to bother him with yet another question. But he explained, putting his hand on her shoulder, "Inner vision is the ability to see the truth about yourself. Ordinary people can't do that, but blind people can."

He had not lied to her. When she went blind, that gift indeed had become hers. The truth about her was that Hal had been the entire focus of her life. She could now neatly divide her existence into four distinct phases. The first was their childhood together, the second the time Hal was away in the army and in Chicago, the third was Paris. The fourth was when she saw the truth about herself.

The first phase did not start at birth but began on the day her father killed himself. His death had freed her to look at Hal as the center of her universe. When he left home when she was twelve, and he barely seventeen, that phase ended. Life, which she had greeted each morning with expectations and excitement, ceased to be interesting to her. So dull, in fact, that she often went around without her glasses. Without them, she saw everything in blurs and developed good hearing.

The second phase of Yolanda's life began on the day she received the first of Hal's letters from Italy. With its arrival Yolanda's existence resumed once again, only to end when the letters stopped. In that first letter he told her that he had made a great discovery about himself and life:

> I never knew that the most important emotion is fear. It far surpasses love or hate. It's the thing within us that lets us judge ourselves. But not only that. Fear, I believe, is the strongest of our enemies, and the fight against it is the most worthwhile of all the fights.

He had chosen her to confide in. He wrote her of the waves of fear that would come upon him "like oceans," of how he fought and always won. How he, unlike some others, would never drown, never surrender to this presence. . . .

> Fear must have followed all men into all wars. What I find curious is that no one has really written about this raw power fear has. I shall one day. One day I will write about that and about other things never written before.

He described to her the battles he witnessed, for he thought of himself as a "witness," not a participant. Not since he had decided to be a writer. And then came the letter from the hospital with the brief description of his wound.

> It must be like that for a brave bull in Spain's bullrings. When the

·30

It must be like that for a brave bull in Spain's bullrings. When the bullfighter's blade goes honestly and cleanly into the beast, he does not feel death come over him, nor the mortal wound. I was unaware of being wounded and unaware of passing out. The moment of truth holds no fear. Fear is conquered then.

Also from the hospital she received a letter that she cherished above all others, for it seemed to her prophetic:

When I come back, I shall go and live in Chicago and work on a newspaper, for I must make a living at my chosen craft. But that will be writing for a living. I intend also to write for my pleasure. I want to do for the novel what Mr. Shakespeare had done for plays and poetry. I want to bring it up for air. Out of its musty construction, its limitations. I want to use the language like it has not been used before. To match it, the language, to the times we live in. There have been so many changes. Industrial revolution and all that, and the novel has not kept up. And there will be changes to come. Undreamed-of changes, and I want to be within my time and also ahead of it. I want to invent almost a new form for fiction that will serve other writers for at least a century to come. I want to take the novel away from the place it has been and put it out into the sunlight. I want to be remembered for changing the very language of fiction long after I am dead.

I have a master plan all worked out. I've gone into training already. I've been writing poetry, for without writing poetry first no writer can call himself that. I guess what comes first is love and then poetry and then all the rest. Oh yes, I've fallen in love, and it will be, like all first loves, the fuel for my life. Nothing will come of it, but it will serve me well. Then, while holding down the newspaper job, I shall begin on short stories. I shall attempt to do one a month. A perfect, true sentence, or two, or three, or four each day. They'll be chiseled like sculpture. After I am twenty-two, I will have polished up the form, and I will move on to the novel. It will be like turning from amateur to pro.

I often think of writing as if it were boxing. What I am doing with my poems is shadow-boxing. What I'll write for the paper will be like skipping rope. With the short stories, I shall be sparring and entering amateur competition. And with the novel, it will be like the first time in the ring with a professional. I shall be a contender when I finish my first. Once I get the title, I will have to meet all the challengers to keep being a champ. I want to be a heavyweight champion of the world.

From Chicago, for he did not come home on his return, she received a letter telling her that he had gotten a job on *The Chicago Tribune* and that he was working on his short stories. "God, Yol," he wrote,

> it's so great when it's going well—the writing. But when it isn't, it's like nothing I've known. I get so depressed when it's not going well and so damned elated when it's going where I want to take it. The act of creating something good on paper must be a sort of sin against God, for you take even Him on when you do something good and true. You move in on his territory.

When her mother became sick and was thought to be dying, she wired Hal and hoped the news would bring him home. But when he arrived, he had little time for her and spent the few days at his mother's bedside. Alone with her, behind closed doors. He had changed. He was no longer a boy, and she was timid in his presence as she would be in front of a stranger.

After he left, there were fewer letters from him. In one, he mentioned having met a girl whom he liked very much. On her seventeenth birthday, she asked her mother for a trip to Chicago. She wanted to see him. And the girl.

She thought she would be jealous of her, that she would hate her. But she found Lee just perfect for Hal. She was older than he by four years, and maybe that difference in age made her seem serene. She was obviously in love with Hal, but her love was more full of respect than giddiness.

They all met at Hal's one-room walk-up apartment. They sat on the floor, for the place was empty but for a mattress, a large kitchen table with an old typewriter on it and a chair.

"How can you live like this, Hal?" Yolanda had asked him.

"It's all I need at the moment," he said. "I'm not here all that much anyway."

They dined on wine and cheese and freshly baked bread, and Lee brought a checkered tablecloth and candles, and it was like an indoor picnic. They sat and talked for hours. She said little, for they were dreaming aloud, the two of them.

"If only we had some money," Hal said at one point. "I'd marry Lee, and we'd go to live in Paris."

"Wait until I inherit my grandfather's fortune," Lee said, "before you propose."

"The old man will live forever from what you tell me."

"Everything he has is tied up in his lumber business, and he will never sell it, never stop running it."

"We'll wait. Not for him to die, but for me to finish the stories, and the money from that will get us to Paris."

"Why do you want to go to Paris?" Yolanda asked.

"It's been his dream for a few months now," Lee said. "Ever since I met him, that's all he wants. He wants Paris more than he wants me."

"I want you in Paris with me," Hal said and put his arm around her. She cuddled up to him, and Yolanda realized that she loved them both, equally. She didn't know why this sudden love began then, sitting on the floor, watching them and listening to them. All she knew was that now she had two people in the world to love.

"But why Paris?" Yolanda asked again.

"I need Paris. I need two years, maybe three, there. I need it now. In a year's time, I would have all my stories finished, and then I would start on my first novel. I'd write it there and come back to the reviews. I know I can take them on, all those who are writing fiction. And they're all there because Paris is the capital of the world for writers. I want to meet the competition. I want to drink at the same cafés where they do their drinking. I want to breathe the same air they're breathing. I can do better than any of them if only I could invade their turf, and their turf is Paris. But there's nothing I can do now. It will be something for later, going there. It will have to wait. But if I wait too long, it might never happen again."

"It will happen," Lee said. "It will happen for you."

"For us," Hal said. "It will happen for us."

Going back home, she thought of ways she could help them make their dream come true. What would it take to give them two years in Paris? She had forgotten to ask; so she didn't even know the sum of money she would have to have. She loved their dream and was angry at herself that she was not old enough to get some impossibly high paying job and save and give them the money they would need.

On her return, she began to do some volunteer work in the hospital. It was required in her senior year to spend some time "doing good works," as the principal of the school would say. During her second week at the hospital, an old man who was dying asked her if she would marry him and take care of him until he died. "I want to die in my own house, not here," he said. He told her that he had some money saved and nobody to leave it to, that if she became his wife she would be well taken care of. The house and furnishings were worth at least fifty thousand dollars, and he had no debts.

At first she thought he was joking, or senile. He was well over seventy and terminally ill. But he held on to her hand and pleaded with her.

"Why don't you hire a nurse and go home?" she asked him.

"I want you to come home with me—as my wife."

He was small and wrinkled, and his hospital gown revealed hollowed shoulders. His breath smelled badly and his head was bald, and yet while she looked at him, she thought that he might be an answer to her prayers. If she married him, Hal and Lee would have Paris. She could give Paris to them.

"Why would you want to marry me and not someone else?" she asked.

"You look like my wife when she was your age. She was barely eighteen when I married her."

She desperately wished she could talk to someone, anyone, about this crazy thing that had been proposed to her. She thought about it night and day for a week. Then she told him that she would marry him, but that the marriage must remain a secret. Summer was coming, and she would tell her mother that she was going to Chicago to find a job. Before fall, he told her, the doctors said he would be dead. He showed her the new will he had made, leaving everything he had to her.

Before she told her mother the lie about Chicago, she wrote her brother a letter:

Dearest Hal,
 I need your help desperately. You know how mother is and how she expects me to stay home. I found a rare opportunity to do something worthwhile, but I cannot tell you or mother any details. I have to ask you to lie for me, if occasion arises. You must corroborate my story

that I have found a job in Chicago. I shall write mother letters which I want you to forward to her so that she will think the letters came from Chicago. If you wish to reach me for some reason, please write to me at Box 58, Wayne, Illinois, and forward mother's letters to me there. Please don't ask me what I am doing, but be of good faith, it's something very worthwhile and I will be well paid. By Christmas time, at the latest, I might even be rich enough to give you enough money so that you and Lee could go to Europe.

Love, Yol

Yolanda, as a child, was secretive, and as she grew, she found it easy to lie and cover her tracks so intelligently that she was never caught.

As Mrs. Martin Lath she was subjected to the indignity of having to share a bed with an old, dying man. She had hoped that this would not be asked of her. She developed a sinus condition in her husband's musty, dark house and spent a lot of her time with her eyes closed. She was saving her good eye, she thought, by not using it when she didn't need to. Her husband's health improved slightly by July, and on the fourth of that month, "to celebrate," as he said, he asked her to perform what to her seemed a very unnatural act.

"Just hold it," he begged her. And, dutifully, she did. She did not see it, for she kept her eyes closed, but she felt it getting bigger and pumping blood under her fingers. A few days later, in the middle of the night, she was awakened by her husband with a new request.

"Kiss it."

She thought of Hal and how she was going to make it possible for him to become a great writer. She hoped that his first novel, the one that would enter him into the class of heavyweights, would be dedicated to her.

Beginning on July 4th, Yolanda diminished the dose of medicine that her husband was to receive for his failing heart. She did so on her own without the doctor's consent, but in full knowledge that his health was improving. By the middle of August, he asked her to put it in her mouth, and she could not. He threatened to cut her out of his will and leave everything he possessed to charity. She did it because of that and spent the remainder of that night on the downstairs couch—not sleeping, but alternating between reading from the Bible and the two letters she had received from Hal.

> Yol,
> I can't tell you with what mixed emotions I read your letter. You, who never deceived anyone, want to enlist me as partner in deceit. Of course I'll be your partner. But what on earth are you doing? I have a strange feeling that you are marrying some old bastard who's about to croak and will leave you a fortune for the simple privilege of sharing his bed. If that is the right guess, all I can say is that you must not let him wear socks to bed. If it comes to the choice of socks or you, I'm sure the old coot will take the socks and leave you untouched. In case you are indeed going to make a fortune, let me know if I could borrow some money from you. I'd repay you a hundredfold and take off for Paris. If you want to tell me everything please do, so I won't have to worry, but if you want to keep all that a secret, so be it. Lee thinks you're the greatest.
>
> Love from both of us,
your Hal.

The other letter arrived toward the end of August, in response to hers advising him that there might be a delay in getting him the loan, would $20,000 be enough?

> Darling Yol,
> I had wished to write you a hundred times to ask you to reconsider whatever it is that you are doing. A few days ago I had a nightmare about you. In it you had robbed a bank and had been shot. Lee and I had seen a gangster movie, and she said that I was still under its influence when I went to sleep.
> If you really, honestly, might be making a fortune, $20,000 would give us four years, at least, in Paris. Within that time I would have repaid the whole loan, and for the rest of my life I would be paying you the interest part. I will make a will, leaving you everything I have and won't change it until I have paid you back the total of $20,000. But, for God's sake don't do anything foolish, and Paris can always wait. I've sold one of my stories to *Saturday Evening Post*, and they said they might be interested in others, and I expect a book of my stories to come out shortly.

So you see, I might be able to make it to Paris on my own. Lee and I have decided to get married on the ship, and not before. Please take care of yourself, and don't do anything foolish or anything that might endanger your life or health, or your future.

Your loving brother, Hal

P.S. There is one problem. Lee says that unless you are on that ship sailing to France, on which we expect to marry, sailing with us as her bridesmaid, she won't marry me. She says that you'd love Paris and must come along. What do you say? Lee reminds me that it is up to you whether she stays a virtuous woman or becomes my concubine.

Although she did not feel "in good conscience" that the reduced medicine had anything to do with Martin Lath's death, she poured the rest of it down the kitchen drain and stuck the empty bottle in a garbage bag. Afterward she went upstairs and uncovered his body. The organ that she had never seen was tiny, wrinkled, and much more brown than the rest of his body. It was then that she offered God the gift of her virginity.

She had thought that the will would be probated by the end of October. But a problem arose. Martin Lath left a sister in California who contested the will. She hoped that by Christmas she would have the money and could make it a Christmas gift for Hal and Lee. The lawyer said it would probably not happen until January. So she spent that Christmas in the empty house, making an inventory of its contents. Hal went to see their mother while Lee spent the holidays in Montana. Yolanda ate a soft boiled egg alone in the kitchen on Christmas day, and it was the first time in her life that she had no tree to decorate. That made her cry.

Martin Lath's will was finally probated on January 18, and she sold the house to a real estate man who knew she was in a rush. When everything was sold and bank accounts closed, lawyer's fees paid and inheritance taxes covered, Yolanda Hubbard stood inside the empty house for a long time and thought of her life. It was just as empty. The thought that she was going to France with Hal and Lee had kept her going during the long months she lived there alone. Each night she had been petrified of falling asleep, for she had nightmares about her dead husband. She ate very little and grew emaciated, and when she appeared at her brother's door in late January, he did not recognize her.

"Don't say anything," she said to him, placing her hand on his lips. "And don't worry about how I look. I'm fine." Then she placed on the typewriter a cashier's check for $20,000 made out in his name. At first he didn't want to take it, saying that his book was coming out and although the advance was miniscule he expected good reviews and good sales, and then he relented and told her that he would take the loan if she told him the whole story, what had happened to her. Lee came in shortly afterward and they gave her no rest, wishing to know what she had been up to. So she came up with a story that they both believed.

"I was part of an experiment," she told them. "It was conducted in a hospital under doctors' supervision and paid for by a research fund. It had to do with a very strict diet and induced sleeplessness. They gave me a clean bill of health. My right eye was going bad anyway, and it had nothing to do with the experiment. I have sixteen thousand dollars and would love to go to Paris for a little while. Will you still want me to be your bridesmaid?"

Lee took her in her arms and held her for a long time, and Yolanda had trouble controlling her wish to cry and hold on to her. Hal was pacing the floor while the two women sat down on his bed, their arms around each other.

"I can't believe it," he kept repeating, but he did believe her. To his questions, Yolanda found easy answers. Two of her companions in the experiment were prison convicts, and two others, like her, were there for the money. She had forgotten the name of the scientific research group who underwrote the expense. "But they're writing a paper on it. I didn't give them the right to use my real name, though. I will be called Miss Lath when the paper comes out."

They celebrated by drinking champagne and eating caviar, and Hal kept picking them up and swinging them around. They laughed a lot and made plans.

"Does mother know?" he asked at one point.

"She only knows that I've been living in Chicago and the job was so interesting I decided to stay," she laughed. "Oh, how I lied about what a great apartment you have!"

"What will you say to her about going to France?"

"I will tell her that you are buying me the trip."

He hugged her against his chest, and her body pressed against his felt a hardness. She moved away then and began to say she wouldn't be in their way. Once in Paris, she would stay in some small hotel, and they wouldn't even have to bother seeing her. She intended to sketch, perhaps become an illustrator of children's books. They protested that she must live with them, but she was adamant. If she were to go on the same ship with them, she wanted them to know that she would keep out of their way. They could all meet for a few minutes a day, but otherwise they must understand that she wanted her freedom and that they must have theirs.

They didn't go to bed at all that night, but talked and talked. Hal read both of them his latest Slim Taber story.

"Slim," he said to Yolanda, "is really what I would have liked to have been as a boy."

Yolanda was disappointed that Slim had no sister.

At six in the morning, the three of them walked out to wait for a travel agency to open so they could buy their train tickets to New York and their passage to France. The ship departing earliest would go to Marseilles rather than Le Havre. On the train to New York, they decided that Hal and Lee would walk, or hitch rides, or whatever from Marseilles to Paris and that Yolanda would take a train and during the time it would take them to join her, she would find an apartment for them.

The first day out at sea, Hal and Lee were married by the ship's captain. Yolanda did not cry during the ceremony, but she did cry alone in her cabin that night over their happiness and over the memory of her own marriage. The food on the ship made her regain the lost pounds, and she began to look better. Hal devised a schedule for his writing, from eight until noon. During these morning hours, Yolanda and Lee would go out on deck and talk or read huddled in blankets, inhaling the cold sea air, fortifying themselves with hot bouillon and tea. She found out that Lee was brought up in Montana by her grandfather. Her father, when she was very young, had gone off to China or India and had died there before she was ten. Her mother had remarried and moved to Chicago where Lee had hated to live. Until she met Hal.

"He changed my life so completely," she told Yolanda. "Before I met him, I gave myself one more year working as a secretary, then I was going to go back to Montana to be with my grandfather. All I wanted was to be back there and help him run the lumber business. I love the outdoors. I love it in Montana, but I know I shall never go back as long as I'm with Hal. He's all I want."

Another time when they were talking, Yolanda found out that Lee had one fear.

"It's his writing," she said. "I'm afraid that somehow it will destroy our marriage. I know he has a great talent, but it will take a toll in the years to come. How will he take fame, for he will be famous. What will it do to him? And to me? Will he come to feel that I'm not growing with him? How can I grow, me who has no talent?"

"You have a talent. You make Hal happy," Yolanda told her. "I've never known him to be happy."

"He gets so depressed when his writing is not going well. I can do nothing against that private misery of his."

She tried to keep out of their way in the afternoons and evenings. She had her meals sent to her cabin, for she was afraid that they would get tired of her, but she cherished every moment they were together and delighted in their love. She tried to memorize everything about them, every line in their faces, the way each would look at the other, the way Lee would brush Hal's cowlick, and the way he would blow a strand of her hair away from her eyes. She wanted to become familiar with their very bone structure so that she would remember them and see them even if she went blind. During the ten-day trip, she got to know instinctively how well Hal's writing was going and could tell if they had spent the night making love. Lee so often would seem aglow with such happiness that Yolanda tried to imagine how they were in bed, what they said to each other, and how they made love.

The night before they docked in Marseilles, Hal read to Lee and Yolanda a new Slim Taber story. They both thought it was wonderful, and he was pleased with himself.

"I don't know why it is that I want confirmation from someone else that what I have done is good. I'm my own best critic anyway," he said. "I have an instinct, a sort of sixth sense that's built into my brain that tells me when I go wrong that I went wrong. Sometimes I'm stubborn and chase the thing down all the way to a dead end, which is a dreadful waste of time, but in some way, when I'm there, at the dead end, I feel that I can discard those pages. Otherwise, I think I would keep the untidy stuff, and I've got to have it all lean."

He was generous in telling Yolanda all this, and she was thankful that often they would insist she join them for dinner or for drinks afterward. She had begun to keep a sort of journal at the beginning of the trip, and on the morning of their arrival in France she tried to analyze her own thoughts about those stories Hal was working on.

> What I think Hal is trying to do is invent a shorthand. In Mr. Taber, Hal created a man he wished father had been. But I don't like Mrs. Taber much. I wish he had tried to portray mother with her warts and all. As she is.

Yolanda, unlike Hal, admired her mother, for she guessed at some great inner strength in her reserve. She romanticized her mother's lack of affection as a coverup for the unlimited love she was afraid of showing. Her mother's Calvinistic faith, which Yolanda did not share, was not only a shield against the ugliness of the world but a shield as well against all the world's beauty. To Yolanda, Clara Hubbard was a heroic woman. But she never talked about her to Hal, for she knew that he resented her and maybe even blamed her for their father's suicide. He, in turn, never talked to her, or in front of her, about their mother. Lee wished to know what, if anything, had happened between Hal and his mother, but Yolanda could not tell her.

They saw Yolanda off at the station, reminding her that she should look for an apartment for them only on the Left Bank, not too far from the Seine, and she promised she would do her best with her high school French. They were, themselves, going to try to walk as much as they could. "We shall approach Paris, the Holy Grail, on foot," Lee said laughing one day, "and I might never recover from this."

On the train, apart from them, Yolanda tried to remember what Lee had said on another occasion: "It is in Paris that he will enter the ring of literature. It will be there, among this generation of gifted writers and artists, that he plans to find the depth and width of his talent. Oh, Yolanda, I just hope I will be of help to him. I hope he will need me for the encouragement I can give. I love him so very much, and sometimes feel so afraid he'll leave me. If it were not for the loan you made us, I would fear that he'd leave me for someone rich...."

"He will not leave you," Yolanda said. "He loves you as much as you love him. Or maybe more. I've never seen him so happy, so at ease. You are good for him, and he knows it."

"Oh, I'm just being silly," Lee said then, "and insecure. And it's all because I'm older. That's what it is."

"You look so much younger than I," Yolanda said.

That was the truth. At eighteen, Yolanda appeared to be in her late twenties; at almost twenty-eight, Lee looked eighteen.

On her third day in Paris, Yolanda found a studio for Hal and Lee. It was perfect in all ways as long as they did not have a child. For it consisted only of a very large room with a skylight and a kitchen and a bath, but the room was partitioned and Hal would have his privacy.

One large window afforded a great view of the rooftops and the Right Bank beyond the river. While she was looking up at the skylight, she noticed a tall building whose top-floor windows overlooked the studio. She pointed out those windows to the concierge and asked what building it was. "That's the Hotel Martinique," the concierge said, "it's around the corner on Rue Sirène."

After paying the month's rent on their apartment, Yolanda walked to the Hotel Martinique and insisted on renting a room on the top floor. "But they are maid's rooms, Madame," the manager protested. "They are small, and you would not like them."

"I would like to rent one," she said firmly.

"There is one unused, but. . . ."

"Please let me see it." The room he showed her had a window overlooking the studio. It was small, but she said she would take it. The room was narrow and built on top of the roof, and there were two other windows on the opposite side. Yolanda hung the bedspread on the window facing the studio and pushed the bed against the window. In this way, even lying in bed she could see them down below, and anyone coming into her room would not suspect that there was a window there.

For the next few nights, she saw the moon reflected in their skylight. She bought a pair of powerful field glasses and could, during the day, see the studio quite clearly. With their help, she would be able to see Hal and Lee whatever they were doing. She knew now that she would go blind one day, if not because of an inherent disease of her eyes, then as punishment for what she planned to do.

Two weeks after Yolanda had come to Paris, Hal and Lee arrived. It had been arranged before that Yolanda would leave a note for them at American Express. They, in turn, would leave a note for her where they would meet. Yolanda had been checking her box at the American Express twice or three times a day. When she finally received the note, they asked to meet her at Les Deux Magots. She arrived at the café before they did.

Lee was enchanted with their studio, and Hal kept looking around and muttering, "A goddamned love nest!" or "What a great place to work!" depending on where he stood. During their dinner, which consisted of wine, bread, and cheese in their new studio, they told Yolanda they were going to live "most sensibly." That they had budgeted the twenty thousand dollars in such a way that even if Hal did not make any money, they would be able to live and travel for years and years without worrying about anything. In their budget, they had included, they told Yolanda, a weekly dinner with her, in the restaurant of her choice, for as long as she remained in Paris.

"What evening a week would you like to reserve for us?" Hal asked her.

She had thought she would see them each day. She lowered her head, not wanting them to see her eyes filling with tears.

"Pick the day," Lee urged, "and I shall put it on this big calendar." She was unfolding a three-foot calendar and pinning it next to the kitchen wall.

"How about Tuesdays?" she managed to say.

"Fine. Each Tuesday shall be Yol day," Hal said.

She had picked Tuesday because this was Monday. But on the following day, when she came to Deux Magots at six, which was the place and time they agreed to meet, they were not there. She sat alone over two apéritifs, and at half past seven went back to her attic. She did not turn the light on, but went directly to the window and looked down on Hal's studio with her field glasses.

They had left on the light on the bedside table, and through the falling light rain, as through silent distortion, she could see them quite clearly. When she was fourteen, she had imagined for the first time what it would be like to make love, and in imagining it found it unexciting. At fifteen, a boy in her class had slipped his hand under her sweater while they were skating by moonlight, and she had let his hand stay there as they glided away from the others. He had skated

43·

her around the lake's bend and tripped her on the bank, and his hand had gone under her skirt. She pushed it away, got up and, crying, skated to the other side of the lake.

Between that incident and the unspeakable, unseen horror of the acts she had been asked to perform in the dying man's bed, there was nothing for her to remember. What she saw through the skylight was somehow what the creation of the world might have been. Out of turmoil, moving, heaving, raising and falling, turning and rolling, something splendid was being made.

The scene below her shimmered, and she realized she was crying. Then, through her tears and the rain, she saw him rise away from Lee. She brought their faces into focus: Hal's as he filled two glasses with wine and brought them to bed, Lee's as she looked up at him. The wine was forgotten, and they were back with each other again. The very rhythm of their happiness seemed suddenly contagious, and Yolanda placed a pillow under her stomach and moved with them, reaching toward them with her empty arms and crying, sometimes loudly, sometimes softly.

By the time she met them for dinner the following Tuesday, she had watched them make love several times at night and in the afternoons. She knew every curve of their bodies. She knew that they began a routine that started with Hal waking up at six, getting himself breakfast while Lee slept, and being at his typewriter by seven. Lee would tiptoe to him and kiss him on the back of the neck and tiptoe away while he worked until past noon. Then both of them would leave the house to return again after lunch to make love, take a rest afterward, and wake to the falling evening. They would go out again by six, and sometimes she had to wait past midnight to see them return.

With her binoculars she could read what they had written on their large calendar. The first week had large letters across it: LIVING IT UP; EATING OUT. On the following week's pages, there was only one dinner entry: YOL DAY under Tuesday and under that, WEEKLY DINNER OUT. She knew that as long as she was in Paris she would be their unseen companion and was both tremendously pleased and terribly ashamed of herself at this fact of her life.

They took her to the Café Athenée for dinner among all sorts of apologies for what they called their "decadent living." "We've been eating out," Lee said laughing, "but as of this week, as of tomorrow, we're tightening our belts. It will be bread and cheese for us."

"And a little wine," Hal added, then laughed and said, "Or a lot of wine."

"Yolanda," Lee said, "you should see the budget I've made. And I intend us to toe the line." She looked at Hal with brilliantly joyous eyes, the kind of look Yolanda thought was reserved only for their lovemaking.

They questioned her during dinner. What had she been doing with herself? Oh, she'd been busy. Walking mostly, wearing down the heels of her shoes. Oh, yes, she'd been to the museums, would keep on going until she had seen everything. Parks? Yes, parks were her favorite, too. Next week she was planning to take a tour to Versailles. She'd love to go with Lee to the stores. As a matter of fact, she'd been too busy so far to have gone inside any of them.

She fielded all their questions with lies. She told them she might be changing hotels or moving to Alliance Française and when she did, she'd invite them over. But hotel rooms are hotel rooms, not much to see. If they needed to get in touch with her, they should leave a note in her box at the American Express. She went there every day. Oh, she was fine and not lonely at all. She was thinking of getting a sketchbook and sketching some.

Their proximity throughout the Tuesday evening was painfully infuriating. It was as if she preferred to see them through the skylight making love rather than to dine with them. She could not understand why they did not act like fevered lovers. Before dinner was over, Hal told her that they were sorry, but on next Tuesday they would be dining with Gertrude Stein. They had tried to make it another evening, but that was the only evening Miss Stein seemed free. "And I must meet her and Alice Toklas," he added, "I hope you won't mind." That night, while looking at them, she noticed that next week's Yol Day had been crossed over and the name G. Stein written over it in big letters.

The idea that she would like to be close to them, invisible somehow but close enough to see them outside as well as inside their apartment, entered her head when she went with Lee to visit the department stores. The following day she bought a wig and two large-brimmed hats. The day after, she bought some old dresses and a fur coat at the Marché aux Puces and a large shawl. She also bought a man's suit. And some make-up. She carried all these possessions to her room.

By the time she began to dress in her disguises, the hotel help thought of her as a recluse and an eccentric. She bought rolls, cheese, and milk, which she consumed in her room. Before she began to dress in the old clothes she had purchased, she had gone out rarely. But now she was seen leaving the hotel often.

She would follow them wherever they went, keeping well behind. She would often wait for them in doorways, trying to imagine what was said by them inside. At first, she kept at a distance from them, but she longed to hear what they were talking about in cafés and restaurants, and she grew bold. Her face was always hidden by the large floppy hats. When she was disguised as a man, she even risked sitting at a table close to them.

It was as if she were a part of them and they a part of her. At night, even if their lights were out and she could not see them, she would hug her pillow to her breast thinking of what they might be saying to each other.

One morning, while Hal was working at his desk and Lee was sewing, she went out, undisguised, and walked the banks of the Seine where artists painted and where old books were sold. She bought two sketchbooks from an old man who was partial to children, dogs, and horses, and brought those sketchbooks to dinner, which she was having with them at their studio that night, and claimed the sketches as her own. They were pleased that she was keeping busy sketching and enjoying her stay.

"But don't you feel lonely?" Lee asked.

"Oh, no," she protested, "I really don't know where the time goes!" She knew they both worried about her, but now that they had proof that she was busy sketching, she hoped they would stop.

Whenever they dined out now, someone would join them, for Hal and Lee had made many friends. Hal would always introduce her as "my kid sister Yolanda," and they often would say that they must find a young man for her. Sometimes they would have one join them for dinner, but none of them interested her. And each time Lee would look at Yolanda with sadness and say she was hard to please and if she didn't give young men a chance, she might end up an old maid. "She has time," Hal would say, but he, too, would look expectantly at Yolanda whenever someone "suitable" was with them.

Twice they took her to parties where she felt lost and was tongue-tied and uncomfortable. When she told them she hated parties and would rather not go, they stopped insisting. Several times she broke a Yol Day dinner with them, and the few times they broke it, she felt glad. It was increasingly difficult for her to be with them now. The demands on her seemed insurmountable. They would no longer be put off. They had to see where she lived. Yolanda was forced to rent a room at Alliance Française. She brought some of her things there. Finally, she bought an easel, some canvases, and paints and invited them over for tea. But the questions did not stop. Those questions had to be countered with lies that became ever more difficult to fabricate. When she was following them in her various disguises, she did not have to cope with lying. As much as she loved them, she didn't like being with them anymore because being with them meant she had to pretend to be herself. And she no longer knew who she was.

Inside her dark hotel room, she had begun to make up life stories about each of her disguised selves. She now liked to fantasize about herself. She was Lord Byron grown old, she was Mata Hari. She could be an actress or a millionaire's wife or a famous courtesan now almost deaf and blind, abandoned by her lovers and admirers. And taking turns being anyone she wished, she kept on observing Hal and Lee through their skylight. In this way, she was no longer Yolanda Hubbard spying on her brother, Yolanda who knew she was doing wrong and would go blind because of her sin.

They were going to go to England late in spring, and she planned to follow them, looking forward to that as to a great adventure. She had decided to travel as a man, but she caught a very bad cold the day before they left. Without them, Paris became a nightmarish place for her. She would look down on their empty studio during the day and at night would go out in one of her disguises because she could not bear the dark and empty studio below. She had filled her diary with everything Hal and Lee had done, eaten, or said over the months she had watched them. And now, each day, she would make entries of what she imagined they were doing, seeing, and saying, but the words were jumbled and meaningless, like her days.

They came back in July, and her life resumed the rhythm of their lives. One afternoon she followed them to the race track. During their months' absence, she had forgotten the sound of their laughter, even how they looked, and now she feasted her eyes on them as she sat alongside them and even went to the betting window behind them. She was wearing her old woman's disguise—a large felt hat with flowers, a gray wig beneath, and a coat with a large collar in spite of the summer's heat.

"I've seen that old woman several times," she heard Lee whisper to Hal.

Hal looked at Yolanda and then said, "I wonder who she is. She must have been somebody when she was young."

Yolanda realized with a start that she was still only nineteen years old. It seemed to her that she had come to Paris years ago, that she had lived several lifetimes. After the races, in the departing crowd, she lost them. When she spotted Hal across the street, she ran toward him—and into the path of a car.

Her hat, her wig, went flying as she fell to the pavement. Before she lost consciousness, she saw Hal's face above hers and the word "Yol?" echoed in her brain. Then, mercifully, everything was quiet.

They tried to guess at why she had been disguised. They found the keys to her rooms in her purse, and Hal went to the hotel alone that night. He was surprised to find out that she had lived not at Alliance Française but only a block away all along. Lifting the bedspread hanging over the bed, he found himself looking at his studio down below. He also found the binoculars, then the other wig, strange clothes, finally the diary, a laundry list of his activities for all the months they were in Paris. This filled him with a white anger that later changed to an unspeakable dread.

Some inkling of evil had invaded his life and his future. Leaving her room, he felt himself dirtied by his sister's obsession.

He could not speak about what he found in Yolanda's room but gave Lee the key, and she went there alone to discover what he already knew. "I don't want to talk about it," he said to her when she returned, her eyes disturbed. He gave her a letter for Yolanda and asked her to take it to the hospital. "I don't want to see her," is all he said.

Yolanda kept her eyes closed during Lee's visit. She did not answer the questions as to why she had been doing the things she had done. The doctor came during Lee's visit and assured her that the minor concussion would leave no complications, her broken arm would heal in time, that she could be discharged in a few days.

Yolanda did not cry when she read Hal's letter after Lee left. There was a check inside the letter for fifteen thousand dollars:

> I shall repay you the $5,000 within the next year, plus interest. Perhaps you should seek professional help. Lee thinks that your diary, which we both have read, is an indication of some terminal case of loneliness or some complete lack of identity. I fear something darker there that should be cured. Thinking back on the years we spent together, I seem to remember that you had not much ability to assume any coloration of your own. Even if you hate yourself, that is not an excuse to try to steal someone else's life. Lending us money did not entitle you to take our lives for your own.
>
> Hal

A year later, when she was back home, a check from his publisher was sent to her with a note:

> Upon Mr. Hubbard's request we enclose a check for the sum of $7,000, which constitutes repayment of a loan.

She read everything he wrote and knew that he would always be the most important person in her life. Even before she went blind she never tried to get a job. She lived with her mother in the old house and did gardening. Hal was paying all the expenses for his mother, and when Yolanda became blind he took on the additional burden, paying for a part-time chauffeur and a housekeeper. The woman was a "fan" of her brother's books and would read and reread everything he wrote to Yolanda and her mother.

Hal came to visit them twice over the years; once with his three children and once with Sally. The visits were short and somehow uneasy for everyone. Yolanda knew he resented the memories that the house held for him. On the last visit he asked after the old gun with the long barrel, and it was brought down from the attic. He wrapped it in a blanket and took it away with him. He never talked about Paris, and Yolanda never told anyone what her life had been there.

There was an interruption coming, lunch on the way. He heard the approaching voices. Why did they always have to open doors and announce there was a surprise? It was always lunch at 12:30, not Santa Claus.

Of course he had made a mistake by not watching his parents more closely. He could have seen Yolanda's conception. He could have been more careful and less careless because he could have seen them, heard them, watched what happened that night she was conceived. He had been five and he did not have to sleep, but he had been asleep when it happened because at that age he was not all that smart. He didn't know how important it would be. Knowing. Yolanda, after all, might have been useful to him. As he had been useful to her. Of course, it was one of those things that he could not forsee. But now he was being careful, and watching everything.

"Mr. Hubbard, you must not push the tray away so hard. The tomato soup spilled over my hands, and it was hot."

"I'm sorry," he said. "I must have been thinking."

"I understand. Writers do get lost in their own thoughts, don't they? I took a creative writing course at the University of Albuquerque once, and that's what the teacher told us."

She might be a fellow writer, another Dr. Robinson perhaps. He smiled at her warmly, and she grinned back and put the tray closer to his chin. If he was to be careful, he must not give any of them trouble. He was being watched. The dark television over his bed was watching him, and somewhere, in some room of the clinic, there would be young writers who wanted to discover his tricks, observing him. What were they making out of the spilled tomato soup? Was one writing a thesis on him, and the nurse would represent Lee and the spilled soup what he had done to her?

"As my lawyer you must forbid them to use Lee's name in vain." That's what he had said the day before they took him away, and the connection had been cut off. By Sally, or the FBI, or perhaps by those who were using Lee's name in vain. There was nothing he could do, and yet it was his job to protect her. From them. She had never been at fault, and yet they were writing about her without his or her permission. They were writing about them, and nobody but he and she knew about them. He had kept her out of his stories and his novels. There was not one character that was based on her. That was a point of honor. And even remembering Yol's visit to Paris had been a break of trust, but he was doing the remembering. And this was a private affair. He would try, even when thinking of Larry Dort, to keep her out as much as he could, because he didn't trust them. During those sessions, the shock therapy, he was sure they were extracting his thoughts with as much ease as a dentist can extract teeth. He was jumping the gun with Paris and even Chicago, he wanted to start with Slim. No, not with Slim, with Hal, as a boy.

The boyhood had to be gone over for buried treasure. There were some buried treasures there, of that he was sure. The real ones, not the ones that came out from going down the hatch. Not the times most people remember, not the Christmases and the Thanksgivings and the Easters. They contained no treasures of memory because something happened that he would never know, that had not even been his fault, as far as the family went. That was, of course what had been wrong all along, what would not make anything right. He had no base. No rock, no foundation on which he could rest. There was to be no beginning for him, of that he was sure now. So he had to do the best he could with what there was.

But there had been magic in his boyhood. There had been rain and the way it fell on the big oak trees outside his bedroom. The noise of it, and the smell, and the way it gave off this strange light. The rain changed things. Not lives. But it changed the leaves and the sky and the earth and everything that grew and breathed oxygen. Not humans, nature. And he could have been a painter, had he wished to have chosen that work. He would have been good because he noticed light. Turner painted light better than anyone. And the Renaissance painters. Maybe from the start there was something educated inside the retina of his eyes. It retained, it delighted, in the changes of light. Most people were aware of seeing the different light during sunsets, a few during mists. But he could see other lights, less spectacular, and what they did with the outside. Inside it was not the same. Electric lights were not magic. The light outside was.

And his boyhood had treasures having to do with the wind. The sound of it. The feel of it. He had been good at appreciating the winds during his boyhood. He could not blame himself, in all conscience, for having been careless about the wind. He was not. He had written some about the wind, but not as much as he could have. The wind had always been a friend. There was nothing, ever, scary about it, except to bullfighters. They would have to wet their capes and their *muletas* to cut down the wind. The wind was dangerous to them because it would expose them. But he was not a bullfighter. He wrote about them, and he wrote about the wind. He had been a writer, once.

He put the tray on the table by the door. There were no flowers although some were sent to him. By those who knew where he was, but he had asked that the flowers be removed. He was sorry now, even cut flowers were better than no flowers. But with the years he had gotten to the point that he preferred weeds. Maybe it was a symbolic preference. More a reminder of mortality than a death symbol. He walked to the window and opened it. The bars prevented him from putting his head out, and without his head out he could not feel if there was any wind. It might be blowing, but from another side. But the wind in Albuquerque was probably no good. Nothing much was good in Albuquerque. He missed the wind in Santa Fe. If he lived alone in Santa Fe he would not have to be here. Living alone he could hide everything, there would be nobody to think he was ill.

He walked back to the bed and took a roll with him. He had not eaten anything, but they would notice he had eaten the roll and maybe they would leave him alone. He needed to lose another twenty pounds to be at his best "fighting" weight, 178 pounds. Except he wouldn't be fighting again. His legs were gone, the knees stiff. And his punches, what of them? But he must not think forward or even slightly back. He wanted to return to the treasures of his boyhood. He wanted to be on schedule. Get it over with Lakeland and his immediate family and move on to his cherished friends.

There had been the time he went to the poolroom at twelve. It was the first time for him, and he had skipped school and wanted to hide. He had thought the movie house would be open, but it wasn't, and he had walked inside the pool hall and found a different world, different treasures there. What was his name? A burly man with a red beard, who took him in tow and gave him a stick, taught him how to chalk up and showed him how to hit the ball. "Go straight at it, that's the secret, whether you hit the cue ball low, in the center, side or high, it all makes sense of a different kind, but nothing unless it's hit clean and followed through makes sense." Hitting clean. He tried to do that all along, even with his women. But women be damned, there would be time for that. He wanted to see it again, the pool hall with the lamps throwing a circle around each green island. He would, twelve years later, see the Van Gogh painting of a pool table just like the one he had seen for the first time in Lakeland. But it brought nothing but sad memories then. His memories of boyhood would not be sad, not today.

"Oh, Mr. Hubbard, you didn't eat much of anything again! What will we do with you?" Indeed what will they do with him? He gave the nurse a smile and showed her the empty roll plate. He had eaten most of it and thrown the rest in the wastepaper basket. Then he pointed to the glass of juice, empty. He had thrown the contents down the bathroom drain. He wanted some good wine, or maybe he didn't. Good wine brought back painful memories. Bad wine, then.

"I'm sure you'll enjoy dinner tonight," the nurse said from the door. "We're having a very crisp chicken, finger-licking good." They were now used to his lack of response. He waited until the door shut tight before resuming with his boyhood.

There was a funny kid in the third grade. He couldn't remember his name, those damn shock treatments took names away, not the names that were the feeders' names, others' names. The kid dressed funny, especially the caps he wore, old baseball caps. His father had been a second string baseball manager and moved a lot around the clubs, and the boy had a dozen different baseball caps. And he talked funny. He called everybody asshole, even the teachers, but there was no meanness in the kid. He guessed that all third graders—since the beginning of indoor plumbing—went for toilet jokes, but this kid's very funny mind resided somewhere near or around the toilet bowl. Shit this and shit that. But the kid was a laugher, even when he had his mouth washed with soap he blew bubbles. "What the shit do you expect?" his father once explained to the principal, "the kid was brought up among baseball players, the best assholes in the world." The kid didn't last long, his father was only passing through Lakeland between clubs. But the nameless kid left behind good memories.

Fifth grade had Peggy Schneider, his first true love, not as true as Lee, of course, but he didn't know Lee was alive, not then, so he loved Peggy Schneider as if nobody had ever loved anyone before him. Of course he couldn't tell anyone about how he felt, certainly not Peggy Schneider. But he followed her home one day because he wanted to know where and how she lived and who loved her beside himself.

He should not have thought of her in spite of the fact that she had been one of the treasures of his boyhood. What he saw and heard that night was worse than he knew from watching his own parents. Mr. and Mrs. Schneider were not a loving couple, unless he was wrong all along, and love could be mistaken for physical violence. That night, watching them from outside, through the small space in the drapes, he saw them hit each other, with viciousness. And Peggy, the next morning, came to school with a bruise under her eye. It was not the first time. What had attracted him to her was her good nature in spite of the fact that, as she explained, she was "accident prone.' She would laugh about those accidents when asked whatever had happened to her this time. "I fell out of a tree," she would say, "and I wouldn't have if I had listened to my parents." "I was trying to reach for my kitten and fell out of the window," she said once, when she came to school with her arm broken. He had loved that about her, her adventurous spirit and good nature, before he loved her for her red hair and for the brightness of her blue eyes. After that, knowing what he knew he began to pity her and love did not stay. Someone else came between her and his pity for her, and that one he kissed. But did not love.

There had been days, and even a few nights, when treasures of his boyhood rained on him, but always, forever it seemed, he had wished that those treasures could have some beginning within his family, within the home. But that would not be so, not until he had his own.

He was growing up "special," in the meanwhile. He never took the measure of that specialness, never really understood when it all began, this attraction he would have for people. It might have grown out of that difference that he tried to pinpoint, that barrier between him, unhugged, and them, hugged. He had no beginning in love. But he would find himself loved. Or that's what he thought. Of course he did not figure that it could be counterfeit, and on finding out that it was he would end it, terminate it like some hypocrisy. The sad truth was that he had never been really loved more than once. By Lee. That should have been enough. The other stuff was admiration perhaps, or their need to be near him, to rub off his talent, to rob him of it. Sharks, vultures, hyenas—whatever they might have been, they were after the scent of his fame, and then after him. Like Larry Dort. He was the first of an army of many.

Larry Dort

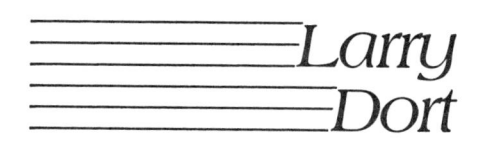

THEY first met at the offices of *The Chicago Tribune*. By the time Larry began to work there as a copy boy, he had a degree in sociology from the University of Chicago, which he got after two years of concentrated studies. While waiting for a job in his field, he answered an advertisement and became the "lowest peg on the paper," as the personnel manager put it when he hired him. "But the compensating factor," the man added, "is the romance of the newsroom." He laughed uproariously at what he must have considered a good joke. Larry found plenty of romance in the newsroom. And all of it centered around the person of Hal Hubbard.

His first day on the job, Hal offered to buy him a beer, which gesture was to endear him to Larry. If he could have chosen the way he wished to look, he would have looked exactly like Hal Hubbard. From the top of his light brown hair down to his scuffed shoes, Hal Hubbard, in Larry's opinion, looked like a winner. He favored turtleneck sweaters rather than shirts and ties, and often wore an old beat-up raincoat cut like a British officer's jacket.

During that memorable first day, Larry learned that Hal wanted to be a novelist. "I'm putting in a couple of years on the paper to learn how to not be caught up in all that descriptive crap novelists get caught up in," Hal said. "And in the meantime, I'm also writing stories."

"If you ever want me to do any typing for you, I'm plenty fast at the typewriter," Larry offered one day. He was taken up on it immediately because Hal liked to write in longhand and he had trouble typing all his copy.

Within the next week, Hal had given him a story to type. Larry took it home and read it in the bathtub. He got goose pimples reading it. He thought it was the most exciting piece of writing he had ever read. That night he told his parents that he knew a great writer who would become the most famous novelist of the century.

"If that's so," his mother said, "then you should become his Boswell."

The idea did not seem too farfetched to Larry; actually he got hold of it as a dog would a bone and chewed on it for over a year. During that year he kept a journal of what Hal said, and to whom, and his own reactions to the stories he was typing for him. He also fantasized himself to be the only person in the world who would know, from the beginning, about Hal's genius, and how, years later, he would be asked to lecture at universities about his friendship with Hal Hubbard. When he received an offer of a good job in his field of sociology, he turned it down without hesitation and continued working on the *Tribune* as a copy boy, a position that allowed him to be near Hal.

He was filled with admiration for Hal's ability and ease when he talked with strangers and acquaintances, either in the newspaper offices or in the bars where Larry often would follow him. Hal seemed to have definite opinions on every subject and did not hesitate to express them. Larry would repeat those opinions as his own during dinner at home. He also greatly admired Hal's physical abilities. On weekends, Larry would often watch him play tennis, and sometimes in the evenings would follow him to the midtown gym and watch him spar and work out at the bag and jump rope. Hal could do two hundred pushups and get up without breathing hard.

Hal never seemed to resent Larry and never told him not to hang around. He accepted him as one accepts his own shadow. Perhaps it was because Larry never competed with him in any way, remaining silent and somewhat colorless, so that often Hal would not even notice his presence. Larry changed profoundly. His need of being useful to someone was fulfilled by the mere fact that Hal Hubbard was in his life. What had once been a compulsion to be helpful, to inject himself whenever he spotted a solvable difficulty, to anticipate people's wishes, to be thoughtful in innumerable, small ways—all that was being kept in reserve for Hal. He was happy at the slightest notice from Hal and waited impatiently for anything Hal wished him to type.

"I've got to pay you," Hal said each time he received a neatly copied story, complete with two carbons.

"Forget it," Larry would tell him. "I couldn't think of anything I'd rather do."

"When I'm rich and famous, I'll hire you as my secretary," Hal would say, laughing, and slap Larry on the back.

Once, on Larry's twenty-first birthday, Hal took him to his "favorite whorehouse" and bought him his favorite girl for the night, Lola, a Mexican woman past her prime. Larry spent the night talking with her about Hal and left, a virgin. He began to think that perhaps there was some homosexual attraction he felt for Hal. But during Christmas, when Hal was away at his mother's, Larry met Carole Scolfield, the daughter of a wealthy investment counselor. She had made her debut that fall. Having met and dated all the eligible young college men, Carole had decided that they were all bores and snobs. When Larry delivered from his father's shop a reproduction of a Victorian loveseat for a servant's room, she mistook him for a workingman. She had read some Karl Marx and had become infatuated with the working class, or at least that's what she told Larry. She asked him, on impulse, to escort her to a dance that very evening. Larry rushed home to get the money to rent a tuxedo and presented himself at her door bearing a corsage. But Carole changed her mind. Her parents were out for the evening, as were the servants. She brought out a magnum of champagne from the refrigerator and put some jazz on the phonograph. They both got drunk between cheek to cheek dances and ended up on the loveseat Larry had delivered earlier that day.

He tried to tell her about Hal. He even read to her out of his notebook the list he had made of what made Hal Hubbard a special human being:

> He has the kind of class that only special, memorable people have. It's in his demeanor, in the way he talks, so self-assured. There is a magnetic quality in his voice and in his eyes. His talent for writing is beyond question, and he knows himself to be talented and thinks he owes dues to that talent. . . .

"I really don't want to hear that much about him anymore," Carole told Larry the third time they saw each other. "Do you want me to think you're more stuck on him than you are on me?"

"But he's—when you meet him. . . ."

"I don't give a damn about him, or you, for that matter! I've had enough!"

He wrote her a letter saying that she didn't understand friendship among men; that he loved her and wished to marry her. But she didn't answer the letter and would not come to the phone when he called. Larry decided that he would adore her from afar, that he was destined to be unlucky in love as he had been unlucky in friendships. But he was immensely grateful to her. The three times they had seen each other, they had made love, and his doubts about his masculinity had been dissipated. He knew now, for certain, that what he felt for Hal was deep admiration and the kind of love he need not fear. He began to refer to Carole as "my girl" although she remained invisible and unreachable. Hal, when he came back, was told of their brief affair and how Larry intended to carry the torch for her. Hal was ready with advice.

"A woman, any woman, will grab your balls if you don't watch out. There isn't a woman alive who doesn't want a man to be her slave. The more, the merrier. With or without marriage that's what women were created for. To trap a man. Good luck, Charlie, you've been made a fool of and have joined that large society of suckers that I'll never belong to."

"Have you ever been in love?" Larry asked him.

"Only briefly, when I was in Italy. I go to a whorehouse each month to keep a clear head about sex."

Two weeks later, Hal met Lee Rand, and Larry Dort watched what love did to him. There had always been something more vital in

Hal than in anyone else he knew. But now everything he did and everything he said was invested with excitement and importance. His streak of cynicism receded out of sight. Hal exuded a generosity of spirit. His laughter came easily, and even his eyes seemed to change into a lighter brown. There was a new urgency in him, as if there was not time to enjoy life, to taste experiences. He looked to Larry like a kid at a Christmas feast knowing that the presents were all safe in the closet and he was going to get at them.

Lee brought out in him a sense of a real future as a writer. What Larry knew all along became actually believable to Hal. He was going to make a difference to fiction. He was going to change the novel into a new art form. These were no mere dreams, he knew he could do it because now he had Lee.

She was older, by four years, and yet in love she seemed much younger than Hal. When she first met Larry she turned to him with a question: "You've known him, am I wrong? Is he or isn't he the most exciting human being in the world?" And with that question and the answer he gave her, they became friends, allies. Although Hal never confided in him about the changes that love brought, Lee confided in Larry. It was from her that he learned they were both frightened of having imagined too much about each other, of having created themselves perfect without any blemishes. They feared that what was happening to them was unearned, that they had been too reckless in loving each other. She told Larry that they had long discussions about how they cherished their freedom, how they did not wish to fall into a trap. They play-acted, promising each other not to lose their heads, confessed to being over-emotional and immature, and then, when they reached an understanding that they must, above all else, be rational, they would burst out laughing and would fall into each other's arms.

Whenever they decided to stay away from each other for a day or two, "as a test," Lee would seek Larry out and talk to him about Hal and about how impossible it would be for her to lose him. Larry would see them when she came from work to the newspaper office, and he felt that nobody but the two of them looked and acted like lovers and he would feel dizzy with the enormity of their happiness.

They talked often of going to Paris. They were both going to save their money, but it would take them years and Hal felt that later might be too late. He wanted to be there now, to work on the novel that would somehow, he hoped, speak for his entire generation, that generation which considered Paris the landscape of its collective soul. Unlike the preceding generation that came to Europe to tour it, the people of his generation, he felt, went there out of a necessity to find their roots, and they looked for them in Paris with a curiosity and a hunger that Henry James would have been ashamed of. Their own sophistication was different, it was more physical than emotional. Emotionally, they were children, and Paris was their playground. He wanted to be part of it all.

Hal also felt that in some ways those young Americans flocking to Paris in the twenties were like some unorganized Olympic team of artists and writers ready to take on the Europeans, to engage them in competition. They were, or so Hal thought, a vanguard of future American superiority in the arts. If they were to bring all the gold medals home with them, then the United States could continue to prosper materially, scientifically, and technologically without feeling guilty culturally. This vision of the future was very real and inevitable to Hal. When he talked about all this, it was not in some symbolic or patriotic way. He felt himself part of a generation that would be freeing America from her bondage of inferiority as an immigrant country. The sons and daughters of the poor, the wretched, the sick, were returning to Europe's shore. And they were nothing like their forefathers had been when they sailed westward.

But both Lee and Larry knew that ideas and ideals were not all that Hal was after. He lusted with all his youth and physical impatience after enjoyment. His dream of Paris was filled with hungers he wished to appease, joys he wanted to discover, foods he hoped to delight in, wines he planned to taste, experiences he would store. He wanted to live life to the fullest, and he hoped to be enriched by others like himself. He was most eager to "go into the ring" with those already writing in Paris. And above all, at twenty-two, he wanted to forget that his father and grandfather had taken their lives. He wanted to deal a death blow to his own lingering doubt that life was worth living.

When they suddenly left Chicago in January of 1923, Larry felt totally lost. Without them, life ceased to exist. He began to think of how he himself belonged in Paris and what his function might be. He decided that more than anything he would like to become a publisher. A publisher in Paris. He would publish books of merit and quality written by still unknown writers, and maybe have a monthly or quarterly magazine where excerpts of works in progress would appear. He needed money for that, and his father was his only hope. But his father was not interested in being "famous as an investor, as a new de Medici." He wanted his son to work for him in what had become a very profitable business. They finally made a deal. Larry would work with his father for two years and would earn his own money for what was considered by his parents to be "a useless pursuit of a pipe dream."

The idea that he might publish something of Hal Hubbard's, that he might be part of that world of expatriates, kept Larry going. He worked long hours and squirreled away every penny. He lived at home to save money. He didn't go out, didn't have time for anything, felt himself growing dull. But at the end of spring, he was ready to leave Chicago and his meaningless life. He had accumulated only two thousand dollars; far from enough, he felt. Lee had written him several letters, but he kept from her the dream of coming to Paris. He talked his father into letting him go to Europe to buy some antiques. He had written his father a letter and mailed it from Le Havre.

Dear Dad,
  You might want to send the police after me. I am not going to buy any antiques with the $15,000 you entrusted to me. And I will not be coming back to America for a couple of years. I shall use your money to establish Ariel Press and publish the best American writers who now live in Paris. I promise to repay this money to you within a few years. If I don't you can denounce me as a thief and I shall gladly go to jail for the rest of my life. Or you might consider that money my legacy, my inheritance. I do not expect anything more from you. But I have to follow my vision. It has been with me for a long time, and I must make it come true myself. It's not only my friend, Hal Hubbard, who would be published by my publishing house, there are so many others in Paris who would give me their books to publish. They all have the best talent available in this century. You did not want to play a Medici to all that talent. I won't be either, perhaps. But this will be a business venture, and I expect to get rich from it. It's a grand idea. I wish you had

believed in it. But you didn't. So I am "stealing" your money. If you decide to prosecute me as a common thief, do it in secret. I don't want mother to know.

You hated the fact that the emigration people changed your name Dym to Dort. You told me how our last name meant "smoke." I don't want my dreams to go up in smoke. I want to make them come true. You married a Jewish woman in spite of everything that must have been said against such a move. But you never regretted it, did you? I am sorry, sorry you gave birth to such a funny child. I provoked kids, when I was growing up, into not liking me. I was a victim of their cruelty, their jokes. I can't tell you how many times I was told to get lost. "He's like some damn glue," some kid would say. "Stop hanging around!" was what hurt me most. I could never choose my friends from the most interesting, the best kids. I began to seek out the dregs, the ugliest girls, the most flat-chested ones with greasy hair and bad skins. But even they would turn away from me. I would approach boys who were physically stunted or not too alert mentally, the ones with terminal cases of acne. But even those friendless creatures would tire of me. And I needed people as I needed to breathe.

Hal Hubbard is my dearest friend, but I will make others, among the best, the brightest, the most talented writers of my time. Will they like me only because I will be their publisher? I will never have to hide the fact from them that I am Jewish on my mother's side, because writers don't care about such details. I was miserable working with you, not because I don't love you or did not like being around you. The months I worked for you I spent dreaming my dream to be in Paris, back with Hal, my best friend, of being a publisher. I am grabbing at all of it now. It's my life. Without it I'd just as soon be dead.

Your loving son,
Larry

He went directly from the Paris station to their studio. The welcome he received from Lee was very warm, but he wanted to see Hal. She told him that he was having drinks with Scott and Zelda Fitzgerald and urged him to surprise them at the café. He hurried there, excited beyond his wildest dreams at the thought of being in their presence. He had read both of the novels that Fitzgerald had published. He had great hopes that Fitzgerald, along with Hal Hubbard, would belong in the constellation of his star writers. It took him a while to gather up the courage to approach their table. When he finally did, with his arms outstretched toward Hal, there was a moment when he thought Hal's eyes failed to recognize him. Then they narrowed, as if forcing memory.

"Zelda, Scott, this is Larry Wart," Hal said. And then, laughing, he corrected himself, "Larry Dort, for Christ's sake!" He got up and bearhugged Larry, slapped him on the back and ordered him to take a seat. "Larry is the first to believe in me as Numero Uno." He laughed and didn't bother to explain. "He worked on the *Chicago Trib* with me."

"I was just...." Larry began, but Hal waved his arm, stopping the explanation.

Neither that day, nor the following night when he joined Hal and Lee for dinner with Ford Maddox Ford, did Larry dare mention why he had come to Paris, what he hoped to do. Something inside of him told him that Hal would make fun of him. He did not tell Hal about it until a week later.

"Americans published in Paris?" said Hal. "It's a crazy idea. But you were always attracted to the dregs of society, weren't you? I remember how we couldn't walk down the street without you chasing after some wino to give him a handout. Is that what you intend to do here for writers of little talent?"

When he found out that in Hal's opinion nobody from the good writers would want to be published by him, "and that sure includes me," he abandoned all plans for starting what was going to be called Ariel Press. The magazine idea was something else, Hal said. He thought that if it were limited to "works in progress" and included drawings of young American artists as well as poems and stories, he could "get the best to contribute." And with his encouragement, Larry embarked on his only slightly aborted dream.

He asked Lee to be his assistant editor, hoping that she, through Hal, would help him attract contributors to what was simply to be *Ariel*, a quarterly publication. As in Chicago, she talked to him about Hal, for he filled her life and she was just as much in love with him as she had been then.

"He seems so strong, so self-confident," she said to Larry one day, "so self-assured, and yet he's very vulnerable. He hopes after finishing *The Slim Taber Stories* to start on his novel, but he's behind his own schedule and sometimes he seems to me like a frightened little boy whose father shot himself. Do you know what that can mean to a child? Do you know how a wound like that can fester? At times when he is very alone, and it could be in a crowd, a shadow comes over his eyes. Sometimes I think that he must know the dread his father knew and I wonder if he will ever get over it. Oh, Larry, he's as strong and as brave and as confident as you think, but somewhere inside he's very frightened."

"Not Hal," Larry protested. "He's not afraid of anything. Never was! Never will be! That's one of the great things about him, his lack of fear, his courage."

"Would anyone have to cultivate courage the way he does if he wasn't frightened?" she asked Larry once after Hal had taken a friend's dare and raced him in a car and cracked up and could have been killed in the crash, but escaped with only a concussion.

Because they both loved him, they blamed the accident on his sudden mood changes, the vicious words he had for other writers, his many unkindnesses. When the doctor declared him free of any effects of the concussion, they thought the change in him was due to his eagerness to have the stories come out as a book. They all expected great reviews, but the book was being delayed. When the writing went well, Larry and Lee agreed, no one could be as charming, as entertaining, as funny as Hal.

When the galleys of *The Slim Taber Stories* were sent off to his New York publisher, Hal decided to celebrate by going to Spain. He had already outlined his novel, its background was to be an international car race from San Sebastian to Madrid. He wanted to arrive there a week earlier; get the feel of the atmosphere, interview the mechanics and car owners before the races. On the evening of the departure Larry was having dinner with them. He was feeling very depressed over their leaving and over the fact that he would be unable to publish anything of Hal's in the first issue of *Ariel*, which was coming out in September.

"That beaten-dog face," Hal suddenly said. "Would it brighten up if we asked you to come along with us?"

Even before he could reply, Lee was urging Larry to come with them. He had to have a vacation. He needed a rest. The first issue was ready for the printers, he had no more work to do. He'd never been to Spain. They would have fun. They would go to Pamplona for the bullfights and see more of them in Madrid. And there was the

Prado they all wanted to see. Although such an invitation, coming from both of them, would have delighted Larry at any time, some instinct told him he should not go. He began to make excuses. But they dismissed each of them and, like children who would not be denied, chanted him into submission to their wishes. The presentiment of disaster receded slowly for Larry, only to return as he settled himself in the back seat and they were taking off for Spain. It was early morning and there was little traffic and Hal was driving over sixty miles an hour and taking curves at only a little less than that.

"Ezra Pound told me the other day," Hal said, "that all Jews are afraid of speed. Is that true, Larry?"

A few times back in Chicago, Hal had tried to elicit information from Larry about how it was for him, being a Jew, and each time Larry had protested that he was not the proper person to ask. For some reason he did not feel Jewish. Neither he nor his mother ever went to the synagogue, and she never observed any of the orthodox practices. Besides, he told Hal, his father was not Jewish, and maybe, because he had been brought up in the agnostic atmosphere with few references to Jews, there was nothing in his life that made him feel a Jew.

Years later, thinking back on that day, and he thought of it often, he wished he had asked Hal to stop the car. He should have gone home instead of to Spain.

"I didn't know you were Jewish," Lee said, turning back and looking at him. "Now I can use that great cliché and say without lying that my best friend is Jewish."

"I'm only half Jewish, on my mother's side," Larry said, hoping that would close the subject, which made him uncomfortable.

"You're a Jew. That's the law. If you were Jewish on your father's side, it wouldn't make you a Jew." Hal put his foot down hard on the accelerator and looked at Larry in the rearview mirror. "Ezra wasn't wrong! You do look scared!"

During the trip Larry felt as if he had somehow returned to his childhood and was the victim, once again, of a bully.

The painful fact was that Hal, his idol and friend, was the bully this time. Two years later, while reading *From Zero to Fifty*, Larry saw himself monstrously distorted as an unpleasant young Jew, a coward and a bore, in love with the hero's girl. In the novel, he ruins the trip to Spain for both protagonists and ultimately causes the death of a car racer. Although few of the details of the plot paralleled the details of their trip, there was enough shock of recognition to make the pain very real and lasting.

For the next thirty years, Larry was to live with that pain and the realization that Hal had betrayed his friendship. Then he wrote his own account of the trip to Spain. *A Recollection,* when it finally found a publisher, appeared to cutting reviews. In *The New York Times,* the critic ended his review with these words:

> To summarize finally what is wrong with Larry Dort, both as writer and man, it is his affinity for suffering and forgiveness. In his book, *A Recollection*, Mr. Dort is no more exasperating than Howard Dull in Hal Hubbard's *From Zero to Fifty*. But that is small comfort to the reader and probably no comfort at all to Mr. Dort's friends.

The act of cowardliness in Hal's book, Larry thought, must have been based on the incident that occurred on a moonlit night as they crossed the Spanish border. They were driving past a ranch of brave bulls. Hal had been telling them what he had learned about bulls from books he had read, how the animals are bred and raised and what happens to them after they enter the bullring, on what he called their "deathday." They had stopped the car and watched the bulls standing in groups or alone against the sky. Suddenly Hal jumped out of the car, vaulted the fence and began a race toward the biggest of the animals standing near a tree. Taking off his sweater, he began to cite the bull, and managed to get the giant animal to charge. Since neither Lee nor Larry had ever seen a bullfight, at this range they could not tell how well Hal passed the giant bull, nor how much courage it took to do so.

When he returned to them, glowing with pride, saying that he had chosen the seed bull, the biggest of the lot, one that must have weighed well over a ton, that he thought his *naturales* credible, that he had brushed himself against the bull's flanks and to prove it, he picked several black hairs off his pants, Larry said that it looked pretty easy. Hal looked at him with cold eyes and said, "I'll bet you a thousand francs that you couldn't do it."

They had consumed a lot of wine during dinner, and maybe because Larry felt high, he was able to take the challenge. Grabbing a blanket off the car seat, he vaulted the fence and ran toward the bulls. One of the youngest and smallest of the animals charged toward him, and in the moment that he waited for the bull to reach the blanket, Larry realized with great panic that the animal was a bearer of sharp horns. The fear that gripped his stomach, his throat, his mind, was like nothing he had ever experienced. He did not run away but stood as if paralyzed, unable to think or move. And yet, without his knowledge or will, his hands holding the blanket did move as the bull approached and the sharp horns followed the moving target. The idea that the bull was after the piece of blanket and not his body enabled Larry to receive two more charges, but he extended his hands as far as he could and the bull's closeness was no longer there. He could not hear the exhaled breath of the animal, nor the sound of the hooves against the earth. He thought that he could go on doing this forever, but on the fourth charge, the bull tripped on the blanket and Larry let go and began to run away from the horns, away from the danger, scrambling and falling over the fence. When, from the safety of the road, he looked back, he saw the animal attacking the blanket again and again. He had not needed to run.

"That was wonderful, Larry!" Lee had exclaimed as he got into the car. "Now Hal owes you. . . ." Before she could finish, Hal's words, cold, unforgiving, cut her off.

"You're a coward! Only a coward could have chosen the smallest bull. And that bull will kill some poor bastard in the bullring. You'll be responsible because fighting bulls are never fought on foot before they reach the ring."

"But you . . ." Lee tried to say, but again he cut her off.

"That was a seed bull, and it will never be sold to a bullring." Hal looked at Larry, his eyes cold, forcing Larry to look away. "Only cowards drop their lures and run away like you did. I did not bet that you'd be a coward. I bet you wouldn't fight the seed bull. You owe me."

And then Hal went over the fence again and slowly approached the bull that was still tossing the blanket around. Pushing the bull away, he retrieved it, and as the bull stood watching him, he calmly walked back to the car, got in, and drove away. It seemed to Larry that from then on, and for the rest of the trip, Hal could not bear to look at him without disgust.

Several times in the next few days Larry wanted to talk to Hal about that night. He tried to tell him that he had been terrified and didn't know what he was doing. He tried to get Hal's reassurance that he would not be responsible for some bullfighter's death, but Hal would only say, "What's done is done." Hal himself mentioned the incident only once, when they were dining with the young bullfighter, Manolo Olivar, one night in Pamplona.

"My friend, here," Hal said, pointing to Larry, "fought a bull once. He must have weighed all of two hundred pounds, slightly under the weight of my friend, who offered the animal a blanket of mine to sleep on."

The young bullfighter did not ask any questions, but Larry saw a chance to put his fears to rest. "I only gave that little bull four passes. Is it true that I've spoiled that animal? Will a bullfighter die because of what I've done?"

Manolo Olivar smiled and placed his hand on Larry's shoulder. "There is no need to worry. A bull learns all there is to know in about twenty-five minutes. You gave him too short a lesson to become a man killer."

In the first moments of relief, Larry failed to notice the expression on Hal's face. When he did look at Hal, it was to say, "You see, you were wrong!" He thought it was these words that made Hal seem so furious. He had hoped that his relief in the fact that he would not be responsible for some unknown bullfighter's death would be shared by Hal. But the same news that brought happiness to him seemed to have brought only merciless anger to Hal.

The rest of the trip was pure hell for Larry. Without saying anything, Hal made it plain to him that he wished he were not around. Incidents from Larry's childhood seemed to keep repeating themselves. Though he was now taking the same punishment as he had been used to while growing up, it hurt more now. He could hear inside his head the words of so many who had said "stop hanging around." And yet he hung around.

Both he and Lee pretended that Hal's black moods could be explained away by the fact that he was not writing and was drinking more than usual. Hal's obvious dislike of Larry, his silences, his looks of contempt, Lee would dismiss as "indigestion." One afternoon, while she went shopping in Madrid, Larry begged Hal to tell him what was wrong. "What have I done?" But Hal looked at him as if not understanding and came back with a puzzled question: "What the hell are you talking about now?"

"He needs to write," Lee would say. "When he's not working, there is some wildness in him, some hatred. It's not you, Larry. It's not me. It's something inside of him that seems to eat him up. Once we're back in Paris and he's working, it will all be like it once was."

But it wasn't. After their return to Paris, whenever they would see each other, Larry felt mocked by Hal. He was in the habit of introducing Larry now as "the young *torero*, also publisher of unknown talents." And it was difficult, or impossible, for him to look Larry straight in the eye. Was it something that would have happened anyway, in time, Larry often wondered. Or did it really have to do with that night? Was it possible that his crime was simply jumping the fence and approaching the bull? He came to feel that this was what Hal could not forgive him for. He should have known better. He should have been satisfied to let Hal do the caping. He should never have invaded his turf of courage.

In September Hal's book of stories was published, and the reviews began to arrive from his publisher. They were very good, but Hal was not happy with them. On September 18, Larry gave a party for all the writers living in Paris on the occasion of the first issue of *Ariel*. The morning of the party, a batch of reviews included one from *The Cleveland Plain Dealer*. Lee called Larry to tell him that the review made Hal so angry that he would not be coming to the party. She read the review to him.

> In Slim Taber, the young author, Hal Hubbard, seemed to have reincarnated himself as the perfect American boy. The Taber family is the ideal American family. Their lives the American Dream come true. Although there are disappointments and minor tragedies, what this reviewer misses is the tragic sense, the despair and the uneasy dread, with which we, living in this country are often familiar with. The stories are excellently written, and Hal Hubbard is definitely one of our most important writers. He might even be said to have reinvented the English language, shortened it into a most manageable tool, but as a man he has obviously not become personally acquainted with the gamut of human emotions, and that includes the seamy or tragic sides

of life. Possibly war, personal acquaintance with it, would have given him that dimension that is lacking in this book.

"He left raging mad," Lee told Larry, "shouting about the man being a goddamned liar, that he would sue the pants off him for defaming him. He did go to war in Italy, you see, and he has known tragedy. My God, what bigger tragedy could there be than seeing your own father commit suicide!"

The party in honor of Larry's magazine went well, everyone said, even Lee who came without Hal and worried because she did not know where he had gone. But neither for her nor Larry could the party be a success without Hal. The presence of Joyce, Pound, Hemingway, the Fitzgeralds, Stein and Toklas, among others, could not make up for the fact that Hal was not there.

A few months after their return from Spain, Larry got an unexpected letter from Carole Scolfield. She was bored in Chicago. She had been thinking of coming to Paris for some time. Would he consider living with her, giving their "relationship" a try? She didn't have marriage in mind, just "an arrangement that would be mutually profitable." He wrote back that whatever she wanted, he wanted too. He moved out of the one room apartment and rented a small two-bedroom apartment with a view of the Seine and filled it with flowers for her arrival.

The day after she came, Hal and Lee gave a party. Later that night, while lying in bed, Carole began to ask him about Hal as if she had never heard of him.

"Don't you remember," he reminded her, "how furious you'd get whenever I'd talk about him?"

"All I know is that he's the only real man I've ever met. What I mean," she pushed her face against Larry's shoulder, "is that like nobody else I know, he's totally male. It's not just sexual, it's as if all the instincts of a male were alive and working in him. And I don't mean he's a primitive, either." She lay back, her eyes on the ceiling, thinking. "You know what it is? What Hal has going for him is the kind of supremacy that animals have. You know, when one male has a whole herd of females and the other males just watch and know they can't challenge him? I mean lions and wild horses are like that, and I think elephants and other animals, like seals or otters. Sometimes the head male is challenged, but the fight always seems rigged because that real one, that male that all females gravitate to, he's better than the others."

She had changed, too. She had never talked like this, or this much, and had never seemed to think things out aloud. She used to be sure of certain facts and just stated them, but now she was trying to formalize concepts in her head that fascinated her. She was no longer the dumb, pretty debutante, she was a woman. But did she think Hal the man for her, Larry wondered.

"At the party tonight," she went on, "there were what, a dozen men? They were all attractive, some much more handsome than Hal Hubbard. But Hal was the head male there. It had nothing to do with what he was or what he said. It's just that he didn't lose it, that essence of maleness, and they don't have it anymore. I think it's disappearing from the species. Evolution. Maybe one day it will all turn around, and the females will be like that. Some will be more dominant than others. Maybe he's the last of the true males, and that's why he's so special."

"I think," Larry said, "what makes him special is that he has a great talent."

"For writing?" Carole asked.

"Yes, for writing."

"He might have that, but he's got a greater talent. For living."

During their lovemaking that night, she still talked of Hal. Larry asked her what she thought of Lee, but she dismissed Lee with, "She's not good enough for him."

Larry said that Hal loved his wife very much and to that Carole said, "He will tire of her." By then, Lee was pregnant. She told the news to Larry before she told it to Hal.

"It happened in Spain. The night you and Hal jumped over that fence."

"How do you know?" he had asked her.

"I know," she said. "And that's why I wanted you to know first, because it was that night that seemed to have affected your friendship. But it gave us a child."

In a strange way he felt connected to them even more strongly now, and he wished desperately that Hal would forgive him for whatever he was guilty of. He was glad that Hal seemed to like Carole. The four of them saw a lot of each other, playing bridge once a week and going out to dinner, but whenever they were together, that barrier between Larry and Hal was still there. Larry was Lee's best friend now and Carole was Hal's.

By the time Lee was in her seventh month of pregnancy, Carole replaced her as Hal's tennis partner. It was she who brought the news to Larry one day that Hal would be going to hunt in Africa if he sold an article about Paris to *The Saturday Evening Post.*

"He's so damned poor, and he won't take any money from me," she said.

"Did you offer him any?" Larry asked.

"Of course! He wants to go to Africa, hunting, and I could take him there."

"He isn't used to having ladies pay his fare."

"Damn those stupid conventions! He's starving, almost. He counts his pennies and doesn't have fun being poor."

"He'll make it on his own," Larry said.

"Why waste time? Why didn't he want to take even a loan from me?"

"Maybe because he knows that you'd want something in return and considers the price too high?"

She was angry although he did not say directly to her what he thought—that she wanted to buy Hal away from Lee. And because he was sure this was her intent, he added, "I don't know if you've noticed, but Hal is very much in love with his wife and she is very much in love with him."

"Being poor together doesn't guarantee a happy marriage," she said. And then, reverting to her spoiled little girl tone of voice, she said, "I don't see why he'd want to drag her, pregnant as she is, to Africa on a hunting safari."

A few days later, she got the idea that Larry and she should go along if the Hubbards went. She begged like a child, repeating endlessly, "Please, please, let's go!" It was impossible for him, he told her. He had too much to do. But she kept insisting until finally he told her how disastrous his trip to Spain had been. "I'll never take another chance at traveling and being mistreated by Hal," he said.

"If your trip with them was so terrible, it wasn't Hal's fault. It must have been yours. Or Lee's."

He had learned, in the months they had lived together, about her inability to be critical of Hal, her blindness to his many cruelties. He had accepted the fact that she had a crush on Hal but was sure that it was a case of unrequited love. Hal, with his writer's insights, could see through Carole. Her shallowness must be obvious to him. Larry felt sure that she presented no threat to Hal's marriage.

A week before they were supposed to leave for Africa, Lee asked Larry to have lunch with her alone. She looked exhausted and her face was pale.

"I can't go," she told him. "And I can't tell Hal I can't go. I think he's throwing some sort of challenge at me, a challenge to some duel that he wants to take place between us and I don't want to rise to the bait. What should I do?"

'Don't go," he said.

"But he wants me to. He bought me a Manlicher-Schoenaur 6.5 and a pair of very large man's pants with pockets all over, and he claims that even if the baby was to be born prematurely, I'd be able to carry the child inside one of the pockets. He's so looking forward to it. In the summer it would be too hot, he says. This is the perfect time. He wants to go before the baby is born. He says he'd write wonderful stories about Africa, and when I said that he'd be better off going without me, he said he could neither write nor enjoy the trip without me. He won't hear about my not going. God, I wish I could go into labor now."

She began to cry then, putting her face in her hands, and Larry tried to console her. The trip didn't matter, Hal loved her enough to understand if she would only tell him to postpone it. And then, through tears, stopping often to blow her nose, she told him that she and Hal had had a fight. He'd had a bad morning, his writing was going nowhere, he was behind his schedule. Hal had lashed out at her when she suggested that Larry's *Ariel* magazine should publish a chapter of his novel. She had leaned her head over his shoulder and he had shouted at her, "I will not be disturbed by you or anyone else! I will not have you hanging over my shoulder while I write! The most important thing in my life is to be left alone in the mornings. I must have that time. I will not have you destroy my life!'

Larry listened to her as she went on, saying she feared that things were going wrong with him, with their marriage. She dreaded that, with the baby coming, what was wrong would get worse until there would be no defense, no knowledge of what was happening to his gift. She said she could never bear it, being with him at that future date when he would stand among his own ruins and not be able to build his way back.

"I sometimes see him, not in a dream, but as if this was reality and he were an old man. Not old in years, but in lack of a future. Sometimes I see in his eyes some desolation, despair. You know, Larry, there is a great dread in him, some damnable stain. I'm sure it's his father's suicide. He thinks he will kill himself one day like his father, like his grandfather, and I can't bear the thought of it. . . ."

Larry put his hand on hers and waited until she composed herself. He had always believed her to be strong and able to cope with everything. Now she seemed vulnerable and very much in need of help. And he didn't know how to help her.

"You see," she said, trying to smile, "my problem now is to be happy in spite of everything, because I believe that the baby feels what I feel. So I've been doing everything, short of standing on my head, not to think about those things. The future and what I see ahead for him. I love him very deeply, but I would not hesitate to leave him if I thought that he was starting on some irreversible downward curve. Damn it, Larry, can I see into the future? Why is it that I have nightmares about Hal when I'm awake?"

"You're worried. About money and the coming baby. . . ."

"No, it's not that. I'm worried about Hal. The other day while we were having lunch with Gertrude Stein and her Alice, and darn it, I'm always uncomfortable there, Miss Stein doesn't like me or at least always ignores me, and I'm abandoned to Alice's care and we talk recipes. Anyway, at one point, I overheard Hal say, 'What do you women write with since you don't have sperm?' I was so frightened, so surprised by his question that I didn't hear what she replied. All I could think of was, does he think our lovemaking somehow diminishes his writing talents? Larry, I'm losing my innocence when it comes to Hal. He can be so mean! I wasn't going to tell you, but you might as well know. That same day at Miss Stein's, you know what he said about you?"

"Don't tell me," Larry said. "I hurt easily when it comes to Hal."

She didn't tell him then, but later he asked her, saying that he would not be hurt, that he wanted to know what Hal had said to Miss Stein about him. And she told him that he had said, "He's a horse's ass. He has some crazy idea that everyone needs help. He's appointed himself to bind the wounds of writers of little talent, to dish out hot soup of a publication to the literary derelicts. He preaches his own brand of salvation. I shall save you through publication in *Ariel*! He's dangerous as long as he's got enough money to publish and give false dreams to those who'd be better off as bricklayers than writers."

By then Hal and Carole were in Africa together. Carole managed it somehow; on the day before Hal and Lee were to leave, she replaced Lee on the trip as she had replaced her at tennis. During the time they were gone, Larry spent most of his time with Lee, talking with her, holding her hand, and trying to quiet her fears of the future. She showed him a letter Hal had written her once after a fight when she left the studio to walk in the rain:

> You're my kitten, and I had thrown you outdoors in such nasty weather and that was cruel and unmerited punishment and I shall not do it ever again, because my kitten is too small and her fur too thin. There will never be a punishment for anything, Ever again. I understand and I hope my kitten does too, that the writing is not all that important. It's been a bad day, but the night will heal all wounds. Wounding each other is something that we will never do.

Hal, before leaving for Africa, had decided that they would stay in the studio after the baby's birth because they both loved it and the rent was cheap. But that instead of working at home he would work in cafés, parks, museums, wherever, and would come back home after lunch "for loving and warming his kitten." She believed now that the worst was behind them and showed Larry a note Hal had written her before he left.

> I know my kitten will be well while I'm gone and will take care of herself and what's ours. Kittens don't understand everything, but they forget and forgive and have faith.
>
> I need this trip. I need it for my writing and for you. We'll start again where we started before, and our only fear will be that we love each other too much. We can live with that.

They were supposed to be gone for a month, but they stayed for almost two. Lee shared Hal's letters with Larry, Carole having written him none. In the first one, Hal told Lee about the excitement he felt when he shot his first lion and his first rhino, and how they were going to go after a bull elephant the next day, how the country looked and how many ideas he had for stories, even novels. In another letter he wrote:

> Carole is a good sport and a good soldier. Never complaining and putting up with the pace we are setting. She got an ibex with a clean shot through the heart and is no trouble, for which I am grateful.

He mentioned her only once more, in his last letter, saying that he had made a deal with her:

> I wasn't going to keep any heads as trophies because they are so expensive to mount, but Carole, who has filthy rich parents, wanted everything I shot and will have them all mounted. I told her she could do that only if she were willing to sell them back to me when, and if, I have the money. She offered to give them to me, but of course I refused. She's been a good girl, only spoiled by the way money can spoil one.

"Do you love Carole?" Lee asked Larry one day.
"Before I met you I thought she was the most wonderful girl in the world."
"You're not in love with me?" she said, laughing.
He shook his head.
"Do you love her?" she insisted.
"Yes," he said, lying again. For her.
Lee never said aloud what they were both thinking: that Carole was in love with Hal. Larry knew he was running out of luck with her, but he was still sure that Lee's future was not threatened by Carole. He knew them both, Hal and Carole. He thought that maybe they would have an affair, maybe that was inevitable under the circumstances, but Hal, having had Lee, could never be happy with another woman.

They kept hanging on to the idea that Hal, once back, would be changed. For the better, to what he was in Chicago.

"He won't talk or care about the competition so much," Lee would say. "He kept judging himself against other writers rather than himself. He keeps thinking that the novel will make or break him, but I'm sure he will acquire a longer range view of his career as a writer. After all that killing that he'll have done in Africa—oh God, Larry, why is he killing all those beautiful animals? The way he was so excited, so happy to be going to Africa. But what for? To slaughter!"

A week before her delivery, she began to talk of not caring about anything in the past or present. She wanted to concentrate all her attention on the future. She made a list of all the things she and Hal had in common, all the qualities he possessed, and all the things she loved about her life with him—and she included "being poor."

"How rich is Carole?" she asked.

"I don't really know," Larry said. "Their house in Chicago is nice. . . ."

"I shouldn't worry about that. Hal hates the rich."

Sometimes Larry felt that she indeed could see into the future of her marriage. Once she said, "If he has an affair with Carole in Africa, I won't think of it as adultery. He will be thinking of it as appeasing lust, as manly behavior, a pleasant, carnal interlude. But I don't know what I'll do if he continues the affair here. What if Carole is really after him? Will she get him, will she take him away from me?"

"If she tries, fight for him."

"No, I couldn't do that. She won't get him unless he wants her. And if he does want her, I'll leave him to her."

She kept hoping they would return before the birth of the baby. But they did not. Larry was with her throughout the birth pains, through all her talk of Hal.

"If things get impossible for me or for him with me, I shall go away. I'll take my baby to Montana and live there with my grandfather. I hope it's a boy, and Hal hopes it's a girl. If it's a boy, it will be good for him growing up in Montana. He will love growing up there just as I loved it. You know, Larry, there is something about those men who work as lumberjacks and loggers that is very fine. They are part of what they do, sure of who they are. They have an advantage

Hal doesn't have, with all his gifts. He doesn't know yet who he can be."

And her first words, after a difficult birth, even before she asked Larry if she had had a boy or a girl, were about Hal. "Did he come back?"

Larry had a strong presentiment of disaster now. She was not like him. She would not be around to watch Hal turn away from her. He, for himself, had decided not to leave Carole unless she left him. But he would be cautious with both of them, on guard against unnecessary hurts.

When Larry saw Carole at the railroad station, he knew that what he had expected had happened. There was a softness to her eyes that had not been there before. He had thought she would let him know right away that their love affair was over, but she did not choose to do so. She was good at pretending that nothing had changed between them. When he asked her, "Do you want to go to the apartment?" she said, "Of course." In bed that night she told him she wanted to "get educated." She intended to spend most of her days at Sylvia Beach's bookstore reading books that Hal told her she must read. After they made love, Larry asked her if Hal had made love to her because he thought it was important for them to be truthful, but she only looked at him wide-eyed and said, "How could you ask such a thing?" He felt ashamed for everything: for her need to lie, for his to make her lie, and especially for the sadness that he now felt.

For the next few months Larry worked harder and stayed away from the apartment as much as he could. On several occasions, he detected signs of Hal's presence there; once his pipe had been left on the table, another time his scarf lay near the bed. He himself was missing his key from his key ring, and when he asked Carole for hers so he could make a duplicate, she found excuses not to let him have it. "I'll be home by the time you come back from the office. You don't really need a key." What he disliked even more than her deception was his own feelings. He almost took pleasure in the fact that Hal was bedding down his girl.

Once he saw Hal and Carole enter a hotel when he was on his way to lunch. He was afraid of talking to Carole about his knowledge of her affair with Hal, afraid that it would bring things to a head. He hoped that Hal would tire of her. He didn't want to do anything to endanger the marriage. He avoided seeing Lee. He hoped she was too busy with the baby to know what was going on. She sounded cheerful when they talked on the phone, telling him that Hal was writing well, going out in the morning to do his work in a nearby café. The baby made it hard for her to meet Hal for lunches, and he did not like to come home to eat. She saw little of him, she said, but he seemed happy. "How's Carole?" she would ask. "Fine," he would say. "She reads a lot of books, trying to improve her mind."

"Hal told me he had given her a whole list of books she should read."

He was cautious with Lee as he was with Carole and Hal. He felt uncomfortable with the three of them now, awaiting some disaster, while distrusting himself and his own feelings.

Hal had been writing ever since he came back. While in Africa, he had drafted a couple of short stories and, within five months, had four of them ready. He asked Larry one day if he would "for old times' sake" type his stories during a long weekend that he planned to take with Lee and the baby in the country. They wanted to get away from Paris and the summer's heat for a few days and Larry was only too happy to oblige. He met them at the railroad station because Hal planned to work on the stories until the last moment.

Years later, he thought of it as the only unnatural, perhaps supernatural, thing that had ever happened to him. He lost the manuscript. He had stopped in a bar and then had gone back to the office. From there, he went to a restaurant for dinner. Somewhere, somehow, the hand-written manuscript got lost. He knew Hal had no copies, and he had even destroyed the notes for the stories, and Larry was in an absolute panic. Again and again he retraced his steps, asking everyone, looking everywhere. And after midnight, he walked into the office of *Paris Soir* and bought a full page advertisement offering a very large reward for the return of the lost manuscript.

Hal was to return on Monday, and on Sunday, in total despair, he had a wild hope that if Carole knew the stories he could somehow reconstruct them, a notion so foolish that Carole laughed at it.

"If you think you could do this, you're really an idiot. And Hal must already know what I'm only now finding out." No, he had not read anything to her while they were in Africa. She kept asking Larry again and again, "But how could you have lost them?" until she brought him to tears. There was no logical explanation, except that he was born with some damnably destructive streak that now worked against his best friend. It was Carole's idea that he go away rather than face Hal.

"Where will I go?" he asked her, for by now he was ready to do whatever she suggested.

"Go back to the States. No, better still, why don't you go to Poland? You once said you wanted to live there for awhile, to dig up your roots."

She packed his suitcase and saw him off an hour before the Hubbards were to arrive. "Don't worry about anything," she told him, "I'll explain everything to Hal."

He felt like a coward. He made her promise she would wire him at the Hotel Europejski about Hal's reaction to the news. She promised she would. The next day he received her wire.

> HAL SAID HE WILL NEVER BE ABLE TO WRITE THE STORIES AGAIN. YOU BETTER STAY AWAY.

Within two weeks Larry received a letter from Lee. She said in it that she was leaving Hal.

> Don't blame yourself for the loss of the stories. He used the loss to make our lives unbearable, but it's really Carole. She wants him. And I must let him go. Because he wants her.

She was going back to Montana with the baby and would be getting a divorce.

Carole wrote him a short note in which she explained that Lee was leaving Hal because "he didn't come home one night. She's a very possessive lady, that one." That day Larry went back home to Chicago. He went back to work with his father to repay him for the money he always felt he stole from him. A year later he read, in *The Chicago Tribune*, the review of Hal Hubbard's first novel. In the review a character called Howard Dull was described as "one of the most unsavory characters in modern fiction." He knew, even before he read the book, that Hal had taken his revenge on him.

When the short stories were lost Hal found it easy to go back to work on *From Zero to Fifty*. He had had a very hard time writing the book because of Howard Dull's character. He didn't know how he would face Larry. The day he came back from his long weekend to discover, from Carole, the loss of his manuscript, he wrote:

> There are some people who stain lives with the poison they were born with, and the stain is what is dangerous about them. They do not know, they never see how they are able to stain others with whatever their own lives are stained with. Howard Dull brought with him the stain of destructiveness wherever he went, to any life he touched. But they were no longer near him. He was gone from their lives. What they did not know was the fact that his stain was to remain with them, like cancer, unseen and undetected. They themselves might have helped ruin their lives later on, but it was Howard Dull who had marked them all for ruin.

That was how the novel ended, and when he wrote those words and reread them he remembered what Larry had once said to him in Chicago, "Lee is the best thing you'll ever have. If you ever lose her, you'll have made the one fatal mistake in your life."

The phone rang, and he let it ring. It sat by his bedside, and the ringing entered his brain with the sharpness that his ears did not allow. A nurse knocks at his door and he pretends to be asleep as the door opens, but she knows all the tricks and tells him Sally wants to talk to him. He waits for the nurse to go out of the room, and now he lies to Sally, his biggest death-wisher, his mistress, his keeper.
"I was taking a walk," he says.
"I just wanted to tell you that everyone will be there for your birthday party. I thought it would make you glad."
"I'm very happy," he says. "You've been a good soldier. Was it hard to round them up?"
"You sound wonderful!"
"I feel great."
"Do you really, darling?"
"Never better." He makes his voice tired with sincerity.
"Am I interrupting something?" she asks.
She has interrupted the most painful memory yet to come. The ruin of his life, his fatal mistake.
"Just a walk."

"Not down memory lane," she says and laughs, gently so as not to hurt any wounds.

"No, just down the corridor."

"I am sorry," she says.

"It wasn't much of a corridor."

"Don't you walk outside? The garden's pretty around the clinic."

"Today I walked inside, but later I'll probably go outside." He feels at the end of his rope and wishes she would take all the right signals and be hanging up soon. "How is everybody?" he asks so she would not take the signal to hang up, not from him.

"Everybody's fine and wishes you well, and they can't be happier about being invited."

"You're not too tired from preparations, I hope. Don't tire yourself out, just a simple party. Have everything catered."

"Darling, you know I'll love this work," she says and laughs gently again. "I think it's such a super idea you had. And I'm so glad the doctors feel you'll be just fine in time for it."

"I'm doing the best I know how," he says and then laughs himself. "I want the cake and to eat it too, with old friends. No resentments, no bad memories, just fun and some good food and fine wines."

"I've ordered your favorites, didn't want to take any chances locally so called Sherry's in New York." She waits for him to object to the cost. To get angry perhaps and accuse her of trying to put them "in the poorhouse," but he doesn't take the bait, he makes her wait a moment for him to bite.

"I was going to suggest exactly that," he says and smiles at her surprised response. She must be surprised, she takes a quick breath.

"I thought you might be mad about how much. . . ."

"Not to worry," he interrupts and smiles again. "Money is to be spent. That was part of what went wrong, me worrying. Never again. Never, as long as I live," he waits a second, "and I hope I'll live a long time," he says, and this time he has to help the corner of his left lip and puts a finger to enlarge it, and then laughs. "We have enough to last us a lifetime even if there won't be any left to give away after we're dead."

She laughs loudly and merrily now, having swallowed his bait, and he wants to reel her in all the way to the boat that is sinking, but he doesn't dare, he's getting a headache.

"Maria said this morning that she had offered mass for your health. I will too, it works miracles."

"It's always good to have God on one's side," he says. *Hang up* he wants to yell and knows he won't.

"I better hang up now, darling," she says. "I don't want to wear you out with my happiness."

"Happiness doesn't wear me out. From now on that's all I want."

She is beginning to cry and will keep crying by the phone after hanging up.

"Goodbye, dearest," she says, and he can even see her tears run down her cheeks. Her cheeks are suffering in the desert dryness and now are getting watered.

"Goodbye, darling," he says, and then, taking a chance at heaving, he sends her a kiss into the receiver. And he hangs up, gently. She will be calling back the doctors, or maybe she'll stay on to talk to some of them. What happened, she will ask. That was the best conversation we've had in years. She'll want more. And they might play along. They might want him out. They might even have stopped spying on him. He would do the clinic no harm by leaving for a weekend. Or forever. He goes to the TV and turns it on. A game of greed is on, and when the TV is on maybe they can't watch him, can't spy on his thoughts. He had to be alone now because it's important to get the sequence of events leading up to the fatal mistake of his life.

The car accident starts those events. He is never the same after that. He begins to think there is less time. He has to hurry now. Writing has to be speeded up, and instead of one finely honed page he thinks he must do at least five each day before noon. It doesn't happen. And he's trapped by his haste. He writes fast, and continuously, and Lee is always there, in the room. Yolanda is no longer spying on him from above. She's back in the States. But he feels that she is still looking at him through the binoculars. He isn't letting Lee know that what he writes in such haste is crap. But he loves her and tells her and makes her suffer the pain he feels. His talent was meant to be used slowly, and he wants to speed it up. And speeded up it disappears. And he doesn't know what to do. He can't slow down because he's a marked man. He drinks more, which doesn't help. His head is soaked with wine, his brain swimming helplessly, drowning. It's just a matter of time. And the others are forging forward. Zelda is good for Fitzgerald. He can write best when facing the dread of what she is doing to him.

Hemingway was working well and seemed happy in his marriage. Among all of them, the promising and the proven writers, he mistrusted, and later got to dislike Ernest Hemingway the most. They were alike in so many ways. Both attracted people with whatever it was in their personalities that seemed to act like a magnet. Both had lost their fathers to suicide. Both had wives they loved. And yet he resented him most because of the fundamental difference that existed between them. Hal felt that life was worthless, and Hemingway had already convinced himself that it was very much worthwhile. When Hal began to suspect that he had reached his peak and everything from then on was going to be downhill for him, he began to envy Hemingway, who was just starting out. It seemed to Hal then that Ernest could have been a much younger brother and not at all his contemporary. Hal began to look on him and the others as belonging to a generation that would somehow get ahead of him, writing about a world he would never know.

Hal hated thinking of himself as outside whatever they were doing, those writers making their mark. He found himself daily filled with an anger directed at himself and everything and everybody, except Lee. It's the writing, not her. It's the others, like Larry, who'd come to Paris to spy on his talent just as much as Yolanda.

Larry begged him to show him a story, one that he was happy with. He was grasping, like the publishers, waiting for the promised Slim Taber stories, and he couldn't come up with them and finally had to write the publisher that there wouldn't be any more. Nobody knew he had made all his rough drafts by the age of twenty-one, that he was rewriting, polishing, editing out of his head, what he wrote inside his head, or jotted down on scraps of paper, but he hadn't come up with a single new one. Was he finished at twenty-one?

Spain was going to fuel the first novel. It had to knock the others down on their collective asses, or he'd be finished as a writer of fiction. He had it outlined pretty well, except he needed a villain. A cloud seeded with disaster. The bull pasture incident provided him with that. He would use it to create the coward he needed to offset the brave. And that night he begged Lee's forgiveness for the deed of treason he would commit, by making love to her. She would never know that the begging for forgiveness turned inside her into a seed of life. They would have a son, conceived the night of his deception. Yolanda deceived, his father deceived, and his mother deceived. All traitors. It ran in the family, bad blood, bad genes in him. And maybe the bad blood would also run in the veins of his son. It would take years to find out. But Lee, who had no bad blood, no poisoned genes, she would give the child purity, straining out anything that had come from him.

"Ready for your session?" They always sneak in, stick their heads inside the door as if the very air in his room were poisoned with deceits that they want no part of. They always claim that they had knocked and he had not heard. He will not quarrel with them again, too much is at stake. He's been an exquisitely good patient, so he can leave for his birth-death-day in Santa Fe.

"I've been waiting for the therapy session," he says and smiles without having to use his finger to help the mouth and puts on his robe. He looks old but not quite finished. He has to bullshit this afternoon in a group. He will join the others and tell them about what, today? Perhaps a little about high school and how he always wanted to be a writer. After all he had goals from the beginning. And later they will all go to the recreation room and make a leather wallet. Busy fingers, etcetera, etcetera, etcetera. The noise of his slippered feet follows him down the corridor, and his mind shuts tight.

Carole Scolfield Hubbard

TWO years after her divorce from Hal, when she was forty-two, Carole found that she had cancer. She knew it had something to do with what went wrong between them. She thought she would have to die of it, not cancer but of what went bad. When did it begin, things going wrong between them? Her doctor said her cancer was three years old. Three years before, she had written the damnable play. Did she write it because she was so good at playing games? Her whole life had been spent playing games.

When Carole was small, her mother was not well, so she learned the game of being a good little girl, quiet and understanding. For the first few years, she knew her mother expected her to tiptoe into her room each morning and each night and gently kiss her pale cheek. With her father, she played the game of doing whatever he wished her to do. He wanted her to become a champion swimmer, something he had failed to be. She had hated the water from the moment he threw her into the lake, and yet she swam for him, bringing back medals, making him believe she would become an Olympic medal winner. But, at fifteen, she began to get cramps each time she went into the pool, until finally her coach had to tell her father that she could no longer compete. It wasn't her fault, she had tried her best. She had played that game to the end.

Later came the game of finishing school, a boarding school that taught her manners and the value of good grooming. When she was eighteen there came the game of making a choice between all the young, eligible men. The parade, during the year of her debut, was endless. She would put each to a test: "The one who won't bore me, I'll get engaged to." But they all bored her, looked the same, danced the same, talked the same, and she knew she could wind each one around her finger. She was looking for a man who would want to wind her around his finger.

The only man Carole met who was different from the others—but whom, like the others, she could dominate—was Larry Dort. She did not find him boring because he talked not about himself or her, but about someone else, a friend. Although she didn't want to give her hand to him, she lent him her body.

In college, she fell desperately in love with one of her professors; he was married, so she learned the game of being a mistress. But he was Catholic and the guilt he felt about her was greater than her attraction. He left Chicago to take a job teaching in England.

Carole had heard that European men were more dominating than the Americans, and she asked her parents to send her to Europe with the understanding that she was going there to find a husband. She was twenty years old, and her parents wished her to be "settled and happy." From all she ever learned, that was to be her final game. And the rules were to stay married. And happy. That was all a woman's life was about.

When she went to Paris, she was going to play the game of being Larry Dort's girl, which was okay because he did make her happy in bed. But bed, she had been told, was not all there was to a relationship. For her, the man she would settle with had to be stronger than she was. When she first saw Hal, she knew he was the one. The game now was for him to leave his wife without appearing to have been taken away from her.

Carole had to guess at the rules, for he never told her what they were. In Africa, she was very good at guessing what the game was: He was the great white hunter. His maleness had a perfect setting.

Hal with a gun in his hand, sighting a charging rhino; Hal naked, washing himself in the river; Hal with the black porters, giving orders; Hal writing in longhand by the setting sun, a glass of gin in his hand; Hal on the cot under the mosquito netting. She was like a shadow, a camp follower, a female presence to look pretty even in the heat and dust. She knew he did not expect more of her than to smile and listen and adore being where he was. She was to be a "good sport," which included not being afraid or complaining and not closing her eyes when she sighted down her light gun at a waterbuck. He told her none of these things, but all of the rules were self-evident.

By not talking much, she would not appear stupid, silly or ignorant—all the things she felt herself to be. By not flirting, she would seem not to lure him. By her silent, supportive presence, throughout the day, by keeping her eyes on him, she would not see all the things that frightened her, and he would never know how much she hated Africa. Where were they anyway? Nairobi? Kenya? If she had only had a chance to look at a map of Africa, perhaps she would not feel so dreadfully lost. The hardest struggle was not to break the rule of seeming not to hold on to him for support. She knew that would be wrong. He hated weakness, and she had to learn to simulate strength. If only he would make love to her.

He didn't for the first three weeks. They went to their separate tents after bidding each other good-night. She had nightmares of wild, charging animals, of colors, of unbearable heat, of thirst and hunger and her flesh rotting in the sun. She thought of bedding down the professional hunter or any of the black gun-carriers, but he would have hated her if she did. So she waited. Each morning she greeted him with a smile, ready to endure anything for him, seeming peacefully content with this life which he so loved and she so detested. And then, one night, she heard him outside her tent, like an animal, breathing hard, clearing his throat, pacing up and down, saw his shadow on the tent walls. She almost forgot all the rules and wanted to cry out to him to come and take her in his arms and hold her and tell her it was all right to cry. But she pretended to be asleep and knew him to be looking at her, deciding to be strong and leaving her untouched. Until the next night, when he knelt down at her side and she opened her eyes to his burning eyes and went quietly into his arms. While everything inside of her was shouting, she remained passively submissive, for that is how he wanted her. It would all be easy with no guilt, no obligations, no morning-after looks of longing.

The unwritten rules of the game in bed were for her not to speak because if she talked, she would give away the secret that she knew how it would all end. What she had to do was to allow him to mold her as if she were a piece of clay and he the sculptor. She waited for him to give her some identity, and each night he allowed her a little bit more until she could moan, then hold him a little, and then he allowed her kisses, but when the passion ebbed there was to be no cuddling. He would get up, as if from a job well done, and leave her to sleep alone. But he wanted her more and more and took her once in the bright sun in the tall grass under the stare of a sleepy lion. Another time, they both climbed up a tree and, in what had been a chimp's bed the night before, they made love. And later still, it became like shooting, for he collected their lovemakings like trophies. In the water which she had hated so much, she made him cry out, "God, you're good!" and she smiled up at him and said, "You made me good."

But it was when they got back to Paris that he himself realized how much work she needed. She read nothing that he approved of; he made her read Dostoevsky and D. H. Lawrence, Huxley, and Sherwood Anderson. While he was working in the mornings, she was to be at Sylvia Beach's bookstore, "boning up" so that they could talk "like human beings together." She let him shape her mind as she had let him shape their lovemaking.

He was in complete charge of her life. He expected her to continue living with Larry "as if nothing had happened." And he would go on living with Lee. They would spend as much time with each other as they could in the afternoons, after he was through working for the day and while Larry was busy at his office and Lee busy with the baby. They would make love in some small hotel, for he now preferred not to use Larry's bed. Going together to a hotel seemed to him decadently French. He told her once that she was his mistress, and another time he told her he needed her. She did not tell him she needed him because she was being careful not to seem dependent on him, not to tie him down, understanding his need to feel free. They never said "I love you" to each other, knowing that by saying it they would make something final that was not yet final. And each knew this because each was playing a game by unspoken rules.

The hardest thing for her to do was to stay on with Larry. After she came back she began to pretend to him that she had caught something in Africa. Something like malaria, except without its symptoms of fever, that left her headachey and nauseous in the evening. She would fall asleep early, now using the other bedroom, often skipping dinner so that she would not have to be touched by him or even talk to him. Everything about him began to irritate her, and if it were not for the afternoons, when she knew she would see Hal, she would have been too miserable and Larry would have known that everything was over between them. But she kept his illusions that she was "out of sorts," and he asked her to see a doctor. "I'll be all right," she said. "They don't know anything about this disease in Paris, but in Nairobi a lot of people suffer from it and recover." Larry believed anything she told him because she was very good at lying.

Larry's losing Hal's manuscript was like a blessing to her. She had no trouble convincing him to leave Paris, for they both knew Larry was too weak to face Hal's anger. She loved and respected the way Hal took the news of his loss from her.

"If it means losing Larry, it was worth it," he said. "Will you miss him?"

"I couldn't bear him," she said.

She moved out of the apartment and into the Plaza Athenée Hotel despite Hal's objections.

"It will cost you a fortune," he said.

"I have a fortune," she replied. She wanted to see him the day she moved into the hotel, see him in the splendid fourposter bed, eating in it the special dinner she had ordered and drinking champagne with her. He was like a child with a new toy, loving the great big bathtub with gold-plated swans for faucets, the sheet-size bathtowels. But by the end of the afternoon, he was berating her again for living in such luxury. And it was then she said to him: "Aren't you tired of being poor?"

"I hate the rich," he said.

"Do you hate me?"

"I love you."

Maybe he hadn't meant it, but he had said it and she clung to those words and knew he would say them again if only they lived together.

The next day she rented an apartment in an old, beautiful building on Ile St. Louis and had the heads of the animals he had shot in Africa delivered from the taxidermist. She spread the skins on the floors and furnished the apartment with antiques, but not opulently, just enough of them to make her feel at home again. The first time he came to see her there, he stayed the night.

Two days later, he called her and told her that Lee had left him, and she was very careful in what she said while her heart beat wildly. She was careful not to express her relief and her great happiness.

"I'm terribly sorry for you," she said.

"It's all right," he told her. "I saw it all ending some time ago." He did not say "when I met you," or "in Africa." He wanted to concentrate on the novel. "I need to finish it now. I know I can if I'm not disturbed. I might not see you for a while."

"That's fine," she told him. "I'll be here. Busy. Reading."

He wanted her exactly as she sounded—undemanding, understanding, and patient. Had she gone to him during the next few weeks, she would have lost him. She knew this instinctively. But she gave him those weeks as she would give him a trap.

When next she saw him, he asked if he could move in with her. The studio he had with Lee had served its purpose. He had finished his novel *From Zero to Fifty* there and didn't want to see it anymore.

From their windows, they could see the Pont Neuf and the statue of Henri Quatre, the Ile de la Cité and the Seine beyond, and Notre Dame. They both loved the apartment more than they thought they should. "I don't want to be enslaved by things and places," he said, "but I've never loved any place more than this and I've never cared about things, but I love those skins and the heads and the furniture. I love it all!"

The narrow streets of the island enchanted them. There were little shops where they would get their wines and breads, cheeses and fine cuts of meat and fish. He enjoyed eating well, and she had learned, in her finishing school, to cook well, and they would have picnic lunches on the banks of the Seine. He would fish, and she would read. Once or twice a week they would go out to dinner at the Tour d'Argent, not far from their apartment. They did not miss the Left

Bank and he did not miss his friends. The island enveloped them and they embraced it, for their world was both large and small now and they were its boundaries.

When it finally came, the presence of mutual love, it came like the torrents of spring. Unexpected, drowning them both, invigorating their bodies and enchanting their minds. They both thought it a miracle. She knew that the possibility of it had existed ever since that first evening he saw her. She had waited for it to come out, recognizing it when it did as an old friend. He was overpowered by its newness.

They hungered after each other and were drunk with the enormity of what they felt. All the games ceased, and she discovered this fantastic reality, much better than any fantasy she had ever had.

"Let's never worry about it lasting," he would tell her, and she obeyed him.

And later, out of their isolation, their insular world, they bravely ventured forth. "Let's never be afraid of people. They can't take what we have away from us." And she believed him.

He would put her and himself to tests. Sometimes, the darkness would overshadow him and, in that mood that always translated into his father's message, he would watch her to see if she could guess at some future dread as Lee could. But she seemed oblivious of the future. And that's what he loved most about her, and told her so. That she lived in the present and damn the past and the future. So she learned all that was expected of her: to never let anything from the past, or any presentiment of the future, infringe on the territory he had mapped out for her.

He loved being her teacher and took her to the Musée of Luxembourg and the Louvre and Jeu de Paume and the galleries. He explained to her what made great art and how the artists, the great ones, didn't give a damn about what people thought and always followed some inner light of genius and how the future generations would always discover that light. Often, she thought, he was talking about his own genius while explaining to her other geniuses, but she would quickly dismiss all speculations that came from her own head and concentrate only on what was on the surface and visible, for that's how the present was and he loved her for her ability to reside only there.

They were married the day the divorce papers came from America. By then, Hal was reconciled to the fact that they need not be poor. "Poverty has its limitations," he said. "I think I would write better if I knew we could go skiing in Switzerland, and that once in a while we could afford a very good bottle of wine. What the hell, once I start making money, I'll set up a special fund for you. It's not as though I'm willing to live off of you. It's a loan toward our future." On the day they walked inside the Mairie for their license, he said, "We're a partnership, and we might as well legalize it."

She was the silent partner and was glad of it whenever they were among people. Although his many friends frightened her, she would not show her fear, as she had not shown the fear of animals and insects in Africa. He could tell her, as he could not tell anyone else, what he really thought of Scott and Zelda Fitzgerald, Miss Stein, Joyce and Lawrence, the Hemingways, even Pound. He could say nasty and petty things to her and she would not judge him, her eyes would not change their color or expression, as Lee's used to. She would hug him and wait as the envy, hatred, or fear drained out of him.

They decided to put away all the earnings from his writing—the royalties from the collected storeis about Slim Taber and the advance for *From Zero to Fifty*—in a special bank account.

"It will be our nest egg, what we will have when we go back. And I want us to go back to the States one day. I'd like to buy a house on Martha's Vineyard and plant our roots and be good citizens. And parents."

He held out that future for her and she feared it, for she had been ordered to live in the present and she was obeying his orders. What she loved now was the fact that he no longer resented her money, he was not being "stingy" anymore. So she wrote her father and asked if she could not have "a sort of dowry" put aside in the bank at Martha's Vineyard. She did not tell Hal about it and listened to him when he said one day, "I don't ever want to be rich, because I hate money. But I'd love us to have all the good things money can buy. And sometimes it can buy peace of mind if your mind doesn't resent the buyer." He would explain to her the difference between inherited money and money "earned truly by the sweat of your mind," which to him was better than money earned by the sweat of the brow.

When the crash came, she wondered what had happened to her father's wealth which had been invested in stocks. She wrote her parents rarely, and when they wanted to come to visit them in Paris, she made up an excuse. One day she received a very formally written letter from her mother:

> I am not sure if you would be interested, but your father tried to jump out of the window of his office. His secretary stopped him, but, just as if he had actually fallen, he underwent what the doctor says is a psychological paralysis. He is confined to a chair.

Her mother did not ask her for money, and she offered none.

Hal was working well on a new novel about the war and wanted to go to Italy for the winter to revisit all the places he had seen during the war. She would have preferred to stay in Paris. They had three cats now and plants that needed her care. She felt herself, by then, a real homebody, and did not relish the idea of leaving the apartment she loved. But she went with him, and it was there, in Venice, on a very cold night, that he told her about his father and the way he had died. She shivered from both the cold and the horror, for he described to her how his father had winked at him just before pulling the trigger with his toe and then said, "I think it's hereditary. I will probably kill myself one day. If there is a death wish in one of the parents, the child will have the death wish, too."

Before she underwent surgery for cancer of the cervix, the cancer she felt she had gotten because she was no longer Hal Hubbard's wife, she thought about that night in Venice and about his words. Her own father, too, had tried to end his life, and now she had planted death within herself, for cancer to her was a self-willed killer.

Did things start going wrong way back there? She often would, on that trip through Italy when he was walking through his own past, say aloud that she missed Paris. But Paris was over for him. He wanted to go back home.

"We should be back there. Things are not going well in the States." By the time they did go back to Paris, she knew that their life there was over. She needed both the past and the future to sustain her, because for her the present was vanishing.

He had chosen Martha's Vineyard as the place where he wanted to live. They sailed in the spring of 1930, forsaking the best of seasons in Paris, giving up their Ile St. Louis, their cats and plants, their picnic lunches on the banks of the Seine, the light that came like a halo through their high windows in the morning, everything that both of them had held dear.

"It was all too good here," Hal said as they both stood in their door for the last time. "Too safe, too placid. We're adventurers after all, aren't we darling?"

She nooded her head and smiled up at him and knew she was lying again to him. She hardly had known a rest from lies. On the ship she lied again when he asked her if she thought it would not be a grand idea if they had a child. They were both aware of having conceived then, on the high seas, another human being who she feared would come between them and he thought would solidify their marriage.

"Not that I'm afraid of us going stale alone," he told her, "but as much as I should not have wanted a child with Lee, I do want a child with you. We're a partnership and we're enlarging the firm."

She was going to make herself love the big, drafty, wooden house standing on the bluffs overlooking the ocean, just as she had loved the apartment in Paris. They brought with them his trophies. With familiar animals' heads and skins on chairs and floors, she would be reminded of Paris and love it here. Having lied so much and so well to others, she now was lying just as much but not quite as well to herself.

He stopped teaching her, and that was what she missed most. He began to see her job as that of keeping the house neat and taking care of herself and the baby inside of her, and "doing good cooking" now that they could not go to restaurants or live on the wonderful French bread and cheeses. He bought a sailboat and because she got seasick, he would go and fish alone in the afternoons. "Why don't you make friends?" he would ask. Because he asked, she made friends with two of their neighbors, a lesbian painter and the wife of a poet. They would get together for coffee on those afternoons when the mists drifted in from the sea and Hal loved to sail.

With the two women, she realized for the first time that she was considered to be the wife of a great writer. She started to play the role, getting better at it with time, but never really seeing Hal as public property. Maybe she could not cope with that. Maybe thinking of him as they thought of him would have betrayed the right she felt they had to privacy, for she still dreamed it could be as it was in Paris. But things were very different. He received much mail and spent a few days each year with his editor in New York City and gave interviews and was asked to speak at colleges.

By the time their first child, Carl, whom Hal nicknamed "Bean," was born, his third bood, *Goodbyes,* was published to great reviews. He also sold the movie rights to *From Zero to Fifty.* During the summer, they were always entertaining. There were house guests not only for weekends but during the week, and it was up to her to keep them company while Hal worked, for the mornings here, as in France, were sacred to him and he would not be interrupted when the writing went well. When it wasn't going well, he would leave his study, which was the room at the top of the house with a widow's walk, and say nasty things about the "competition," as he now called all writers. Also, during those times when the writing was not going well, he would drink too much and would often say things to her that he would not have said otherwise. He called her "dull" and a "drudge." But she knew it was only the liquor talking and forgave him and knew he did not mean he was tired of her.

She had tried her best to be a good mother, but she never liked her own children. The one Hal called "Shrimp" because she was so small when she was born, whose name was Anne, almost cost her her life and afterward she could not bear him any more children. Maybe that too went against her, for he wanted to be a father of a whole brood of kids. In the hospital, before the hard delivery, he had said as much, and he told her that it would be a daughter because he willed it. "But," he had said, "a girl is too fragile for this world, and we shall bring her up as if she were a boy, toughen her up, make her compete with her brother. We will make a man out of her so that she will never fear being a woman."

From the very start he wished the children to possess great strength of character and never to show weaknesses. "We're both liars, but we won't let them lie. Honest seekers-of-truth is what I want my children to be. They will expose all the shams and the shoddy ways of the world the way we two could never afford to do." The babies would cry and he would forbid her to attend to them when they did. "Keep them well fed and warm, but if they cry for other reasons, let them cry. It doesn't hurt them as babies, it develops their lungs, and when they're grown they won't have to cry," he said. He himself would hug them each day, saying, "A hug a day keeps the doctor away."

It was like a religion to him, from the start, believing that liars are the evil people of this world, and she now felt watched by him. Lying would not have done her any good when it came to things he wished she would do with him, such as playing tennis, going sailing. So she didn't lie about such things. She did them. Sailing, though, even on smooth waters, made her seasick. So she got to be a very good cook and baked breads as well as they baked them in France. She bought a goat and made goat cheeses and sewed and cleaned the house. "Don't you ever read?" he would ask, but for reading she had no time. At night she felt exhausted and went to sleep early, always before he came to bed. Sometimes he would wake her and make love to her, but it did not happen all that often anymore. It had to do with her not being able to bear more children, she thought. But maybe it simply had to do with his wanting her so seldom.

If she didn't like summers because summers meant a stream of guests, she liked the other seasons at Martha's Vineyard even less. There was too much rain and too much cold that came from the water and the mists. She would walk around with a long woolen skirt on and two sweaters and socks, lighting fires in the fireplaces. She looked into the flames, preferring them to the water. She hated the water that seemed all around, for the house stood on a peninsula. What she hated, Hal loved. He loved the views of the ocean, and he loved the sound, coming from beyond the beach, of the never-ceasing surf. The sight and sound of the surf filled her with sadness; the ebbs and flows of it filled her with dread that it would always go on, forever, this life that separated him from her.

She knew he had become restless and bored by the fall of 1938 and knew it was just a matter of time before he left her. Yet she was surprised when one rainy afternoon he told her that he was going to Spain to cover the Civil War for *The Chicago Tribune.*

"Is it me?" she asked without thinking, risking everything by the question. But he didn't seem to have heard.

"It's my war," he said, "and I should have gone there the moment it started."

"But you've seen one war, in Italy. . . . "

"I want to see this one," he said. And it was final. No matter what she did, or said, he would go.

She thought that she had lost him as a husband, or, even worse, that he would be killed in that stupid war. She began to drink too much, starting the day with sherry and ending it with gin. She sent the children away to a boarding school, knowing they were too young, but she thought they would be better off away from her and the house, which was an empty, waiting place without Hal.

The lesbian painter that fall had two friends visiting her and the four women would play bridge and cook gourmet dinners together. Sometimes Carole, who was not like them, would cry and one or the other would put her arms around her and hold her and kiss the tears away. They were good friends and yet each, in spite of knowing how she felt and that she would never go to bed with anyone but Hal, propositioned her. She responded each time by getting drunk and insisting that she put herself to bed. Her bedroom had become a mess of unwashed sheets and bottles.

During Christmas the children returned from school, strangely quiet and secretive and not at all like they had been before going away, but as if locked into some conspiracy. It was then, upon their arrival, that she thought for the first time of writing a play about an ideal marriage threatened by two children. She chose the title, *A Marriage,* because Hal was at war and never knew that she was fighting now, as she had been fighting ever since they met, for him. She outlined the plot but couldn't write it, not yet. She developed the characters in her head and began to confuse the two children in the play with her own.

Eight months after Hal left, he came back with shrapnel wounds in his right thigh. He came back to her in the summer of her thirty-sixth year, when she was beginning to feel like an old woman. She played the game of nurse with grace, and he began to call her his "good egg." And because he wanted a hotter sun for the coming fall, and she longed for warmth, they went to Haiti in October. Within a week they found a house they liked and bought it, deciding that's where they would spend most of the year, returning to Martha's Vineyard only for the summers.

But it was far from being Paris all over again. He wanted the children to be with them. He wrote Lee in Montana to send Robert, whom he called "Bobby," and the new house was filled with them, with their chatter, their games, and their busy lives. She began to suffer from headaches and drank rum a lot to keep some part of herself away from them. Hal worked hard, and the children had things to do all the time. The servants—they now had five—took care of everything that had to be done, and she felt useless.

Hal bought a powerboat and whenever he could not write, or whenever he felt like taking off, he would go fishing, now a passion with him. He tried to break records and soon the house was filled up with stuffed fish. He would take the children, who adored boating and were getting the idea that all they wished to become when they grew up were fishermen, and she would stay alone in the house with no one but the servants. She went with them several times, but each time had to stay below deck, not wanting them to see how sick she felt, and hated vomiting when there was nothing left to vomit.

"Why don't you find a hobby?" he would ask, seeing how useless she felt. "How about piano? You played once."

She had told him that she played as a girl, to please her parents. "Would it please you?" she asked.

"That's not the question. I want you to please yourself."

Playing piano would not have pleased her, but she bought one and stared at it a lot. She began to feel guilt for the poverty all around them as if she were personally responsible for it. She would not buy dresses and walked around the house in an old robe. But she didn't feel cold anymore, and that seemed like an accomplishment even in the tropics.

He told her very little about the war in Spain, but he talked about it to the others who came for drinks and dinners and sometimes to stay in the little guest house at the end of their property. It was strange how she learned about him only when there were strangers around. And they were all strangers, for they were not her friends. She had no friends.

She tried to play the game of hostess of a famous writer according to the rules, but she felt that all those people who came to their house were feeding off of Hal and that little was left of him for her. They wanted something from him, an opinion, or advice, or just to hear him talk, and their wants were catered to by Hal who played, she felt, a new game, of an oracle. He was not good at games. And with some, who seemed like leeches to her, he was far too generous with his time, and sometimes, during those months of 1939 and 1940, in Haiti and in Martha's Vineyard, they would have arguments about how she felt about "his" guests.

"Why do you hate them so?" he asked.

"I don't hate them. I just don't like them."

"You just sit there, like a dummy, never saying anything."

"I have nothing to say to your friends."

"Damn it. You never had a friend, except for Larry."

"I don't see why...."

"You don't see anything. What's happened to you? You never grew! Ever since Paris you've been nothing but...."

"A burden? A drudge? A bore? What?"

"Shit! You don't take pleasure in anything or anyone! Not even the kids!"

"I take pleasure in you," she said, but he walked away from what she tried to tell him. That's why she began to write the play. For him most of all. To explain that sometimes it could be perfect to be just two against the world.

The cancer must have started around then, as she began to write. No matter what he said to her about finding a hobby, he had never meant for her to invade his turf. He had written a play himself about the war in Spain, but it never was performed anywhere, and he himself felt that he had failed. For the first time since he was very young he had failed, and the failure of that play made him angry. If she had attempted to write anything but a play, maybe things would not have ended as they did.

She had never written anything before, yet she found it incredibly easy to write *A Marriage*. It took her three weeks when he was away in California on a month's lecture tour, and before he came back she had sent the play off to a New York producer who had come several times to their house in Haiti. She mailed it without thinking that anything would happen, pleased at her own daring and knowing that if she did not send it off right away, she would never do it at all.

The timing had a lot to do with the disaster. The day he came back, he told her that his own play would finally be done by a small college in California, and he sounded very pleased. While he was still talking about it, the phone rang, and he answered it. She went to the kitchen to prepare dinner, for at Martha's Vineyard she cooked herself. By the time she came back, his face was darkened by anger.

"That phone call was for you," he said.

"Who was it?" No one called her. Not even her parents with whom she had ceased to communicate.

"Alfred Burns." He waited for her to speak, but when she didn't, he shouted at her: "Why did you use my name?"

She had expected him to be angry with her for not telling him that she had written a play, but she had not thought he would have resented her using his name. She had sent it in with a title page that read, "by C. S. Hubbard."

"Don't you know," he yelled, getting up and pacing the floor, "that the only reason he'd be producing a play by you is that you're my wife?"

The accusation struck her as funny, and she laughed. He threw the glass that he held into the fireplace and stomped out of the house, not coming back for hours. When he finally did return, he apologized.

"I was stupid," he said. "Out of my fucking mind. You wrote a play! Come here, woman." He gave her a bearhug and ordered her to tell him what the play was about.

He then told her that Alfred Burns thought the play would be produced in the fall, and that they should drink to its success. He tried to make her feel happy, made love to her, kissed her, and asked for her forgiveness although she had forgiven him some time ago. She had never really minded the outburst except for those hours she had sat waiting, as if paralyzed, feeling that now, for sure, it was all over between them.

The next day she let him read a copy of the play, something he wanted to do. But when he had read it, he didn't tell her it was good or bad. He only said, "Is it us?"

"It could have been," she answered. Her instincts to lie when necessary were not at work that day. What happened after that, and for the next few months, was not unlike a roller coaster except it was at a much slower pace.

Whenever someone came into the house, he would introduce her as "my wife, the playwright." He would sometimes bring farmers from the local bar just so that he could tell them about "my famous wife. She'll have a play done on Broadway." And now, he would not answer the phone. "It's probably for you. You're the only one who gets phone calls nowadays."

She tried to talk seriously about the play with him. "I won't let them do it," she said. "I've already changed the name to my maiden name, but I won't let them do it if it bothers you so much."

"At least one of us will make money at my craft," he said and laughed.

He was obstinate in his objections that it did not bother him, that on the contrary, he was very proud of her. Didn't he talk about her to everyone? Would she object if he started on her biography? He could put aside whatever he was doing to do that, if only she would cooperate. "Tell me about you and Larry Dort and how the two of you made love!"

She didn't know what to do, but decisions were out of her hands now. The producer and director arrived one day and stayed for a week discussing changes. Then the leading man and lady came for a weekend, and there were more discussions. Hal sat quietly, as once she had sat in front of his guests, and pretended everything that was said interested him greatly. But in his presence she was tongue-tied and ashamed of what she had done, of the compliments she heard. If she could, she would have stopped the whole charade. But how could *he* be envious of *her*? That was as incomprehensible as it was evident.

He was not working. Once, when he came back home from the local bar, more drunk than she had ever seen him, he accused her of having stolen his "creative juices."

"How did I do that?" she asked. "By writing that damnable play?"

"No! Shit on the play! It's by always wanting to screw. You're the horniest broad I know."

She didn't cry, but laughed instead. They had not slept with each other for over a month, and before that it had been months. He slapped her face then. It was the first time he had ever done anything like that. For a while, for a week at least, he tried to make it up to her by being his old, gentle, loving self, but the slap stayed on both their memories. He had shown weakness to her—his own. He had said several times over the years that only a coward would "slap a dame."

Two nights before the opening of her play, they went to New York to stay for a week at the Plaza. She made sure that he would not feel that this was "her time," as he said. She invited his friends to the party, but they all had read about the play opening and sought her out to compliment her. They made her feel important, something she hoped they would not do. Hal had his arm around her neck most of the time, bragged about her, saying how proud he felt. But there was an edge to his words just as there always was now whenever her play was the center of attraction.

The night of the opening, when she came out from the bath, expecting to see him getting ready, she found a note instead:

> I thought this night would be the least painful for you to accept the news that I am going to England to cover the war for the Trib. I've made my plans some time ago. I don't know how long I'll be gone. Send me all the good reviews. And have fun together with fame. I have acted on occasions like a jealous kid. Forgive me. Competition always brings out the worst in me, but of course you never thought of it as competition. I hope I won't either, being away. Take care.
>
> Love,
> Hal

The morning papers carried the news of his leaving to cover the war on the front page. The reviews of her play were mixed. It ran for two months and when it closed, she wired him: NO MORE PLAY, THREE OF US MISSING YOU DREADFULLY. WE LOVE YOU. A few days later, she received a letter from him.

> Darling, what was happening to me before I left was something neither of us liked. Could it be that war is my element? This one, unlike the dirty, tragic Spanish War, seems to bring out the best in people and I'm beginning to fall in love with people, something I desperately needed. The British are unbelievable. They take to this war like ducks to water, showing their best feathers, so to speak.
>
> Goddamnit, this is the only civilized country left in the world, and maybe when this is over, or even before, we could establish ourselves here. No matter how I feel about the Haitians and the natives of Martha's Vineyard, it is here, in England, that I have discovered that the most important thing in the world for a civilized person is to keep

up a good front and not fall down in some heap, as we tend to do back in the States. Have you been writing? I have. With pleasure and joy and ease which is something that I probably envied you being able to do. All that is behind us. Keep well and give the kids all my love.

Hal

P.S. Get that heater fixed if you decide to stay on in Martha's Vineyard. If you decide to go to Haiti, be sure that Bernard varnishes the boat.

She tried to read between the lines but there was nothing for her there. He did not speak of their alienation, so maybe everything was still all right with their marriage. She didn't know whether to go to Haiti for its winter warmth, or freeze in Martha's Vineyard. With him gone nothing mattered. She thought of going to England, but did not dare. She took the children to New York City for a long weekend over Thanksgiving and was surprised to discover that she no longer thought of them as enemies of her marriage. They were so good-looking and so well-behaved and seemed to enjoy everything so much that, for the first time, she began to like them. She wanted them to come and stay with her, offering them the choice of living either in Haiti or Martha's Vineyard. But both said that they should go back to their boarding school.

She finally decided, on an impulse, to see her parents in Chicago. She was shocked at the way they looked, old and emaciated. They were very cold, but polite to her. "There are certain obligations children have toward their parents." They were talking in circles about their deep disappointment in her. She should have communicated. She should have sent them money. They were living in a one-room furnished apartment. There was nothing left of their antiques, the good things they had had. "We sold it all." Her father had never left his chair. "But there is nothing physically wrong with him," her mother whispered to her while they were on the other side of the room. Carole said she would put five thousand dollars in their savings account. Her mother showed her their bank book. It had twenty-two dollars in it. "We don't want charity," they said together, proud. Strangers to her now.

"I'll send three hundred dollars each month."

"You don't have any money of your own," they reminded her.

"But my husband does."

"We never met him," they said together, proud and hurt.

They had grown so close that they thought the same way and looked the same way; same wrinkles, same pale, lifeless eyes, same words and looks, the same hurts. This was her ideal marriage grown old. Two people feeding off each other. They did not kiss her good-bye, as if such intimacy had to be earned and she had not earned it. They offered her their wrinkled cheeks and a look of such abandonment that the moment the door closed behind her, she cried. Tears ran down her own cheeks, the sorrow for all old people in the world in her heart and a horrid void for Hal and herself. She could never imagine them like that, and not being able to imagine them old together, something vital, something that held her together to the world as she understood it, slid out from under her and she felt herself adrift.

When he came back in the spring of 1943, it was to tell her that he was leaving her, had fallen in love. The woman was an actress and did not want to marry him, but he wanted to live with her. Even as he was telling her this latest news he noticed that she was a shadow now living in the past. She wore dresses she had worn in Paris, too small for her now, for she had grown plump in her despair over his absence. Her hold on reality was very fragile. And whatever hold she had on it had to do with their years in Paris. At first he thought she was playing some silly game with the past. But soon he was to realize that her mind had decided to live where they had both been happy.

"I was at Sylvia's today," she would say to him, "reading *Sons and Lovers,* and Lawrence came in, and he smiled that thin smile at me, you know this thin smile he does so well that it makes everyone who sees it exceedingly sad."

Sometimes she would leave sentences unfinished, and sometimes she would pause as she walked, the walk of someone cut from the world, and would start conversations with invisible people. And she was always in Paris. She called their cats and would hold their invisible bodies to her, and he knew they were very real to her. And he would be embarrassed hearing her tell them secrets, about how happy she was, and she would look out of the windows and see, he was sure of this, not the bluffs of Martha's Vineyard but the Ile St. Louis and Paris beyond.

He was going to leave her, but now he could not. He was chained to her by pity and her needs. He thought she would get worse if he committed her. By summer she became an unbearable drain on him. "I'm your silent partner," she would say with a wink. But she would not be silent. She talked of Africa and of the first time he had come to her tent and was "good," and did not make love to her. "Sense of honor in marriage," she would say and throw her head back, not laughing but trying to figure something out. And then she would lower her head, smile at him, and remind him of the night he lost that sense of honor. She recalled for him what he had thought of Fitzgerald and Hemingway, of Pound and Stein, bringing back too much that he neither needed nor cared to remember.

What he resented most was the fact that his kids were seeing his past through her ravings. They watched her with great fascination as she unraveled Paris. Within her pain, she performed as a great actress might, creating her own validity, her function, in all of this. And he saw it clearly now, what she was and had been all along. An appendage of his life. The play she wrote had been a fluke. She had drowned within his career long ago; the play had just floated by, affording her a moment on a passing raft, but she had let go. He did not like what she was doing to the children, nor to herself. But he saw nothing new in what she was doing to him. He was her life, she had bought it, she had no other. If he wanted her to exist he would have to let her be what she was. She wished no refunds on her purchase of him.

But understanding all this made it no less easy to cope with. Whenever guests came, he would now keep her sedated, but even then she might come downstairs, her eyes crazed with devotion, her gestures those of a sleepwalker, her hair a rat's nest of pins and ribbons, shivering with the cold that was now always the cold of a Paris winter. She looked beautiful, her face peaceful, as she talked of the picnics on the banks of the Seine, of restaurants and cafés. She brought back memories that he now cherished as much as she, and sometimes he felt that she was playing for his benefit, and not for hers, the forbidden game of a lost life. Wearing dresses she had once worn and perfumes she had once used, she was sucking him back when all he had thought he wanted was to move forward now, without her. Her very gentleness seemed awesomely dangerous to him. It would be easy walking into her quicksand, joining her there.

It was because the temptation was so great, the trip to where she was so irresistible, that he finally had her committed and got the divorce from her. After she was in the hospital with cancer, he felt guilty over the fact that he had fought for his life and in the process had destroyed hers. But then she recovered. She had always been clever. It had all been the same game they all played. She was one of the survivors, and he, always, their victim. She had been no better and no worse than the rest of them who had drained the juices without which he could not write, nor live.

"Whatever did you do to your hair, Mrs. Kowalski?" He watched the nurse try to pick out the oatmeal from the old woman's hair, but after a while took his eyes away.

"That's lovely!" The middle-aged volunteer was looking over his shoulder. He had tried to do a sky with watercolors and had been thinking of Turner, and now he was tired of having been in the "day room" and longed to be inside his own night, in his own room. And he got up and shuffled down the corridor of no memories toward that designated room where he was bookkeeping the facts of his life.

Before lying down on his bed, the act of bookkeeping being best done that way, he had a great insight. One thing could be said of Hal Hubbard, but of course nobody else knew this: he had been fully and totally present and conscious of the act of each of his three children's conceptions. With Bobby it came after the destruction of the fear on the pasture. He had kept a careful record of when Lee could conceive and knew this to be her time. But what was he doing now? He was past Lee and was inside Carole's ledger. But with her, too, he had known the moment of the conception, twice. He had never been too sure of her. He didn't want her to wash away the seeds that he planted knowingly, and on those two occasions had kept her with him in bed, talking and making gentle overtures past the time of her excitement, into the sleepiness of her body, so that she would not get up, so she would not eliminate with a douche what he had done. He didn't want his children not to know. They had been willed. No matter what he did or what he had not done for them, he had done that much. The three of them came not from carelessness but from his will. And maybe, in the final accounting, it would count for him.

"We've got some rules around here. We don't divide people by professions, or by rank, or by economic status. We divide them by parents. Not good or bad parents, but those who knew, from the beginning, that they were parents. All the women and the men who knew they were conceiving, please move to the right side." And he walks to the right and looks back and nobody else is following him. He is alone. They are all waiting. Nobody knows what happens next. And an angel comes and gives him an apple. He doesn't know whether to say thank you, or whether he should eat it or just hold it. But it doesn't matter. He is alone. Nobody else comes.

He had to go back to see those years from the perspective of a bird shot in flight. But the birds know shit from money. And the essence of Carole Scolfield Hubbard was money. What was wrong with money was that you had to buy it. Not exactly buy it. You had to trade off. At the beginning it must be the same for everyone. It's practical to have it. Once he had said, when he was tired of not having enough for Lee and himself: "There is one reason why I want to have money." And Lee had asked: "What's that?" And he said: "I would like to have money so I could feel that I am rich." He never felt rich although money came his way. His own, after Carole's. But by then it had been poisoned.

It really all began with the trophies. He had shot the animals and did not wish to leave their beauty behind, not those heads, nor those skins. It all could have been simple. But money always complicates things. It was simple when he made the deal with her: she would pay for tanning and mounting the trophies and keep them until he could repay her the money spent. With interest. She had agreed readily, and they shook hands. This was before he even fired the first shot, the first night they were camping out.

What was he doing when he finally bedded her down? The heat? Her, his, fault or attractiveness? It did not come sinlessly. He had known too many Catholics by then or were they more Protestant and Jewish than Catholic feelings, those of sexual guilts? It didn't matter. The guilt was there although he denied it and didn't want to deal with it. Someone once said, "The only shocking thing about adultery is when you get your electric blanket to short-circuit." But his adultery was for profit. Her money. No matter what one would prefer to think. He had bought Lee a pair of safari pants that cost the equivalent of twenty dollars. Carole spent as much for a scarf. Everything she wore had the smell of money. Even when she was naked he smelled it still, and when he made love to her, even that first night, it was dancing in his head, the feel of it, what it could do, for him, with her. He traded Lee off for it, and that was that. As all trades, it was questionable who got the best of the deal. Lee was not in an Albuquerque clinic, he was, with doctors talking over their dinners about who they were treating and for what. Under the double whammy of paranoia and schizophrenia, he shared what was wrong with the talentless, the lost, and the bad traders.

"We're having a movie tonight." The nurse came in and lowered the light that was shining into his eyes, and the drapes she drew together like lips, touching away the sunset. He had to respond because responding now was trading off for the weekend he had to have.

"What are we showing?" he asked.

"*The Big Sleep*," she said.

"Ah! One of the great ones!"

"Oh, really? I've never seen it. What's it about?"

"He called the cops on me, he should be ashamed," was only one of two dozen great lines that he still remembered. "Great flick," he said.

"I was going to watch T.V. but maybe I'll come down and watch it with you."

"You won't be sorry," he said. And she would be because it was a man's picture. It was a joke, perpetrated by Faulkner against all those who wrote theses on his work. That was Faulkner's best work, and it was hack work. He admired Bill for having written the script of *The Big Sleep*. The original line at the beginning, Bill told him once, was: "You're pretty small, aren't you?" but they changed it to: "You're pretty short, aren't you?" because it would have been too much for the public denied single entendres. And the double entendre was too much, because Humphrey Bogart's answer was, "I try not to be."

He blew it with Carole, trying not to be small or short. It didn't matter who bought sex. She or he. They had some good sex. Whorehouses are not strangers to that either. But he was a whore all along with her. He loved it so at the Plaza Athenée, in that four-poster bed and those crystals and gilded swans in the toilet, that he amazed himself and asked her to move, not to spend the money. He should have gone on whoring, getting better at it, getting more for what he did with richer, maybe older women. He shouldn't have been so goddamn stricken by his whoredom. Maybe he should have whored around more with his writings. Magazines, television, movies, he should have laid them all and taken all comers.

Come one and come all to Hal Hubbard's Writers' Clinic, where without the use of enemas we shall extract from you, ladies and gents, that story that lingers within us all, the immortal story of the kitten who went up the tree and wouldn't come down until the fireman got him down. Ladies and gents, here is a Pulitzer, Nobel prize winner, ready and willing and more than able to assist you in getting down on paper, where it matters, your first date, your senior prom, your visit to your dying father, or mother, or brother, or child, whatever the case may be. We will fashion weepy prose, or moving prose, or sentimental slop for all your relatives. With no charge but the single admission fee, Hal Hubbard will edit long-windedness right out of it and make your story suitable for framing or sending off. Photostatted or mimeographed, inside your Christmas cards to friends and relatives.

Let's send off to editors across the nation, but most especially the New York editors, let's flood them, their desks, their mailboxes, their paneled offices, with stories of marriages, sold and bought marriages. Let's hear it for marriages, ladies and gents, and let's get it all down, down to the smallest details. On paper, soft or hard, whatever the assholes want, the glory and the pain, the smut and the smiles, all of our collective marriages that have seen no print, that have lingered unnoticed, except by the participants, in the musky closets of decaying memories. Let's air our marriages for the whole world to see, with sexual preferences as to positions and frequencies showing plainly. Let's spread the legs of our brains, open up undreamt-of cavities of our minds to the titillating memories of our marriages.

After all, ladies and gents, you have right here, in front of your very eyes, a minor master of marriages. Only two, but what's in a number? Quality here, not quantity, counts. But today, for one day only, and this offer will not be made again until the Second Coming, which happens to be a long way off, we offer you a chance at a novel. Novels, ladies and gents, in case you are not reading or buying any, are written to be reviewed. Short stories do not attract critics by the score, but novels, ladies and gents, like heavyweight boxing, are the cream of the cream of review writing. The craft would go begging if it were not for novels. All of you here have a first novel in you, unless of course that is behind you. First novels, someone wise once said, are like rafts. You pile everything you've got on top, and if you have not left a thing out, you sink. Hal Hubbard is one writer of his generation who was able, through sheer luck and perseverance, to make his first raft floatable.

Should you be having one too many love scenes in your novel, he will take it and use it the way he knows best. He will bed your girl down. How about friends, ladies and gents? Friends make great characters in novels, especially if you give them a few qualities they don't possess or take away a few they do. Friends can be easily turned into enemies if you know the craft of novel writing, and who knows it better than your very own instructor, the great Hal Hubbard himself! Had you not delayed so in coming, we could have had for your benefit, and at no additional cost, a veritable bonus. We could have presented to you, alive and in the flesh, one of Hal Hubbard's benefactresses, the second Mrs. Hubbard. Herself a playwright, she could have instructed each and every one of you in the tender art of the theater. She could have guided you through the murky labyrinth of her playwriting mind straight into the lap of producers and theater critics. A baptism of fire, some might say, or simply a dream never realized by some who long to be taken apart at the fall of a curtain. But you came too late, the second Mrs. Hubbard is no longer with us. No, madam, she did not die, we prefer to say that she has passed on.

What's more important, plot or character, you ask? Let's not quibble here about details or ask academic questions. Mr. Hubbard never took a job teaching before for exactly that reason, he was fearful that someone would ask a question like that. This is amateur night, no professional queries answered. We want to make authors out of you folks who have never heard of critics and would paste over your bed, framed and most probably autographed, any and all reviews, bad, good, indifferent! You will even take a review that does not fit your book and be glad because tonight, and for one night only, we are all amateurs, fans of the English language. The mother fucker is the best mother fucker around, and all of you Italians, Frenchies, Germans, even you Spanish writing amateurs, you better give a round of applause to the great mother fucker herself, Mr. Shakespeare's own, English!

And now, moving right along, what would you like to write about, you, little lady with the crying child in your arms? War you say! A perfectly suitable subject for a lady and her child, I say! You don't have to go to them, you don't have to smell them, you don't have to be shot at, war's what women could write best about. Trench warfare, or aerial, or atomic? Take your pick, dear lady, your time is at hand to say war good-byes to the men who had cornered the market on wars for too long. Yes? the young man wants to do a novel about a famous novelist who, in spite of his fame as maleness impersonated, was a fairy at heart! Anyone we know, by chance?

Let us stop here for a footnote to history, if we may. May we be so bold as to let off a prediction? When fairies start flying out of the closet they'll step on anyone's toes who happens to be in the way. Hal Hubbard himself, whose many and various problems never did include having doubts about his *cojones* and to whom they belong, and who they wish to be next to while in between sheets, inside gondolas, or back seats of cars, wants you fellow amateurs to know right here, and tonight of all nights, that he was never tempted, never felt himself lured, never wished to succumb to what many have called the other side of the sexual coin. No, ladies and gents, take it from me, Hal Hubbard's mouthpiece, there was nothing like that going on inside, or outside, of his head. A few remarks made about the closeted boys of his day should not mislead you and conclude that somewhere in there lurked a homo.

Now how about insanity? Anyone for the subject of insanity here? There is a story there, but not a whole novel perhaps. A chapter? Yes, perhaps a chapter in the ever-continuing story of what is loosely called life....

He got tired, for he had talked aloud, not as loudly as he had wished, but just loud enough to hear himself. What more was there to say about the sell-out? Nothing else that he cared to remember. And now go gently into The Big Sleep.

Robert Hubbard

"WERE you an orphan," the boy asked the old man. "I mean when you were my age, when you were growing up?" "I might as well have been," the old man said. "How come you say that?" the boy wanted to know. The old man didn't want to get into a conversation about the reasons he had said that. Sixty some years was a long time to remember how it was when he was a kid. It wasn't as if he remembered a whole lot. He remembered mostly his mother always complaining about the fact that he was born. "If I didn't have you, I could go to Kansas City or St. Louis. I could do anything, be anything." Sometimes she would speak to him directly and tell him what a burden he was to her and how she had never wanted him to be born.

At about forty, he figured out that not being wanted even before birth was something that discolored and blighted his life. Later he divided all men into two foreign camps: those who were unwanted at birth and those who were wanted. He made friends with the ones like himself and watched out for the ones unlike him. Sooner or later the ones who were wanted would hurt him in one way or another.

He looked at the boy and knew, had known all along, that he was one of the wanted ones. It would be just a matter of time before the boy would hurt him. Unless he hurt the boy first.

from *Two Breeds* by Hal Hubbard

Robert had not known who his father was until Hal Hubbard wrote asking him to come for a visit. He was fourteen by then.

"Why didn't you tell me he was my father," he said. "I've read his books and everything."

"I thought it might hurt you to know," Lee said.

She made it seem as if it was nobody's fault, the divorce, because that's how she thought of it.

"I'll find out," Robert said, "and if he's not the kind of guy you should have married, the kind I'd want for a father, I'll orphan myself. It doesn't impress me all that much, him being famous and all. If he's not a good man, I'll know you left him for good reasons."

"What if you find he's a wonderful man? Will you blame me?"

"No," he said, "then I'll know you're right, and it was nobody's fault. But if he's OK, I'd like to see him again. That is, if he'd want to see me again."

"If he asked you to live with him, would you do it?"

"No, I live here."

"Here" was not only the house at Fort Benton, but thousands of acres of Montana forests, the logging camps and the mills.

"One day . . ." was what she used to say. One day Robert would meet him because he was not dead like the fathers of some children he knew, and she did not hate him like the mothers of some kids hated their ex-husbands. One day he would know him. One day was finally here and he was almost a man at fourteen. He always had thought that the father he did not remember would come to him. Then he could show him his world, and he hoped he would love it and decide to stay. But that wasn't to be. He would be going to his father's world. And he was both scared and excited about it.

His mother knew she had done well by him, and he knew it too. The only thing that made them strangers to each other was his wish to always judge people and her wish to avoid judging them. "They change, you know," she would say. "Maybe today they seem bad or stupid or in need to lie, but tomorrow. . . ."

"Once a liar, always a liar," he would say.

She agreed that he was fair when he did judge people, but she had something he did not possess, and that was compassion.

"You pity them?" he would ask.

But it wasn't pity. It was as if she could take their place and feel for them as she would have felt herself.

He could not do that, exchange places with people. He was who he was, and that went for everyone. So he hated liars and would want her to fire anyone who was a liar and worked for them.

"Don't be so tough," she would say.

But he had to be tough, for both of them. If he was not tough, those who worked for them would steal them blind.

"You have a suspicious nature, like your father," she once said to him. That was enough to let him know that he had something of him, and he clung to that trait because that was the only thing he had of the man who had fathered him.

On the plane he thought that he shouldn't have come alone. If his father wanted him, he should have invited her as well. Robert had never been away from her. They were a team, and now he was separating them as he had separated himself from her when he was a baby. He was ready to hate his father.

But when he saw him, brown and bearded, a big man, much taller than he had thought he would be, coming toward him with outstretched arms in greeting, he went to him with love. They held on to each other for a long time, and he knew that she could not have been wrong in choosing him for her husband. His father's arm was still around him when he introduced him to his "brother and sister." He had not known Hal Hubbard had other children.

He liked Bean right away because the boy came toward him, just like his father, and hugged him. But the girl called Shrimp, who was not yet seven, hid behind her father and would not even shake hands. In the jeep, he heard her say, "I don't want a new brother," and Robert knew he would have to win the kid over if he wanted her for a friend. Yet, he wasn't sure he wanted that. The girl was small, so he wasn't going to be in any hurry to judge her. He wasn't good at judging girls, anyway.

One thing he did not like about that first day in Haiti was the fact that his father decided not to call him Robert or Bob, but began to call him "Bobby." It seemed to him that it was all right to give a nickname to a baby, but he was almost a man. He thought that at some time he would talk to his father about why the other two were called those silly nicknames. Another thing he did not like was his father's wife. She tried to make him feel welcome, but he figured her for a liar. She didn't much want him there, and he was not all that sure that she wanted her own kids there either. Her eyes were always on her husband as if he was the only one that mattered to her. But he loved the big, breezy house and the way the country looked and smelled and sounded. It was unbelievably hot, and he had not known that all the people would be black. He hardly ever saw blacks in Montana. The smells from all the tropical flowers they had growing in the garden reminded him of the way one of his mother's perfumes smelled. He missed her and thought that she would love it here, at least for a visit.

"How is your mother?" Hal asked him in the jeep.

"She's just great!"

"You two get along?"

"Oh, sure," he said. "We get along real well together."

Later, when he was in his own room unpacking, the one they called Bean, but whose real name was Carl, asked him how come he got along with his mother so well. "I don't know any kids who get along well with their mothers," he said.

"Maybe if you have a father you don't have to get along with your mother. I've just met my father, and I think I'll get along with him just fine, too."

He did not go on then about his mother. He had learned to keep private what he felt for her and did not like having to apologize for how he felt. But he did ask Carl about how he felt about his parents.

"I love my dad," Carl said. "I love him a whole lot."

"Why do you love him?"

"Oh, because of everything, the way he is."

He didn't have to ask about the mother, it was not the same thing.

He was tired after the long trip by plane and the waits in the airports. He went to bed right after supper, although his father wanted him to stay up and play some cards with his brother.

"I'm tired," he said.

He noticed his father's eyes narrowing, and there was a mocking tone in his voice when he said, "You're not a sissy, are you?"

"I guess not," he answered, looking him straight in the eye. "I never called myself that, and nobody else ever called me that either." It seemed to him as if they had squared off for the first time and that there would be more of the same, but he was not afraid. "We go to bed early and get up early back in Montana," he added and stood up and excused himself.

"What time is early?" his father asked.

"Five." Then, from the door, he turned and smiled at him and said, "It's all different here, even the time. Maybe I'll sleep late." He had to make it clear to him that he was his own man and not like the other two kids who were so much younger than he.

He woke up to the crowing of the roosters and when he opened his eyes, his father was sitting on the chair by his bed looking at him.

"Hi," he said. "What time is it?"

"After six," his father said.

"How long have you been here, watching me sleep?"

"Not long," he said.

Robert guessed he had come in to see if he really woke up at five, but maybe he just wanted to be with him, to see him sleep, to get to know him somehow, to make up for all the years. He wasn't going to hold those years against him, he decided. It was nobody's fault that he grew up without a father. If he couldn't leave off blaming his parents, he'd be like some of the weak kids he knew and he didn't want to be weak.

"I've got something for you," his father said and reached down to the floor and brought up a gun, a .22, brand new. "Do you know how to shoot?"

"Sure," the boy said. "You've got to know how to shoot if you expect to eat when you're in the woods. And fish, too."

"How good a shot are you?"

"Not bad," Robert said. And then, remembering all the skins and heads of wild animals he had seen downstairs, he added, "But I'm no match for you. I mean, you must have been to Africa and shot all that stuff."

His father smiled. It was as if by offering that smile he was saying, "We might not be equal now, but one day we might be." Or, at least, that's how Robert read the smile. He knew he was going to be asked to compete, to prove his worth.

Hal devoted all that month in Haiti to his three children. They went crock hunting and spearfishing, duck shooting and after tuna.

They played doubles almost every day, Hal and Shrimp against Bobby and Bean. The oldest son worried about the youngest child, who was expected to keep up with them. He would see Shrimp's determination in her clenched fists and her tight-set jaw. The kid, he decided, was not having fun. She was fighting against fears of being a girl when she should have been a boy, fear of not being as good as a boy, fear of her father.

One day Robert spoke to his father about it.

"She's just a little girl. Don't you think she shouldn't be made to compete with us all the time?"

"She'll have a better start in life," his father said, "without time out to be a sissy. Females are treated like men nowadays. I'm giving her an equal start."

"What if she's learning only to hide her fears?"

"No child of mine is a coward."

"I'm not talking about that. I mean all the fears that come when you're competing all the time."

"What have you got against competition?"

"Shrimp is too young to compete with me or you, or even Bean."

"Leave Shrimp alone and speak for yourself," his father said. "What have you got against competition?"

"It doesn't prove anything. If you win against someone who's not as good as you, you haven't proven anything. And if you don't win against someone who's better than you, all you've done is found out what you already knew."

"Without competition life would be dull," said his father and smiled.

"Mom once told me that everybody has it in himself to get better without destroying someone else in the process."

"Woman talk!" his father said and laughed.

His father was right about competition. It made life exciting.

It was tough on Shrimp, and Bean didn't seem to love it as much as Robert began to love it. The prize was always the same: admiration from their father. That was what the three of them were after, and Robert had the edge because he was the oldest. Their father made it worthwhile for them. The way he would look proudly, the way he would show his pleasure by hugging the winner with a bearhug that would encircle him. They were hooked on it. And only Robert knew that it held some danger for all of them.

·120

He loved to stretch the boundaries of his endurance and courage. Over the years they would, the three of them, ski together, and they would each make a parachute jump, climb mountains, and take long camping trips. They would canoe down the Colorado and the Rio Grande and hunt in the private preserve of one of Hal's rich friends in the Carolinas. And whenever they were together, doing what his father called "the manly arts," life would hold a special excitement unlike any excitement he had known.

Shrimp loved it best when they were aboard *The Maria*. There she was almost their equal, except when a giant fish would go for her line. Then the fear would come into her eyes. But when she was not dreading whatever impossible thing might be asked of her, she was making everyone laugh at the stories she'd tell. Tall stories that were not so much lies as flights of wild imagination.

Bean was the quietest. Robert noticed he was happiest when left alone, dreaming or thinking. Robert loved the way Bean was protective of his smaller sister and also protective of his mother and father. He was the one who guessed at his father's moods and was attuned to them as a weathervane is attuned to the wind.

In Haiti, Robert disliked being inside the house because of Carole. She tried too hard to find "amusing ways" for them to spend the time. It seemed to Robert that what she was doing was killing time until she could be alone with her husband. Whenever their father was working, they were left to their own devices. Robert wanted to go outside the enclosure of their garden and see the people, the marketplace, and the harbor. But Shrimp would say that they might get kidnapped.

"Where did you get such a silly idea?" he once asked her.

"Well, our father is famous, and kids of famous fathers get kidnapped and killed sometimes. They hold them for ransom, you know. And besides, I look like him, exactly like him, and the kidnappers would know I'm his daughter."

Shrimp derived a great deal of pleasure from the fact that she resembled her father most. In her room there was a framed photograph of him at the age of seven, and it was amazing how very much alike they looked. She wore her hair cut like a boy's, and people would often take her for a boy. She also had an album she was hiding under her bed, which she showed Robert. It was filled with photographs of her father as a boy and a young man. Shrimp saw in this physical resemblance to her father a reason for being favored, but there was no favoritism. If anything, his father seemed harder on her. Robert had the advantage of being a visitor. His father, who sometimes seemed cruel to Bean and Shrimp, was never cruel to him. But Robert knew all along, ever since his first visit, that a time would come when they would confront each other in what his father called a moment of truth. Hal talked a lot about that moment, when the choice made under stress "shows the nature of the beast."

When Robert was sixteen, he saw Bean in his moment of truth. Shrimp was snorkeling. Robert and Bean suddenly sighted a shark and before Robert could react, Bean was in the water, going after Shrimp, pulling her out and climbing aboard with her. It had happened so fast, and yet his father termed it "a moment of truth," and hugged Bean to himself and congratulated him on his presence of mind. Robert's moment of truth was to come on his last visit to Haiti, when he was eighteen.

It was the winter when his father had finally decided to place Carole in a private sanitarium. He was under great stress, having to finish a book he had been working on, worrying about his wife, and at the same time knowing that a divorce was inevitable now that their life together was finally and irrevocably over. Yet he was not quite able to explain all this to the children. The first night, the two of them stayed up late and Robert tried to find out from his father as to what had gone wrong with his second marriage.

"When we live with another," his father said, "we risk inflicting hurts without knowing when or how. It's the chance we take. Maybe she's suffering from hurts received or from hurts given. The best we can hope for is that we will never willingly, knowingly, hurt our mate."

Robert knew that his father had been hurt by this marriage, as perhaps he had been hurt by the marriage to his mother. And he admired him greatly for being able to take care of his own hurts alone, not unlike an animal. He stayed in his studio more often now and from what Robert had learned, his work was not going well. He let the kids use the boat alone except for Bernard, who took care of it. "I've posted a hundred dollar reward," he told Robert, "for the biggest marlin. Why don't you try for it?"

The three of them were going after the prize marlin, not for the money, but for the glory of catching one. And it was Robert, at the end of his second week, who brought in the record fish. Bernard had used the ship-to-shore phone to advise Hal of the catch, and Hal met them at the pier.

"How long did it take you to land him?" he asked.

"Over three hours," Robert answered. "I couldn't have done it without all the advice you've given me over the years."

"Don't give me any credit," Hal said. "I wasn't even there." He reached for his wallet and brought out a crisp hundred-dollar bill. While a photographer from the Haitian paper took a picture of Robert and the record-breaking marlin, his father suggested they go out that night and get drunk.

"The drinks will be on me," Robert said. And then, indicating the photographer, he added, "Stand with me." But his father refused. He remained out of the range of the photographer's camera. That evening, during dinner, Robert noticed that his father was getting a head start on him and drinking pretty heavily. At one point, Hal said, "I wish I had caught that marlin." And Robert had felt bad that he had caught it instead of his father..Hal sent the two kids to bed earlier and said to Robert, "Let's get going. I want to see you drunk."

"It's about time I got drunk," Robert said. He had never been drunk before.

They did not go to the Olaffson, but to a small bar that was also a whorehouse. The whores were Dominicans, his father informed him. "They all are. The Haitians don't do that for a living. They do it as part of living." After they ordered the first round of rum sours, Hal looked around the place at the half dozen whores lining the walls and pointed to the prettiest. "How would you like to take that one on? My treat."

"No, thanks. I don't go for the pros," Robert said.

"Never?"

"Haven't had to yet."

"Wouldn't do you any harm."

"Thanks all the same."

They drank their rum sours in silence for a while.

"How come you're not in the war?" his father asked.

"You know I help run a business that's classified as essential to the war effort," Robert said. He wasn't getting drunk as fast as he wished, in spite of his father. There was something about this place, about his father's tone of voice, about the whole idea of getting drunk together that seemed to him to be leading to a squaring-off. Maybe it was the damned fish, he thought, or maybe all the troubles his father was having. Maybe it was Carole's illness, or the coming divorce. Whatever it was, he looked dangerous, challenging.

"It wouldn't stop me, running a business," his father said after a while. "I'd want to get into this war if I were you."

"I also have flat feet," Robert said. "I tried to join, but they wouldn't have me."

"The Navy would take you," his father said.

"I wanted the Army."

"You got a girl?" his father suddenly changed the subject. "Besides your mother, I mean?"

"Not yet," Robert said.

He suddenly began to wish again that his father had told him something about how it was between him and his mother. Did Carole come between them? From her ravings, sometimes he thought she had. It was hard to tell for sure. He would listen to everything she said. She talked about Paris and often would mention Lee's name, but he couldn't make sense out of the words and snatches of conversations that she seemed to be carrying on, mostly with Hal who was more real to her when invisible. Maybe there was a chance for his mother and father to get back together now. The mere thought of that possibility filled him with a warmth that was familiar, for he had often thought over the years that they must have been very right for each other, those parents of his. He knew that somehow, in some mysterious womanly way, his mother was still in love with Hal. And the way he liked to listen when Robert talked about her, Hal might be in love with her still.

"I've got a girl," his father was now saying. "Crazy about her. She'll be here tomorrow. It was to be a surprise, but what the hell. Met her in England a few months ago. Was covering the war, you know. Good war. One of the best. Probably the last, best, fucking war. Last, best girl."

For a silly moment Robert thought that maybe he was talking about his mother, that she was coming. But they hadn't met in England. He asked through a mouth that seemed suddenly filled with cotton, "Who's coming tomorrow?"

"My girl, maybe you've heard of her, her name's Peggy Smith."

Could he mean Peggy Smith, the actress? He had seen a few of her pictures and had read something about how she flew her own plane over Germany and something about her racing cars. She was more an adventuress than an actress and she made more headlines than movies.

"Intend to marry her, if she'll have me. After the divorce." He motioned the bartender for two more drinks, and two girls detached themselves from their chairs and came over. One tried to squeeze herself on Hal's lap and the other put her arm around Robert.

"Want to take them on?" Hal asked.

"No, thanks."

Hal waved the girls away and then took a good look at his son. Robert looked back at him and knew that the next thing his father would say, he would not like. He was looking at him the way he'd look at Shrimp when he thought the kid was being a sissy.

"You sure you like girls?"

He had done nothing to provoke the challenge and yet he expected it. He was drunk, but not so drunk that he would give his father the satisfaction of not responding.

"You go ahead," he said. "I don't have to bed down a whore to prove I'm a man."

They were still looking at each other and the way his father's eyes went cold, Robert knew this was not to be the end of it. The moment of truth was at hand.

"It seems," his father said, "that I read somewhere that the most distinguishing characteristic of all fairies is that they love their mothers. You love your mother, don't you?"

"Leave mother out of this," Robert said slowly, looking into his father's eyes.

"I've left her, but if you hang on to her, you won't be able to screw a female. They will all seem like mom. You will just become another classic case of a guy turning into a fairy."

There had been times during each of his visits when Robert felt that his father was on the verge of saying something hurtful to him, but each time he had retreated. And yet, it had always been there, for the last four years, this thing between them like a cocked gun. It had lain in wait for both of them, and now it was going off, and it was ugly. He tried to push it aside with a joke.

"There are more fairies in this world than anyone will ever know. The thing is every fairy knows that he's one." He looked away from his father's steely eyes.

"Want to take me on?" his father asked.

Robert smiled and looked back at him. "What with, dueling pistols?"

"Bare knuckles."

Through the haze of his vision he saw his father get up off the stool, take his jacket off, and square off, like the boxers in old photographs. He was laughing now, his eyes and his mouth were laughing, and Robert thought it was a joke, that he just wanted to clown around a bit. He got up, none too steady on his feet, and started shadow-boxing toward his father.

The blow that landed on his lower jaw hurt. He was rubbing the sting when the second blow, into his midsection, made him reel against the jukebox.

"Come on, throw something my way." His father shouted and danced around him, light on his feet in spite of his added weight, for he had put on fifteen pounds since the last time Robert had seen him.

Robert had not wrestled in high school, nor had he ever boxed, except for the times when as a boy he'd had to fight guys who wanted to fight him. But that was hitting, not boxing. He heard the girls squealing against the wall out of their range of vision, heard the owner of the bar yelling something in Creole. The ceiling seemed to meet the floor at the rear of the bar as Robert stumbled toward his father, who was waiting. He threw a wild punch and felt it being blocked by his father's longer reach. I have age on my side, Robert thought as his father landed a right and a left—not hard, but playfully—on his jaw and again on his midsection.

"Come on, Bobby," his father said. "You're fighting like a drunk. Throw me a right, an uppercut."

They were both breathing hard. The liquor they had consumed seemed to affect their wind; both kicked away the tables and the chairs to allow themselves more room, and the owner and the girls kept up a chorus of chatter, now of encouragement, for the fight was not like the ones in the movies. Nothing was getting broken, and they themselves were not in danger.

While his father was throwing light jabs, Robert saw his first opening, reached his father's face with a right and saw blood spurt on his lip. Before he could say they should stop now, his father hit him over the eye. Now Robert did not want to stop. He wanted to win. He knew that with one lucky punch, he could knock his father out. It was he who had taught him to love competition, and now that love of winning was aroused in his son and he lowered his head and charged, his two fists protecting his head, yet ready to be used as weapons.

"Atta boy, Bobby," his father was saying as they circled each other. "Look for an opening." He lowered his arms and danced around Robert. "Here's one," he mocked, and the boy threw a punch and his hand bounced off his father's arm. "You got to be faster," his father said.

Robert went at him with his whole body, punching wildly, hitting as hard as he could, wanting now to hurt him. Unexpectedly, out of sudden confusion and the sheer exasperation of not really knowing why they were hitting each other, out of the pain of not understanding and the pain that his father's blows had inflicted, Robert began to cry. Soundlessly, but tears were wetting his face, blinding him. The fact that he was crying angered him, but the anger was now against himself, not his father. When his father saw that Robert was crying, all he said was "Oh, shit!" and walked away from him.

Robert stood in the middle of the floor, looking at his father's back while the girls began to pick up the chairs and push the tables back where they belonged. The oldest of them came to Robert and put her arms around him and led him away to a small room where she undressed him and washed the tears and blood off his face. He lay naked against her body, his face buried in her generous brown breasts, feeling drained of strength. She kept murmuring to him in Spanish and brushing his hair with her fingers and he kept crying.

What were they fighting about? Was it his mother? Or did she have nothing to do with it? Was it something between the two of them that had to be settled? It was settled in his father's favor, whatever it was. It was too complicated to be Hal Hubbard's son, he thought. And he didn't want complications. He wanted to be back where he belonged, in his woods with his mother.

He left Haiti early the next morning without saying good-bye to anyone. Before sneaking out of the house, he wrote his father a note:

I think what you were doing last night was trying to push me out of the next. I think it was way past my time to leave it.

Instead of going home to his mother, he stopped in Miami and, while there, enlisted in the Navy. After the end of the war, he married a nurse he met while recovering from a wound he received in the Pacific. He did not tell her who his father was. He never talked about him to his mother. But he read the letters his mother received over the years from Hal. In one of them, Hal wrote:

It was always difficult for me to have Bobby around because he always brought you with him. Our years together were the only good years I've ever had. You were the only true thing in my life. I always knew he loved you with the kind of love I should have, the kind that is unconditional. That's the whole difference, in a nutshell, between most of us poor bastards and God, we can't love unconditionally, and he can't love any other way. We were, in a way, enemies all along, Bobby and I. I never should have wanted him to be born. Maybe in some way, he is what I would have been if things had not gone wrong. Or, maybe, because he is the way he is, I feel diminished somehow.

"How do you feel?" Dr. Jones was looking across his shiny desk straight into Hal's eyes with an encouraging smile. Dr. Robinson was sitting by the window, silent and smiling.

"Never better," Hal said.

"What have you been thinking about?"

"When?"

"Before our session?"

"My oldest kid," he said. Just in case they knew anyway.

"Tell me about him."

"Not all that much to tell. He's a good man because he was a good boy."

"Do you take any credit for that?"

"Not much."

"Why not?"

"Because his mother brought him up."

He winged the rest of the session, artfully avoiding this son and his other kids and wife, making the doctor believe that he wanted to write, that he had an outline of his next novel in his head, that he felt happy about how it was going.

"Do you always think of your plot and your characters for a while before sitting down to write?" Would Dr. Jones also become a writer, he wondered. Out of the woodwork they seem to be coming at him.

"Always," he said. Was this a lie? He couldn't remember how it used to be.

Back in his room that he was going to leave on his fifty-seventh birthday, which would coincide with his deathday, he tried to extract the essence out of Bobby. It was all hers, this essence. Once, that first winter in Paris, while they were lying in bed reading to each other Plato's *The Last Days of Socrates,* he had turned to Lee and said, "You are like him." "Plato or Socrates?" she had asked. "The master," he had said, "Socrates himself." He knew her essence then and told her what it was. "You are my own midwife to the world. You have a skill of bringing my thoughts to birth. That's what Socrates did for everyone." She, like Socrates, had a kind heart that believed most firmly in moral goodness. She knew, instinctively, that it made sense. She used logic to make that deduction. She did not understand all this, as no honest person ever understands the gift of honesty. But he did, because he was dishonest.

Why did he want to punish Bobby, why did he include him on the list of those who ate from within? Because the boy had cried in a Haitian bar instead of punishing his father. If only he had hit him harder, had knocked him down then, but instead he had looked at him and cried. What was it, pity? Or knowledge? Of what?

He put him on the list because nothing was quite the same after that. On that last visit he again brought back Lee. All her goodness. And Bobby, not Lee now, overshadowed that time of his hope. He had thought that he had another chance at loving a woman. Peggy Smith was coming. She was to be his salvation, and Bobby had ruined that salvation for him.

He took down from the shelf above his head *The Quest,* the novel he had been working on when Bobby came that last time. He opened it to the right page and read to himself:

> He was past forty now, and gun-running was his way of life. Maybe

he went into that business because of the dangers. He had nothing to look forward to, not since she had died on him. He didn't expect or want to fall in love with another woman. It had been too costly to him.

And yet, when it happened, it seemed to him that he could start over again. Everything that never seemed possible seemed possible now. What he had not figured on was that none of it was real, none of it had substance.

He had written those paragraphs the night after his fight with Bobby. Maybe what he wanted from his son, and did not get, was some kind of freeing from Lee. Maybe what he was after was the loosening of the chains. But the boy was chained to the goodness within his mother.

Peggy Smith was to be his salvation. He might as well place her here, between his first son and the other two myths. The sequence was as good as any now. The ledger could be filled, but she did not belong in it. Yet she belonged with the clarifying memories of the downslide.

London, 1943. He didn't want to go out into the rain, leave the comfortable, friendly bar. He wasn't interested in attending the press conference of a minor actress, an adventuress, even if she had managed to fly over Germany in her private plane and drop some goddamned leaflets. Why should they be wasting time giving publicity to the lady, if she was a lady?

"You've got to meet the broad," Jack Williams, the NBC correspondent said, pulling him out of his chair. He went reluctantly and in the taxi told Jack what he thought of crazy broads who interfered with the war effort. "Don't be a pompous ass," Jack said. "Peggy Smith could win this fucking war single-handedly if she was given free rein. She made a couple of films in Germany before the war, and it is a well-known fact that the Führer keeps her picture by his bed. He keeps talking about her as if she were the greatest actress since Bernhardt. She's said to have seduced the pants off the RAF brass to let her fly out of England without getting shot at by our guys."

The press conference was held in her hotel's ballroom, and when they arrived, there were already a couple of dozen journalists standing among the sheet-draped furniture, drinking champagne and eating caviar. "That's what she lives on," Jack said, "and if the bubbly and fish eggs could do for my wife's boobs and derrière what they seem to do for hers, I'd feed her nothing but that." Hal was standing by the door, ready to escape, when she came into the ballroom wearing a long, red satin dress cut very low. Her hair was an unbelievable blonde, the kind of blonde he used to dream about as a young boy during his wet dreams. What made him stay was not that she looked better than any woman he had ever seen, but the way her eyes seemed to mock everything. She made them all feel young and foolish and horny. Her eyes seemed to say that she knew all there was to know about how things could be, but rarely were, between men and women.

They began to shout their questions at her, but she was in no hurry. She was enjoying the sight and sounds of them. There was something unbearably sensual about that private enjoyment of hers, about the way she held herself aloof and yet more accessible than any female he had ever seen, including whores. Hal thought that what they were all doing was making love to her, collectively, as she made love to herself.

"Come on, Peggy, tell us. What was on the leaflet?"

"How far over Germany did you get?"

"Were you alone?"

"Did you get shot at?"

She held the leaflet over her head, and they saw it was printed in large German script and signed with her name.

"What does it say? It looks short and sweet."

"Did you write the message yourself, Peggy?"

"You're damned right I did." Her voice was everything he thought it would be. Low and husky and suggestive of pleasures only she was capable of giving and receiving. "It says here, 'If he couldn't get it up with me, how come he's fucking the whole world?' "

They hooted and cheered and laughed, and she laughed with them, throwing her blonde head back and taking pleasure in what she had done and in their approval.

"Have you ever been in bed with Hitler, Peggy?" someone shouted.

"Back in '37 I had the clap and wanted to give it to the son-of-a-bitch," she answered, and a wave of laughter swept the room.

While she told them in more detail about her encounter with Hitler and the details of her solo flight over Germany, he kept looking at her without hearing what she said or what they asked. All he knew now was that he needed her. She could bring joy back to his life. There was more than joy in her, a sense of life that he felt spreading across the room. And they too must have felt it because nobody wanted to leave that room. They asked her to sing, and she climbed up on the top of the piano. They surrounded her, and she seemed to surround them as she sang German songs because, she said, "They're the best among all phoney love songs." Her voice grew huskier and lower and made a mockery of holding on, celebrating freedom from bondage, emancipating love and sex.

It was past midnight when the last of them left and yet he still stood by the door, and she had not once spoken to him nor even looked his way. And now she came to him, and without speaking or looking, she took his hand and led him across the lobby and up the stairs to her room.

In her bed he tried to discover familiar landmarks on the landscape of her face, but all was new. In the way they made love and woke to the air raid sirens and made love again, this time with more shyness and grace than passion. She left him, saying, "Come back, or stay." He lay on her bed, his eyes on the ceiling, his nostrils inhaling her fading smell, and then reached for a pen and wrote a poem on her pillowcase.

> What happened here
> When you were near
> had happened somewhere else before.
>
> It must have been
> The original sin.

He waited for her until it grew dark. Then wrote another poem on the pillow that had been his.

> He wanted more;
> thinking it should never end.
> What was it for,
> he wondered going away
> to fend off the world.

He had not written poetry in years and never two poems quite as bad as these, but it was not the gift, it was the thought. Bad as they were, they said what they had been meant to say. He didn't know where she would lead him, but he wanted to be there in case she wished to take him by the hand. For he had become lost.

For a week he stayed away from the bars where he would have run into the correspondents who had been there, who knew that he had been the one who never left. He scanned the papers for interviews with her and learned she had started a picture. He could have gone to the studio, could have used people he knew. He could simply have called, or gone back to her hotel. But he doubted it had meant something to her and tried to cure himself of what could have been the laughter and joy of her presence. Yet he knew the symptoms well of being in love again. Without her the only reality seemed to be writing poems to her. And he wrote her poems as if they were the only things he could write, words coming easy, as if in poetry they did not have to be chiseled by his tools as in prose, as if they were birds springing forth from an open cage.

> I search for your face in the crowded train.
> I look for your eyes in the barren rain.
> I seek your smile in the last dead leaf.
> And I find them all in this gulf, my grief.

He walked around the London that Byron and Shelley and Keats knew and one evening picked up a paper and read a letter to the editors written by a group of women who were protesting Peggy Smith's "adventures, which, we feel, endanger the war effort." He walked into the nearest bar and on a napkin wrote in her defense:

> Her crime, even as a child, must always have been the same: she laughed and made fun of ashes of doom. One does not laugh at war. Laughers endanger the effort that war requires. Wasted lives are endangered by people like Peggy Smith.

He crumpled up the napkin and threw it into a spittoon. She didn't take kindly to his chosen trade, he thought. He must not use her, she could not be used for his writing. He would use her for his life, if he could, to give him that other breath that he needed to live.

When he came back to his hotel late that night there was a message for him to call Jack Williams. "Where have you been? Peggy wanted to know if you could meet her tomorrow at four at her studio. Told her all about you. She doesn't read books, so you can't impress her with your talent. But she must have been impressed." They talked for awhile, and Hal found out that there was a pool among the war correspondents, and the pool had to do with who'd be the first to lay Peggy Smith. Jack was trying to find out if Hal had made love to her, but he skirted the question artfully.

He walked onto the set while she was doing a love scene with her leading man. She smiled when she saw him and ruined the take. Watching her now, he knew something he had not figured on before, that he could never possess her, that she would always have to be free. But he also knew for certain that he would have to try to make her his woman. And thought it would be possible, somehow, to do that and not infringe on her essence. While she went through her scene again and again, making jokes and faces each time something went wrong, more at play than at work, he was weaving a net for her capture. He would have to map out the future of their affair, making sure that this free bird never knew when the net was closing in on her. Even in captivity she would spill that joy that was now bursting from her, spoiling the director's shots. "For Christ's sake, don't laugh, Peggy!" "You smiled again!" "Damn it, can't you ever be serious!"

Her crime was a talent for being happy. Her mistake was her passion for life. He would write poems to her, each day, but not for publication, and he'd stop writing them only when she was safely tucked in his breast pocket, in Haiti, his to hold and take from that which he did not possess. It would not be thieving, for she gave of it freely. He wanted from her not sex, not even love, he would give her both. He wanted from her the ability to laugh off even the serious side of living. She had a true talent for that, and he would learn from her. Otherwise, he knew, he would start on some very steep, downward curve that would only end in the same way his father's and his grandfather's lives had ended.

They went from the studio to her hotel and made love again, hungrily this time, and she kidded a lot and said she had never read poetry before she read her pillows. Were the poems good, she wanted to know. "Love poems are always good," he said. But he would have to watch himself and not be her teacher. She would be his.

He waited for her to call him because she said that she would, that it made her feel more secure if she made the moves. But she did not call for a week, and when he went to her hotel, he was told that she had gone off to Hollywood. There was nothing to keep him now in England, not even the war.

When he came home he found the doors of Carole's love for him jammed into the past. He came back to tell her that he was leaving her for Peggy. But Peggy was not his. And he decided he would wait.

He subscribed to a clipping service and entered another subscription in her name so that he would know what was being written about her, where she was, what she was doing, whom she was seeing. The clippings arriving together in the mail, his and hers, made him feel almost as if he had a part of her. She was under contract to Warner Brothers. She was doing a USO tour. When she came back from the Pacific, she was scheduled to do a movie in Hollywood. He finally decided to write her a letter. It took him over twenty rewrites, far more than any of his short stories. But he had to be careful so the bait would not show.

> Peggy, I'm back in Haiti. I've got a boat all equipped with torpedoes and guns. Will be going after the German subs. If you find time, and would like some excitement, and if you like the waters around here, I wish you'd come and give us a hand. My three children will be with me during the summer. Wife not well, and not here. Am stocking on champagne and caviar just in case.
>
> Hal

While waiting for her to answer, he attempted to write a screenplay for her, but the form was unfamiliar and after a bad month of trying, he gave it up in favor of a short story. Someone else would turn it into a script. But the story he wrote was for her. It was called "The Hired Hands," and he felt it was the best piece of work he had done in years.

Two months after he mailed the letter, her answering wire finally came: WILL BE THERE AUGUST 15TH. HOLD THE SUBS. PEGGY. He had been able to live through those months, seeing Carole, now in a private clinic, sink deeper into her phantom past, only because he knew Peggy would come to him. Now he got busy, hired workers to enlarge the guest house for her. He had the boat revarnished, bought her the best fishing gear he could find, stocked the cellar with champagne from New York and the ice box with Russian caviar. He did a thousand little things for her, and yet, on the eve of her arrival, he felt nervous and did not want to be by himself.

While drinking in the bar with Bobby he thought of wiping the slate clean of everyone he had ever known, making the presence of the children invisible. He wanted to start off with her on a new life, alone. And in his anger that it could not be done, he attacked his oldest son.

Robert was not there when Peggy arrived, but the other two were. He was glad Bobby was gone, for he would have seen on Hal's face what the other two did not notice. He would have known that Peggy for him meant his salvation. He had taken the children with him to the airport because they would help deflect from her what he felt for her. Seeing her come down the plane's ramp, he knew everything was going to be all right in his world. But he would never burden her with that knowledge. Shrimp made friends with her instantly, and she paid more attention to them than to him. He was glad of that. Glad that neither his son nor his daughter thought him a traitor to their mother.

"Let the bed be our only private territory," she had said the first night. And it was her bed, in the guesthouse, that was his refuge from then on. Outside it she was more a friend than a lover. He would have to watch himself, all the time, so she would not suspect that he wished to lean, to rest against her.

She loved the children and played with them as if she were a child herself. He tried his best to leave her a lot of space, and that space she relinquished with pleasure to them. When the summer was over, they would have to return to school. But only Bean went. Shrimp stayed behind, pretending to be sick, and Peggy, knowing she pretended, told Hal to let Shrimp stay and said she wanted her on the boat with them. She'd come to chase the subs, and that's what they would do. Together, the three of them.

Why did he always feel as if he were walking on glass? He did not want to shatter the feeling of freedom that she had to have. And she was independent even on the boat, baiting her own line, fighting her own fish. Never asking, always coping, even in situations new to her. As far back as he could remember, he thought that the role of a man was to help women, but she was like no woman he had known. She was a grown child, with the same drives that take children away from their parents toward their own ways of doing things, with the same childish fear that interference would diminish her somehow. With Shrimp she was not like that. Shrimp could tell her anything, help her, advise her. She was no threat to her, Shrimp was her peer. And to Shrimp she must have seemed like a mother she always wanted. But with Hal, Peggy was always erect, standing squarely on her two feet, like a bull in his *guarentia,* he thought, proud but distrustful at the same time.

He wasn't going to drink as much as he usually drank on the boat, but he did. What had enchanted him in London—her total lack of awareness that he was a famous writer—now began to bother him.

He had not followed his instinct. He had used her in his writing. He had brought on board the story he had written especially for her. He handed it to her when she arrived that first day, saying he wrote it for her, that he believed it would make a good film with her in the part of the woman, but she kept leaving it in the main house. He tried to make her read it on the boat, but she kept putting it off saying that reading at sea would make her dizzy, and who'd read at sea anyway when there was all that air to breathe, the waves to watch, and the sun and the sky to be glad of.

They were out for over ten days, on the lookout for the subs, but although he spent most of his time on the bridge, scanning the horizon with his powerful glasses, he never spotted one. She made it clear to him that they should not sleep together on the boat; "Shrimp might see us, and it would hurt her. She's got a terrific crush on me, and I have one on her. Student crushes are gorgeous, and we're both students. What a dreadful thing it would be if she knew I was the woman who was bedding down her father." The two of them laughed and joked all day and told each other outrageous stories, and although neither one tried to keep him out, he felt left out.

When would it happen to him? When would she instill in him the joy that she could feel on rising and throughout the day, taking pleasure from the most simple things: a flying fish, a cloud that looked like a face, from cooking what she termed "seaweed stew." Why had life not spoiled her as it had spoiled him? Would it always be like that, almost reaching, catching her, but for the presence of Shrimp or some other obstruction? Would there always be another hurdle? And beyond that, would she always be free, escaping him?

He tried writing poetry, going down to the cabin he had thought they would share, but he could no longer write poems to her. Above on the deck, he would hear her laugh with Shrimp. She even made old Bernard laugh, and Hal, who had known him for years and considered himself his friend, had never been able to do that.

When they came back a wire was waiting for her. She had to reshoot some scenes; they needed her immediately, the delay was costing money.

"Stay," he said, when they were back on their turf, in her bed.

"I'll be back," she said.

He took both of them to the plane, Shrimp happy to be spending another couple of hours with her, for they would fly to Miami together. After they left, Hal drove to the Olaffson Hotel and got good and drunk in the bar and brought a Vassar girl back to the empty house. She had come to Haiti because she was writing a thesis on him and had hoped for an interview. Instead she got laid.

Hal grew a long beard and tried to write, but the writing was not going well. He caught malaria in November. One day, running a high fever, he saw her walk into his bedroom and sit down on a chair. He thought he was hallucinating and closed his eyes. But when he opened them again she was still there, sitting by his side, reading his story, "The Hired Hands." When she was finished, she put it aside, and he pretended to be asleep. She bent down over him and kissed him gently on the forehead, and he opened his eyes and she bent lower and kissed his parched lips.

"You're a goddamn genius," she said. "Why didn't I know that?"

"Will you marry me?" he asked.

"I love you," she said.

"Because you think me a genius?"

"No, because you're sick and grew a long beard. I've got a weakness for sick, long-bearded men."

There was no trap set when she walked into one. She was saying that she loved him, repeating the words over and over again, like a child with a new toy. He wanted to tell her all that he had felt, how long it had been, loving her, but she didn't want to hear anything from the past. "We're born as of now," she kept saying that first day, "we have no past."

He went for his divorce to Reno while she went to Hollywood. She never asked for any rules, but he told her that he understood how it was with her, that he would never hold on to her. That she would be free to be, to do, what she wished, that there would be no strings, even in marriage. And saying all this, making her sit still until he was finished with the declaration of her independence, he wished she would say that none of this mattered now, that she was going into captivity and would love it there. But she listened, impatiently, and nodded her head, smiled and laughed and said that she would not hold on to him either. That they were two independent beings united only by love.

"But freedom is more precious than love," she said. "We both know this, don't we?" And it was his turn to nod his head. "It will be hell sometimes," she said, "but we'll walk through it unburned."

"There will be no hell for us," he said. And then she told him that she'd live with him but would never marry him.

He didn't know that Hollywood could be hell. Everyone assumed they were married, and they did not deny these rumors. They were lionized. There were two camps, one in which he was Mr. Smith, and the other in which she was not Peggy Smith but Mrs. Hal Hubbard. She felt at ease in both, he felt ill at ease in both.

They were living in her rented house, almost empty of furniture, high in the Hollywood hills, and he thought he could work there while she was away in her studio, making "The Hired Hands." She would leave while he was still asleep and would come back home exhausted, after six. She didn't like to talk about her days, and he had nothing to tell her about his. "Let's go away," he would sometimes say, and she would answer, "To hell with it all. Let's go away. To Haiti. Anywhere." But it was just talk. She had to do what she had to do. She had a great sense of responsibility. After two months that seemed like two years, he decided to go to Martha's Vineyard ahead of her.

"I can't live without writing, and I can't write here," he said.

"I know," she said. "Go. I'll come as soon as I can."

He went. He did not get infected by what was hers. She did not cure what was wrong with him. Even when she was tired she could kid about her work, their life. He could not ever do that about his.

The day he came back to Martha's Vineyard, he began his usual routine and wrote well for two weeks, averaging ten pages a day, which was the best he had ever done. He was writing a novel called *The Quest*.

When Shrimp and Bean came for the summer he continued to work, keeping only the afternoons free for them. "When is Peggy coming?" they wanted to know. The kids presumed they were married, and he did not tell them the truth. "She will be here soon." But she never came. Not that summer, or ever again. In the fall he experienced his first real writer's block. It was hell sweating it out, but he understood that it had not been her fault. She had tried, in her way, to send signals to him all along. She needed to be who she was, uncaught, free to roam as she pleased. She never made him any promises, so she would keep none.

With her he had thought that for once, he would be doing the taking, but it was not to be. When he was leaving her in Hollywood she had said, "Tell Bernard to let me know if you are sick again," but Bernard wouldn't know now if he was being sick or well. Peggy Smith was not to be in the ledger. She did not belong. She could not have reversed his fate. She had not in her the power to will his fate away. She had joy in her but it had been too late for him. There were no guilts and no regrets. She passed through him like a sunny day but never belonged to him.

Carl Hubbard

THE young priest was unaware of the fact that the hunter was dying, not of the wounds received, but dying nevertheless of a lack of wanting to live.

"How is it, father, that you make a living?" the hunter asked. He was simply making conversation. He didn't mean anything by the question. Or maybe he did. Recently, everything he said sounded suspicious to him.

"We do what we can. And we eat whenever the people we care for have something to share." The priest's folded hands bore scars. The hunter knew he was not yet used to making a living with them.

"Are the natives ever grateful for having their souls saved?" The young priest did not answer, but smiled gently as if saying, "You are one of those who think missionaries unhealthy to the natives." The hunter suddenly was angry. He had not asked for the priest. He didn't want him around. He wanted to be left alone. He was tired. Dying from want of wishing to live took a long time, and it was a tiring business.

"Son, do you wish to make a confession?" the priest asked. "No," the hunter said. "But thank you anyway."

He turned his face toward the wall. He remembered his last confession when he was seventeen. "Forgive me, father, for I have sinned. I made a girl pregnant. I talked her into having an abortion." The child he never had would be twenty-eight this summer. He wondered if life for him would have been different had the child lived.

from *The Last Hunt* by Hal Hubbard

When Carl was seven, he realized that the less he thought about his parents, the better off he would be. Thinking about them gave him headaches during the day and nightmares during his sleep. Before he went to boarding school, he used to eavesdrop on his parents and there was much that he did not understand. What he did understand was that his mother was more at ease with his father than she was with her children. What he didn't understand was why his father did not make her care for them.

When he was sent to boarding school with Anne, he realized that he had a job to do and that job was to take care of her. He always thought of her as Anne instead of Shrimp, and of himself as Carl rather than Bean. Those nicknames were his father's and they belonged to him.

At home it was easy, protecting Anne. All he needed to do was to take the blame, no matter what. But in school it would be hard. Anne's teachers and the other kids would soon discover all sorts of things about her that he didn't want them to discover. For one thing, Anne was an awful liar. It came very easily to her. It was more natural for her to lie than to tell the truth, and she probably didn't even know when she was lying. He himself lied a lot too. He had to. But whenever he lied, he knew he was doing it and wished he didn't have to.

For another thing, Anne was always scared, and they might start calling her a coward. And if their father ever found out, he might have Anne given up to an orphanage or something. Once Carl overheard his father say to a friend, "The best thing to do with cowards is put them away somwhere where they won't be seen. Once they used to kill them, but we've become civilized. What's wrong with this world is that we let cowards not only run around loose in it, we let them run things."

He tried to explain to Anne, before they went off to boarding school, how she should never show fear of anything. How people who showed fear were called "cowards" and how they were put away in special places. He tried to teach her that you had to be very clever at lying if you were to lie, and the difference between truth and lies, but it was very hard teaching a five-year-old. Soon, at school as he had done at home, he began to take the blame for things he had not done, but which Anne had. She took things that didn't belong to her and lied that they did belong to her. Carl would give those things back and say it was he who had borrowed them, which made him a liar. Then he would have to explain to Anne why it was he had to lie and how he hated doing it. It was no good getting mad at his kid sister because each time he'd get mad, there would be this cowering look in Anne's eyes. Carl's biggest job was to prevent his sister from being recognized as a coward.

Carl knew all sorts of things that Anne didn't know and which he found out all too soon. He knew that his father would try to make Anne do things the kid would be too scared to do. He knew that on her fifth birthday Anne would get a fishing knife and a rod and that his father would expect her to bait the fish and to cut their throats, take out the hook herself and scale and clean the fish. He knew this because he himself had been made to do this at five. At seven Anne would get a gun and would be told how to use it, and his father would expect her not to cringe when she shot, just as he hadn't expected Carl to cringe. He had a two-year start on his little sister and he would teach her how to play all the games their father expected them to play. Most of all, from the beginning it was his job to explain to her that being a girl was no excuse. Their father believed in equality between the sexes.

By the time he was eight years old, Carl knew for certain that his mother would have been much happier if she had not had any children. The way he found out was by overhearing her say so, but he must have known all along. Knowing it for certain, from her lips, made him feel sorry for her rather than angry. She tried her best to be a good mother to them, and he admired her for trying. It did not come naturally as it did with a lot of mothers he knew, being a parent. It was something she was playing at and not enjoying. The same week he overheard her confess to never having wanted to be a mother, he and Anne wandered into a Catholic church. They had never been inside any church before, and what surprised Carl was to see a lifesize statue of a lady. Below her feet was a sign which said, "This is Our Mother." He read it aloud to Anne.

"We've got a mother," Anne said, "and that's not her."

"Well, maybe we've got two mothers."

To Anne, seeing the statue meant absolutely nothing. But Carl became obsessed with it. In the church lobby, he found a pamphlet with the picture of the statue on its cover and read about Mary. He went to see the priest and talked about her with him. He made friends with the priest and by the time they went back to their boarding school, he was filled with the idea that he would become a priest when he grew up. He began to read books about Mary, about the saints and martyrs, and about Jesus. He began to look at everyone with different eyes, hear with different ears. His nights were now filled with dreams, strange visions of martyrs dying for their faith, saints fighting devils. He began to put sharp pebbles in his shoes for the pain they would give him, and he wrote to manufacturers of religious articles for a hair shirt, but he could not find anyone who sold them.

By the time he was eleven and had spent a holiday with his mother and sister in New York City, he was a totally changed boy. He still took care of Anne, but his vision of caring was enlarged to include everyone. Whenever he saw a bum or someone who looked crazy on the New York streets, waves of warmth would envelop him. The only thing he missed were his dreams, and he longed to go back to his familiar school bed to resume those nightly visions. What especially enchanted him was a recurring dream in which he was a fisherman, but instead of fish, in his dream he would pull out men, women, and children on a line of golden thread.

Gradually he became emotionally detached from his family and friends. He lived toward the future when he could become a priest, a missionary in Africa saving souls, talking of the glory of that Mother who gave her love to everyone, and of the mystery of God and the charity of the Savior. When he came home one summer to discover that his mother had detached herself from reality, he was filled with wonder at her ability to do what he often wished he could do himself. She lived comfortably in a world that was not their world, much more real because it was fulfilling all her needs. He did not consider her crazy, as Anne did, and as his father must have. He thought of her as having surrendered to her own visions, something he would one day do himself.

He knew that the only person who could never understand what was happening to him would be his father. Because he was afraid Anne would tell him, he kept his thoughts and his dreams a secret from her. When he saw his father he would act as he had during those years when he was trying "to become a man." He kept shooting, although now to kill anything filled him with shame and disgust. He fished and hated catching the fish and seeing it denied its life. He liked best to have Robert around because when he was around, Carl could relax and retreat into his own world.

He had been writing letters to the priest who first instructed him in the Catholic religion, and to him Carl confided that he was afraid of telling his father about his decision to become a Catholic. The priest advised him to talk to his father during the summer holidays and explain how he felt, and offered to help by being there when he did.

By the summer of that year, his parents were divorced. Carl decided to face his father before Peggy came to join them at Martha's Vineyard. More than anything, he wanted his father if not to approve then to try and understand his wish to become a Catholic. If he did, then he would tell him more, about how he was going to study to be a priest and how he hoped to work as a missionary in Africa. He would also ask his father about Africa because he had been there.

During the first week of his fourteenth summer, he found no opportunity to talk to his father alone. His father had several talks with him and Anne about the divorce, saying that when their mother got well, they would probably live with her part of the time. He explained about things not changing between the "three of us guys." But things had changed. They both saw in Haiti how crazy he was about Peggy, and they liked her very much themselves and had a much better time with her around. Anne would say that she didn't miss her mother at all and that she wouldn't go live with her even if she did get well, which she hoped she wouldn't. Carl wrote his mother every few days, but it was hard to give her any news because there was none. They were waiting for Peggy. And he doubted his mother would have wished to know anything about her.

father came to his room early in the morning, wanting to know if he wished to go sailing with him alone. "Shrimp doesn't want to come," he said, "and there is a nice gale force wind coming from the south. The Coast Guard posted warnings, and the seas look good and rough. How about taking them on, Bean?" It was the kind of day for sailing that both of them loved.

For a long while, they were busy keeping a steady course toward Nantucket. While working the rudder, Carl thought how very lucky he had been to be the son of such a wonderful sailor. His father did almost everything well, and it was from him that Carl had acquired his desire to excel. He had taught Carl how to be physically strong and how to endure hardships without complaining. Over the years, he had laid down the kind of code he himself lived by, but nothing he had ever told him had to do with the soul. It all concerned the body. And now it was Carl who was going to bring that subject up for the first time.

Besides the priest, whom he had seen several times and had written letters to, Carl had not talked to anyone about God and how he intended to get to know Him and serve Him. Although he knew that he had to talk to his father about it, he had not rehearsed what he would say. When his father took the first drink of gin and sat down beside him, relaxed, looking over the high seas and the gray horizon, Carl finally got up the courage to speak.

"What do you think of God?" he asked his father.

"God? You mean G-O-D?" He looked surprised at his son's question. "What would I think of him? I don't know him."

"How about the son, then? Jesus."

"Like in Christ?" His eyes were still ahead, not looking at Carl.

"Yeah, Our Lord, Jesus Christ. What do you make of him?"

"He was probably a good man in bad times," Hal said. "Why are you asking?" He turned to Carl and looked at him hard.

"I've been thinking a lot lately about God and Jesus and things like that," Carl said. "I just wondered if you ever think of that."

His father looked at him, and for a while they were looking at each other. Carl was hoping that it was true what he heard once, that eyes could speak volumes. Then Hal smiled and patted Carl on the shoulder. "Hey, aren't we supposed to have a man-to-man talk about girls and stuff like that?"

He found his opportunity to talk to his father one stormy day. His
"No," Carl said. "We're supposed to talk about God. I'd like to. . . ." He wasn't making much sense, he knew, and his father's attention, which was hard to keep at best, was going to wander off. "I want to become a Catholic," he said quickly. "I'd like you to know that."

"What the hell do you want to do that for?"

"I intend to be a priest," Carl said and hoped that his father would not laugh. But he did. He laughed so hard he spilled his drink over the slicker. Carl didn't hold it against him, his laughing.

"Why would you of all people want to be a priest?" his father asked, growing serious.

"Because when you're a priest, you get as close to God as you possibly can. You're like . . . like His soldier." Carl laughed nervously. "No, maybe even like His officer."

"What's the head honcho, the Pope—a General?"

It wasn't like that, he had never thought of being a soldier once he became a priest. He was messing the whole thing up. He wanted to tell his father how happy he was to have found a real family, having understood Jesus. But he couldn't explain any of this. He was tongue-tied and feeling stupid.

"You're really serious about all this, aren't you, Bean? You really believe in God?"

"I believe in Him because He's very real to me."

"How real?"

"More real than you." He had not meant to say that.

His father's eyes went hard, and he looked away and they didn't say anything for a while. Carl could have said something then, he could have tried to explain. But he had said the truth.

"Would you like to put that to a test, the reality of God?" His father was looking at him again, and the boy knew that look. That's how he looked whenever he was "separating bullshit from the truth and getting down to the bottom line." "Would you want to put it to a test?" he asked again.

"Sure."

"Suppose I threw you overboard. Would you call for help to me or to God?"

"It wouldn't be a good test," Carl said. "You'd be doing the throwing, so you'd be responsible for getting me out."

"All right. Suppose you fell overboard. Who would help you, me or God?"

"I probably would try to help myself, and if I couldn't you'd help me."

"So where was God all this time?"

"Where He'd be if I hadn't fallen, or if you hadn't thrown me overboard."

"And where is that?"

"Inside of me." The boy smiled at his father then." "And inside of you. And everywhere. Where He always is."

"How do you know Him, this God of yours that's so real and who's trespassing inside of me?"

"Through His son."

"Would they know me through you?" The question came loud and stunned the boy.

"I love you," Carl said, "you taught me...."

"I wanted you to be...." Hal didn't finish. He took the rudder from his son's hands and came about and headed home.

"What did you want me to be?" Carl asked before they docked.

"A man," his father said.

"Priests are men."

"Without balls."

He didn't blame his father for not understanding. He didn't really understand all that much at the time himself. He didn't know then that the reason he wanted to be a priest was because it gave him freedom and joy. Freedom to love everyone and joy in serving God. Both of these things were very private, and he could never explain adequately to anyone why he became a priest. There were times in Africa when he was sick with fever and thought he chose the priesthood when so young because he could not cope with his own family. The passage in the Bible that had impressed him most when he read it at thirteen was the one that demanded denying your own mother and father to follow Christ. But it was only in fever that he felt any guilt about his vocation.

He had gone straight to the seminary from prep school, and the hardest thing was taking leave of his mother and Anne, for neither of them let him go easily. His father, he felt, had reconciled himself to the idea that day on the boat. He decided that once he entered the seminary he would not see his sister nor his mother or father because the hold they had on him was still there whenever he was in their presence and the hold had to be broken.

He went to Africa when he was twenty-two. Two years later he saw his father in a Nairobi hospital. He had heard on the mission radio that his father had been killed during a hunt and then that he had only been mauled by a lion and was alive. The radio reports indicated he was badly hurt, and Carl hurried to see him.

He was shocked at the way his father looked. The wounds were healing by then, and the doctors did not think there was any permanent damage, and yet Carl thought that something crucial had happened to him. Something that would never be cured. He seemed as if bloated by some sort of inner despair. He talked in shorthand that made everything he said sound glib.

"Female companion here shot badly," he said to Carl, indicating Sally, a small woman who hovered around his chair, patting pillows in place, adding ice cubes to his drink. "Had to go after wounded lion. Was in lion's embrace for awhile. Many bones broken from too tight hug. How's priest business?"

"Less dangerous," Carl said.

"Didn't go into it because of that?"

"No. Not because of that."

"Missionaries not healthy to natives," his father said.

"We dispense medicine and schooling as well as save souls," Carl said.

"Each man has to save himself."

"Not everyone is as strong as you. Some people need help."

"Priest talk."

Carl stayed around for two days. His father wanted to go after another lion as soon as the doctors discharged him from the hospital. But Sally would have none of this, was urging him to fly back to Haiti to "read the obituaries." It seemed to Carl that his father, whom he remembered as the most independent of men, had grown old before his time, had abdicated caring for himself in favor of being cared for by Sally. It was she who seemed to be running his life now, making all the decisions, assuming the imperial "we."

The night before Carl left, his father wanted to talk to him again about the lion. But what he said to Carl seemed to be symbolic, a metaphor for something else that had a deathhold on him.

In the ten years they had not seen each other, his father had become prone to make pronouncements, as if speaking for all men who were truly male.

"What do you priests do for sex?" he asked Carl.

"We dispossess it of importance," Carl answered.

"Is it true that a lot of priests are fags?"

"I don't think there are as many as you think."

"Do you think it's natural to live without sex?"

"More natural than it is to live without God."

If it had been anyone but his father, he would have tried to talk to him seriously about that giant lack in his life, the lack of an awareness of God. But this was, indeed, his father and he could not do it. Yet he thought that if his father were to make a confession, it would be brief and to the point: "I hate life." What he remembered best about him was his lust for life, which had now turned a hundred and eighty degrees. Or so it seemed to Carl. And seeing him so changed made him want to cry.

Before going back to his mission, Carl carved on a tusk of an elephant his father had shot these words of Thomas Aquinas, and gave the tusk to him:

> This is the earthly goal of man: to evolve his intellectual powers to their fullest; to arrive at the maximum of consciousness; to open the eyes of his understanding upon all things so that upon the tablet of his soul the order of the whole universe and all its parts may be enrolled.

He was near closing the ledger on Bean when Sally's call came through.

"I hear you're writing again," she said. She sounded cheerful, but the cheerfulness was the greed he knew so well. After all, whether he lived or died she'd profit from his work. They had a legal document dividing the spoils between her and his children, share and share alike. He would not accuse her of having protected their unmarried state with the trappings of permanence because he was being "good" and there were but ten days to go.

"Just taking notes for a new book," he told her. "Most of it is walking through my head, am waiting for the running to start." Pitter-pat of nonexistent characters' feet.

"That's the best news in the world," she said in a low voice, trying to sound sexy again. He waited for her to continue, to tell him more, to ask perhaps the name of the new work, whether she should alert the publishers, ask for an advance. She was his manager, and he had once been the champ. She breathed into the phone.

"It will be good," he said.

"A blockbuster?" she asked.

She was never too good with her choice of descriptive words. He would have liked it better if she had the grace to ask how much they could make off of it.

"Coming-out-of-retirement-a-champ kind of thing," he said. And smiled. He loved smiling at her through the phone. It was one luxury he could not afford when they were face to face.

"Should I write anyone, or call anyone?"

"About what?" He pretended not to know, puncturing ever so slightly her balloon, but the pin was so slight that she would never know.

"About you writing again, of course," she said. No hurt in her voice because his was so matter-of-fact. Oh, the games he was playing now, they were all solitaires.

"Not yet," he said. "Give me a little time."

A small guilt thrown her way. Not nice to be greedy around people just recuperating from illness.

"Of course, my darling." She didn't say, "I can wait." One small point he had to give her. She had her wits about her, they weren't shock-treated away. She didn't deserve the small point he gave her. So he took it from her. Fifteen love, if they were playing tennis. His favor.

"You know how it is when I'm starting," he said. "It goes slow in the first stage." He waited and she waited, and between Santa Fe and Albuquerque there was dead air. "I figure, after the birthday party I'll get down to real work." He counted the seconds. On the count of ten, she said what he thought she would.

"I'm sure you'd be more comfortable writing at home."

"Only if I'm well enough," he said and smiled again. It was as easy as blowing bubbles, talking to her today. "I don't want to cause any more trouble, for you, or me, or anyone. I'm O.K. here. I could write here if the doctors think it best." He was looking at himself in the mirror and laughing silently.

"I think they think you're fine now. I talked to the doctors today, and in their opinion you're getting along so well that if you wished, you could come home before your birthday."

That was set. He beat her six love.

"No, darling," he said to her, making a face into the mirror between words. "They might trust me, but I don't yet trust myself." He gave himself the winner's trophy for that.

"You could never . . . " she began, but he didn't let her finish.

"Of course not," he said, very seriously, lowering his lip as if he were Charles Laughton playing Captain Bligh. He left it unfinished, but both knew what he meant. Who me, kill myself? You must be kidding?

"Could I come and see you?" she begged, but she had lost the set, and he didn't want to start another.

"I miss you too," he said, "but I think it's best for both of us if I attend to the job at hand. I owe you that much."

"But I owe you. . . ."

"You owe me nothing, darling."

"You know best," she said and then went on for a few seconds more before releasing him. Iron hand. Did he ever call her that? By now, he must have called her everthing under the sun, iron hand included.

"Love you too," he said and gently put the phone down. He gave her food, himself as sporting liar, and she might not call again for a few days. He wasn't keeping her guessing. He was setting her up. For the kill. His.

He had set her for the kill when she missed the lion. The lion brought Bean back into his life. The boy—not the boy, the priest-man—knew all about him and deserved to be present at the ceremony that would finalize it all. Out of the ten, Bean would hurt the most seeing the old man blow his brains out, but he was best equipped to cope. After all, he was the family priest. He might say the blessing, or whatever it was that priests did over the body. What would he say, this son of his that took all the good qualities and carried them away to the starving blacks? He had been born clean of what was wrong with Carole and what was wrong with him. He had been born poor and rich at the same time. He had been a joy. Bobby was all Lee, but Carl was all his, his true and only son. Not his mother's child, like Anne. Carl made it easy to believe that out of his loins could come something good and fine, as if he had conceived him masturbating, without Carole's help, and what came out was good.

It had been presumptuous of Carl, Father Carl, to give to his father Hal the words carved on the elephant tusk. Lee had loved Aquinas. Carl, Father Bean, should never have touched that wound. Of course he didn't know that those were her favorite words that hung, framed, over their Paris bed and looked upon them making love, making order of the whole universe through their own parts. If Carl had not used those words he would not have been invited. Ignorance of the law is no excuse, no siree! So much for the beloved son, God's servant who looked and saw literature's servant gone to hell. Maybe it wasn't punishment at all that he was after for Bean. Maybe it was simply that he wanted to see him once more. He and Lee were the only two who had been truly loved. Lee he could not bear to see on his death day, because he had died on her a long time ago. But Bean could take it like a man.

Anne Hubbard

SHE was not just standing there on the bridge looking at the view. She was going to jump. The man walked slowly over to where she was and stopped a foot away from her.

"Nice day," he said. The young woman made no response. She was a foreigner, most probably English or American. She stood very still, like a statue, her eyes on the trees across the chasm of the river.

"Most days are nice now that the war is over. Funny, isn't it, days being nice and life being awful?" She must understand Spanish because her eyes flickered with what might have been interest. "It's funny, too," the man went on, knowing that if he talked he would delay the jump, "the way the war made a difference in how we think. If it were not for the war, we might never find out the sorry son-of-a-bitch was even alive among us." He hoped she understood he was talking about Franco.

"My father was a sorry son-of-a-bitch," she said with a foreign accent. "I killed him. Now I'm going to kill myself."

"What will be, will be," the man said and then walked away. You never know, it might be best to die than live in sin.

from *A Day of Shame* by Hal Hubbard

When Anne was five and before he went away the first time, she asked him, finally, the question that had been on her mind for a long time: "Do you love Bean more than me because he's a boy and I'm a girl?" Her father ruffled her hair and said that he loved them equally. That being a girl was just fine with him. She had known for a fact that her mother lied. But she had not known, until that day, that her father was a liar also. Now it was all right if she was a liar too. When later she found out that he did not lie it was too late to stop being a liar. It was a habit by then that she could not break.

She had just begun to hate her mother, earlier that year. Her father was going away to Spain, where there was a war, and might be killed. And that was because of his wife. What did he ever want with her, this woman? Sometimes she wondered if maybe she was not her mother at all. Maybe there had been somebody else who gave birth to her, and maybe even Bean, and this woman was nothing but a hired actress, nurse, or a maid who was paid to pretend to be a mother. Maybe she would get fired, or die, and then the three of them could live alone in the house. Years later, when her mother went crazy, Anne felt glad. That was for a little while, before she was frightened. She began to fear that her father might go crazy too. And later, much later, the same fear came back, but this time it was the fear that she herself might go crazy. By then she knew for sure she was her mother's daughter. For she was a liar, just like her. She had been wrong about her father. He always told the truth.

The bond of possible future craziness was the only bond she felt between her and her mother. She was bound to her father in many wondrous ways, best of all was the physical evidence that she belonged to him, that she could not have been anyone else's child. She looked exactly like him. She kept a photograph of her father always with her. The photographs would change as she changed, but always, as she grew up, she kept resembling the pictures of her father at that age. It didn't matter, when she found out in school that some kids thought Lindbergh, or Babe Ruth, or President Roosevelt more important than Hal Hubbard. She knew this to be a lie. Her father's books would live forever and so would her father. And one day the two of them would live together, alone with each other.

Pleasing her father was all she had ever wanted, as far back as she could remember, but it was always so hard. If she had been older and Bean younger it might have been easier. Then it would not have been so tiring to prove that she was his equal. She grew up afraid of failing at this job. And she was always afraid, of that and of other things, and she knew all along, even before Bean told her, that her father would hate it if he discovered her to be afraid. And being discovered was fear added to the other fears. She lived in the state of fear as others lived in the State of Massachusetts.

Even worse than fearing was hiding her true feelings. She wanted to hide the fact that she often wished her mother dead, that she often dreamt of her being dead. And she thought she had better hide how she really felt about her father. She loved her father too much. Nothing else mattered to her, not even Bean, not even God, not even life. She would do anything for her father, and she did everything, except she would have liked it better if he had simply asked her to die for him. That would have been easy, walking into a fire, or into the sea, or swallowing poison, but living for him was very tiring and very hard. And it was hard waiting for approval, for praise that would not always come because he would not understand that her job of pleasing him went on all the time. When he approved of her or praised her for something she could feed on it for weeks.

The hardest things to cope with were two facts that could not be dismissed. Fact number one: she was a coward. Fact number two: her father hated cowards. Fact number three did not exist. If it did it would be: her father hated her. But he didn't. He loved her. Maybe fact number three was that she didn't deserve to be loved by him.

At ten she decided that tennis was something she could excel in, and that would please him. At tennis she had a chance to be better than her brother who pleased her father all the time. She would practice for hours against the house wall and on the courts with a pro until she was good enough to win a tournament, until she was beating Carl regularly, until she was good enough to beat her father. But she could never beat him. Anyone else but him. Her father was untouchable as far as competition went. He was the best. But she, when she grew up, would be second best.

When Bean learned to read, and she couldn't read well enough yet, Bean read aloud to Anne from their father's books. From then on she believed herself to be the one who knew best about her father as a writer. She could sense whenever he was writing well even before she saw him, by the way he opened and closed the door to his study. And she knew when things were not going well by the sound of his footsteps pacing the floor. If she could, she would have made it possible for her father to write well all the time because writing well made him very happy. Once she asked Santa Claus for that. Her father found the letter she had written to the North Pole and took Anne on his knee and explained to her that Santa Claus could not do that for him.

"You see, Shrimp," he said, "not Santa Claus, nor God, nor anyone else can make that happen. It's up to me alone and whatever juices are in me. Your father's been drinking too much, or getting interested in other things. If the nose isn't kept to the grindstone, the sharpness goes out and with it gone, the writing is sweat instead of pleasure. If writing isn't pleasuring it's no good. But don't worry, Shrimp, your dad isn't going to count himself out. Not for a long time, anyway."

The best of all summers was the summer when Anne's mother was finally taken away to a clinic and there were the four of them, her three men and she. And when Peggy came into their lives it was even better because, Bobby being gone by then, they were equally divided, two women and two men. She loved Peggy at first sight, not only because she was more beautiful than any woman Anne had ever seen, but because she felt no jealousy toward her. And not feeling anything bad, she gave Peggy and herself equal credit, and for the first time in her life felt good about herself. And there was something very new in her life, laughter. Peggy brought that gift along for all of them. Anne began to pray that she would get sick, contract some terrible disease that would keep her in Haiti and out of school so that she could stay forever being warm, feeling loved and loving life.

The night before Bean and she were to leave and go back to their boarding school, she painted her chest with purple spots and rubbed the thermometer until it registered 103°. Peggy knew right away that she was faking, but didn't give her away. She told her father that she knew how to take care of schoolitis and that they didn't even need a voodoo doctor. "What she needs is to go on the boat with us and look for those German subs. That's the only known cure for what ails our Shrimp." Bean, Peggy said, didn't catch schoolitis and he left for school, but she stayed.

Once they were out at sea Anne wrote a note and signed it in blood. The note said, "I shall always love her, and I will never love another woman in all my life." She put the note in an empty gin bottle and threw it overboard. Being with them and old Bernard, going after the subs, learning about how the hidden torpedoes were going to be fired and how to use the machine guns, did not, for once, fill her with dread. Everything now filled her with excitement. Even learning make-up. Peggy told her that she was a growing girl, and she had better learn this "art, which isn't an art at all, but part of a bag of tricks that women have to know."

"Why?" Anne asked her.

"God and men know, I sure don't," she said and laughed. She laughed so easily and so often, and it was that art that Anne wanted most of all to learn. But maybe it couldn't be learned, maybe you were born with it. But she tried, along with making up her eyes and lips, to make a laugh.

They often slept on deck, Peggy and she, and would talk long into the night. She told Peggy a dozen stories of things she and her father did, some real but most made up from that corner of her imagination that was open to the possibility of how it could have been. And now there was another corner opening up of how it could always be, the three of them, brave and true and special people, her father, Peggy, and she. She didn't ever want the trip to end, and if it had to end she hoped it would end by her drowning. She kept imagining herself dying trying to save them from the Germans, or the sharks, and seeing them, for the last time, smiling at her. She would not mind at all if she never lived to be eleven.

But the trip did end, and it was time for Peggy to go back to Hollywood and for Anne to return to school. The only good thing about it was that they were going to fly together to Miami. And her father had promised that they would be together again for Christmas and maybe even Thanksgiving. It never happened. She and Bean spent the two holidays in school. And that summer, although they were all waiting for her, Peggy never came to Martha's Vineyard. Most of that summer she blamed herself for somehow frightening Peggy away. But her loss was also her father's loss because he had loved Peggy. He didn't say that he had married her, but they were supposed to think he did.

The day Bean told her father about wanting to be a priest, then told her, Anne decided she would tell her father what it was that she wanted to be. She didn't want her brother to know, this was a gift for her father alone. While doing the dishes with him, she brought the subject up.

"What do you think I want to be, when I grow up, that is?"

"A nun?"

She laughed with her father because that was funny. "No. I'm going to be a writer. Like you."

"A writer? I thought you were going to be a fisherwoman."

"No, I've changed my mind. I want to write. Except I won't be anywhere as good as you are. I'll be almost as good, but not quite as good as you."

"Maybe you'll be better," her father said.

"I couldn't be better because you're the best."

"Mr. Shakespeare is the best."

"Ugh," she said. She had to read a play by Shakespeare because she wanted a part in it and she did not like it at all, but she got the part. Until that day when she was giving her father the gift of her being a writer, she had wanted to be an actress.

"If you're going to be a writer," her father said, "you ought to know who you're in debt to. And all writers using the English language owe a great deal to Mr. Shakespeare."

Before she went back to school, her father gave her a long list of books she had to read if she intended to become a writer one day. She thought none of them were as good as books her father wrote, but she read them all. She liked a few, Dickens, Dreiser, and some stories by London and Kipling.

Her father was busy writing in the mornings and would spend his afternoons at the Olaffson bar while she and Bean swam in the pool he had built and argued with Haitian boys in Creole which by then they knew very well.

Bean went to see his mother every day at the clinic, which was only a few blocks away, but Anne did not want to see her and stubbornly insisted that she would never see her mother until the doctors made her well. She no longer thought her mother might not even be her mother. She just could not bring herself to face her. And that was because she was a coward. She was afraid that insanity was catching.

Feeling good about herself was something that had happened a year and a half ago. It had been an illusion, like Peggy. Now everything was real, and what was more real than anything else was the fact that at twelve, she was miserable. She had plenty of reasons, for one thing she had two friends at school who were no longer her friends. When she got up enough nerve to ask them what had happened, one of them said, "We've decided that you are not a terribly nice person," and the other one nodded her head, and then both walked away from her. She was not a nice person. She was envious, a liar, a cheat, and a coward, and there was no future for her. She read a book on witchcraft and thought that maybe she was just simply evil, or a bad witch. But that didn't help things either.

"Kids your age suffer from being in their rotten years," a friend of her father's who came to visit said to her one day. "Don't feel bad, it's just a phase. You'll outgrow it."

She felt totally unattractive, and not only because her skin was bad, her hair so greasy that she had to wash it every day. It was something else, deeper inside. It was not a phase, no matter what anyone said.

Before they went back, her father asked her when she was going to start on her "chosen craft."

"I'll bring back a story that you'll like," Anne told him. "I'll bring it with me to Martha's Vineyard when I come for the summer."

She tried every day to get started on that story she had promised her father. She could not begin and without a beginning she could not go on. She got personally acquainted with the hell that was writing. The hell she had heard her father talk about when his writing wasn't going well.

A few days before school ended she read a story in the school paper by an upperclassman. Anne offered to buy it for a hundred dollars which she had in her savings. The boy sold the story to her, and she brought its typewritten original with her to Martha's Vineyard and gave it to her father the first day she was there. She watched his face as he read the story and saw pleasure and pride on it. When he was finished, he got up, walked to her and put his arm around her shoulder. He lifted her face so that she would be looking straight at him.

"This is far better than anything I ever wrote at your age. You were wrong, Shrimp, you'll be better than your old man if you can write stuff like that at your age."

She wanted the story back, but her father held on to it. The editor of *The Saturday Evening Post* was coming in a few days for a visit and her father wanted to show the story to him. She was going to steal the story back, but the editor called and cancelled his visit and Hal mailed the story to him. When Anne went back to school that fall there was a contract and a check waiting for her. The story had been scheduled for publication in the magazine around Christmas time. She brought the check for four hundred dollars to the boy who had written it and told him she'd share the money with him, but the boy said no.

"If it's published at all it will have to be published under my name, or not at all."

She offered him the whole check but the boy refused and demanded that she come clean with the editor. They finally wrote a letter together in which Anne requested that the boy's name be substituted for her name. By return mail, she got back the story and a letter from the editor, asking for his money. The boy became angry, maybe out of pride, or out of regrets over losing the money, and claimed that nobody had a chance in this world unless his name was Hubbard. And, in his anger, he wrote Anne's father explaining what had happened.

Before Christmas, her father wired Anne that she was expected to spend Christmas with her mother in Chicago. Bean went, but Anne decided to stay in school with three other girls who had no place to go that year.

She was seventeen by the time she saw her father next, having spent all her vacations at school or, reluctantly, with her mother. He was living openly with Sally by then, and Anne did not like her. The only thing she liked was the fact that they were not married, and she hoped they never would be. Her father was writing and there was no time for fishing or doing anything else alone with him. He was drinking a lot. They never talked about the story. They hardly talked at all. One night she wrote her father a note and handed it to him, hoping he would not show it to Sally:

> If the incident of the story, for which I'll always be ashamed, is going to ruin what we had, I might as well kill myself.

In the morning, under her bedroom door, she found her father's reply:

> Maybe we never had all that much. When I first realized you were a liar, I should have tried to explain to you why it doesn't pay. It's your job to change, and you must attend to it.

After that the air was cleared somehow. All she needed now was to cure herself from the thick crust of dishonesty that had grown as she grew. But suddenly she felt herself a stranger in her father's house. She thought of nothing but how to change, but as with the story, she didn't know where to begin. Starting might entail asking him some questions and seeing how honestly he would answer. Why did he drink so much? Didn't he know this woman he brought into the house was even worse for him than his wife had been? But everything she thought of, in order to become honest, had to do with others, not herself. How would she cure herself from having always been a liar and a cheat? She was her mother's child, and would end up crazy like her. Except her mother "recovered." It would have been nobler had she died, committed suicide. She, like her mother, was a coward, and cowards were scared even to kill themselves because of the fear. That's when she began to drink. Her father who was not a coward drank, and her mother, who was, drank. Why had she waited so long? Life was quite bearable when you didn't feel it. She acted sober because she had a sort of a talent for acting, but she was drunk each day of that summer.

If Bean had still been at school it would never have happened. But Bean had already gone to the seminary when Anne got pregnant. She slept with the boy five times and each time she had been drunk, and he was younger than she and both were petrified. "You must write your father," the boy kept telling her. But she kept delaying doing what she knew she had to do. She was too afraid of getting an abortion because two girls in her school had; one was dead and the other one went crazy. She didn't know what caused the girl's craziness, she didn't think it was guilt, she believed it was because the abortionist did something to her. But there were other abortionists, maybe her father knew a good one who would not hurt her. She decided to take the boy to Haiti with her. They would talk to Hal, he would know what they should do.

They arrived to find that neither Hal nor Sally were there. Waiting for him in the empty house, the boy began to talk about getting married. "We could both study at home and get our high school diplomas by mail." Where was home? He thought they should live here, in her father's house. "It's big enough," he said, looking, admiring, maybe even envying or lusting after everything that it contained. He was poor, on scholarship in the expensive private school. She saw it all now, he got her pregnant on purpose. He wanted to marry money. She went to bed with him because she had been drinking and didn't know what else life had to offer. Now, watching him looking over the house that he was sure might be his one day, she began to hate him and the child inside of her.

When Hal finally came back, Sally was not with him, she had stayed on in New York for a few days more. The boy talked. He wanted to get married, he was against abortions. He would make a good husband and a good father, except for one thing. His family didn't have any money. But marrying was the only honorable thing to do. He had read Hal's stories and tried to talk to Anne's father as if he were Slim Taber. She hoped her father would not fall for this. She listened to them, not saying a word. Finally, when her fate was sealed between the two of them, and the decision was that she should marry this boy she now hated, she asked, "And then what?"

Her father looked at her with eyes that were very cold, and said, "Bring up the child as best you can."

"Where would we live?" she asked.

"You can have the house on Martha's Vineyard, free of rent," Hal said. "Your mother wants it sold, but you can live there for a year. Then you'll be on your own."

"He can't even get a job," she said, pointing to the boy whose child she was carrying.

"You could always try writing," her father said to her.

They did not spend Christmas in Haiti, but flew to Martha's Vineyard. The boy liked that house too and liked fishing. He already acted as if they were married, especially after he received a check from Hal made out in his name. "Your father's okay, we won't have to worry about money," he said. She told him that she would open an account at the bank and would get a dress to get married in, and he endorsed the check.

She found an abortionist on the mainland and when she came back, weak, and feeling as if she might die, she threw him out of the house. He stood before the house for a long time, shouting at her, swearing at her and demanding his money back. She realized that he was no better than she had deserved and that their child, if it had lived, would have been a horror. She would never have children; she knew this with a kind of certainty she never thought existed.

She didn't go back to school after Christmas, but stayed in the house going over all of her father's papers. She read all the letters in his files and all the unpublished manuscripts, every bit and scrap of paper, in order to know him better. She had only him to hold on to now.

When Hal and Sally came in the spring, bringing with them a few friends, she lied to him and said that she had had a miscarriage and told him how glad she was it had happened the day before the wedding.

"Did you love him?" he asked.

This time she told him the truth. "No, I never did."

She thought that he would speak to her then, ask her questions, say something she might learn from, but he didn't tell her anything. That night she overheard him say, "I'd never bed a woman down if I didn't love her. Except in a whorehouse. Shit, if that's the moral goodness Socrates talked about, then I've got some of it in me."

Anne tried to be helpful around the house, but Sally had everything well in hand. She had taken typing in school and offered to type for her father, but by then he was using a professional typist. The typist depended on this work to make a living. Anne read a lot and entered two tennis tournaments, got to the finals in both and lost both because her father was not there watching her. One night, when the guests and Sally had gone to bed and her father was reading in the living room, she tried to talk with him.

"What do you think I should do with myself?" she asked.

"If you don't go back to school your options will be limited," her father said, not looking up from his book. He had not looked her straight in the eye, she realized, since the story incident.

She sat for a while looking at him as he read, and then got up and went to her room. Nothing seemed to matter anymore. She knew her father neither trusted her nor cared about her. She had been a disappointment to him all along, now she was a disgrace. In the bathroom there were some sleeping pills left over from her mother, and she swallowed all of them.

She must have botched the job because she woke up in a hospital room. Her father was at her bedside. When she focused her eyes on him his face had seemed soft.

"I'm sorry," she said.

"Don't be. Consider it a lesson. And learn from it."

After a moment, she said, "I should have used a gun. Sleeping pills are not for us Hubbards."

"How do you feel?" he said, and he did look at her, now, wanting her to answer straight.

"Glad to be alive." She didn't know if she was telling the truth or lying again.

"Look," her father said then, "I want you to know that I don't hold anything that happened in the past against you. If you want to give yourself another chance, this time, at doing things differently, with honesty, you have it now."

"Don't you ever lie?" she asked him.

"No."

"You once told me you loved me as much as you love Bean."

"When I told you that it was the truth."

"How about now?"

Her father didn't say anything, instead he got up. He looked tired.

"How long have you been here?"

"Too long," her father said. "I need sleep."

She had been given another chance, but at what?

She took inventory then. She had none of her father's talents. She was not good with people. She would never be anything like him, except in looks. As a female version of Hal Hubbard she was a stunning-looking girl now. She did not wish to remain a beggar any longer on her father's doorstep. She joined a small theater in Boston, and in the very first play, although her part was an insignificant one, her last name appeared in big letters and there were two interviews about "Hal Hubbard's daughter." The one in a national magazine appeared with a picture of her father at her age, and the resemblance was commented on. She knew her father would see the stories because he subscribed to a clipping service, and seeing them he would write her.

But he did not write her.

A Broadway producer came to see her because he did spot the stories. She was offered a small part in a play that lasted only a week in New York. During that week several interviews with her appeared, because giving interviews was part of her contract. A Hollywood agent brought her to the West Coast and put her under contract to a large studio. The publicity department used her name often, and each time there was a mention of the fact that she was "the daughter of the famous writer, Hal Hubbard."

She made a few movies but knew herself not to have real talent. She was earning a living, however, enough to drink a bottle of champagne every day, and half a bottle of brandy after dinner. She tried to keep the drinking under control, making it private, but the publicity department wanted her to be seen with all the upcoming male starlets, and each time, every time there was a picture of her in the press, her father's name appeared, and maybe that was why he never wrote her, not once. She tried writing him, but none of the letters she wrote were good enough to send.

She had no trouble with the young men provided by the studio to escort her to parties and premieres. She made each one understand that she was engaged, deeply in love, and that she was going out only because she had been ordered to do so by the studio. They understood, and only a few attempted to seduce her, failing miserably in the process. She needed no sex as long as she was keeping herself on a perpetual alcohol high, but then she discovered marijuana and fortified herself against reality with that, smoking a couple of joints in the morning and going to sleep stoned.

One night, driving herself home from a party where she sniffed cocaine for the first time, her car ran into a lamppost. The accident left her paralyzed.

Within a few days she received a check signed by her father. It arrived accompanied by a note from his New York lawyer. The note informed her that she would continue to receive a similar check each month until she was "back on her feet." It also advised her that her father would be claiming her as a dependent for tax purposes. She decided not to bother thanking the lawyer nor her father. The checks would be sufficient to take care of her rent, food, liquor and drug bills, as well as the rental of the wheelchair.

Her agent got her a part in a television soap opera of a paralyzed wife with homicidal instincts. It lasted over two years and then the writers had her commit "the perfect murder" which, after all, was not so perfect. She was caught and died in the electric chair. When it was over, she had nothing to do. By then she preferred cocaine to alcohol.

He wanted to close the ledger on her, but there was something missing, an inner vision into the truth, perhaps. Should he, or should he not, have guilts about her? Now, not before, now was the important time. He had good intentions about bringing her up. Should he have spent more time with her, had more patience, showed her affection, hugged her more? It would never have been enough, of that he was sure. She, like her mother, needed it all. Down to the bones.

He probably should have told her about Yolanda. It had happened again, with his daughter, as it had happened with his sister. He had allowed a female of the same genes to get too close. A certain kind of closeness in the family was dangerous. It could become obsessive and ultimately enslaving. He failed to protect both from something he should have known instinctively was bad for them, good for him. He let both take him as the center of their beings. What had been good for his ego, had done irreparable harm to both of them. He should have known the second time around. When he finally pushed Anne out of his life, as he had done in Paris with Yol, he was not doing it for her, but for himself.

Maybe that was the one thing a brother owes a sister, and a father owes a daughter, protection from closeness that could be dangerous. Maybe that was the only thing he should have done for this kid. Maybe. . . .

There was a soft knock on the door and he waited. The light was out and it was past midnight. The door opened slowly, and he saw the silhouette of a tall man, a pail in his hands, a mophead sticking out of it.

"You asleep?" the voice asked softly, then the door closed and the man was inside. Standing by the door, waiting. Hal switched on the light over his bed, and the man moved closer and now he saw him. He was black and wearing an attendant's uniform.

"Don't be scared," the man said.

"What do you want?"

"Were you asleep?" the man asked.

"Wasn't asleep. Thinking of my daughter."

"I'll come back some other time." The black man turned as if to go, then said, "I got a daughter, too. Ain't seen her near ten years. She didn't fancy her old man boxin'" He laughed quietly. "She sure wouldn't fancy what I do now."

"You were a fighter?" Hal asked.

The man nodded.

"Did you get far?"

"As far as I could."

"How far was that?"

"Contender."

"Who got to you?"

The man laughed, a deep, satisfying sound that came from somewhere in his memory. "Being a nigger."

The man wasn't a doctor in disguise, Hal thought. "Sit down," he said.

"Ain't supposed to," the man said, sitting, stretching his long legs out as if he had found comfort, the pail at his side, the door closed. "The nurse catch me in here like this, kiss this job good-bye."

"You mind if that happens?" Hal asked.

"Not too much. Kiss this one good-bye, kiss another one hello. They's always nigger work somewhere."

"How'd you get to be a boxer?" Hal asked.

"High school. In Detroit, I was a senior, a man comes up to me, says if I don't mind being a nigger out of the ring, he could sweeten my life."

Hal sat up, propping the pillow behind his head. The man sitting at the other end of the bed wasn't part of the games they play. There is a story in that man as in all the others like him who came out of nowhere to be taken by him, the writer. And he took from them, never paying. But they gave willingly, that was the difference. Like this man was giving now.

"Hey," the black man said suddenly, "you want to git out of this place a while, hear some music, drink some booze?"

Hal didn't answer for a moment, old suspicions rising.

"Listen, man, if we gets caught, you gets back in here, I push a mop somewheres else, nothing to lose, right?"

A lot to lose, Hal thought. They won't let me go home. For the party. The excitement of breaking the rules was too tempting.

"They took my clothes away," Hal said.

"No sweat." The man jumped up. "I get some."

He went out. Hal was aware of his heart beating faster. He would be out! It'd been a long time since he had an adventure. Everything's been so stacked up, planned. Sally left nothing to chance.

"Here, these oughta fit." The man handed him a pair of pants, a shirt, and a jacket. "Forgot the shoes."

"It's okay. I'll wear my slippers." When he first came here and they gave him the slippers, for a whole day he thought of Dachau, expecting his head to be shaved and that there'd be a gas chamber somewhere.

Hal dressed without talking.

They went down the corridor, and there was no one at the nurse's station.

"She's getting laid," the man said. And then down the stairs, and out the back door, and they were in the parking lot, getting into a beat-up black Buick and still not talking much, Hal trying not to figure out what he'd gotten into. He wanted to have faith, trust, and it didn't come easy because both were gifts he never received.

They drove slowly past the gas stations, all of them closed for the night. Hal didn't know where they were going. He decided to make small talk, feel the man out.

"You like what you do?"

"Moppin'? You got to be kiddin'. What I likes is the odd job part, live from day to day, don't worry if the boss thinks this or that."

"Do you like Albuquerque?" Hal asked.

"Not much, except for the sky. Bigger than any sky I thought I'd ever see before I died."

The car stopped in front of a factory-type structure, and they heard it, even before getting out, the music that came from within through the air. One thing he missed in life was knowing jazz as well as he knew bullfighting. He should have known more, listened more, but now hearing it, he was glad he came. But the coming came too late. And knowing this interfered. He tried hard not to make it interfere.

Inside, there were a couple of dozen people listening to the jazz quartet. It wasn't a bar exactly, maybe just a rented place, everyone had his own bottle and the ice came out of an old icebox. They sat around on chairs, most of the listeners. The musicians were black, the few whites college kids. The music, when they improvised, was inspired or maybe magnificent, or just average, but it brought tears to Hal's eyes. Someone passed them some Scotch, and they didn't talk, just listened.

They stayed two hours, then the man said, "We better be gettin' back."

While the boxer drove, eyes staring straight ahead at the white shafts of his headlights on the dark road, Hal thought about the music, the jazz he had missed, that could be that good, that might somehow still finally fit into his life like a small missing piece of a whole puzzle, not an important piece, but now in place because it belonged.

"I want to thank you," Hal said to the man.

"A privilege," the man said, waving it away with a hand. Then, eyes fixed to the windshield as if embarrassed to glance over at Hal, he said, "You're the writer, right? Hubbard?"

Hal thought about that. He'd been a writer.

"I'm not pryin'," the man said. "Just askin'."

"You ever read anything I wrote?" Hal asked.

"No."

"I wrote about boxers," Hal said, remembering.

"That so?" the man said, as they pulled up in the parking lot of the hospital. The building seemed quiet as death.

"I'll go change back to my pajamas," Hal said, "so you can have these clothes. And thank you again. I had a real fine time."

They entered the building like thieves. Hal made it to his room without being seen by anybody. If he told Dr. Robinson tomorrow about his escapade, they'd think he made the whole thing up.

Benjamin and Maggie Horn

WHEN he first saw the first of the black birds, ugly even in flight, he knew there would be others soon. They never traveled alone on their business. The first pair landed gently on the dead tree, and after a short while, more clumsily reached the ground a few yards away from where he lay. They waited although he did not move, and he wondered if there was an instinct in them that told them that it was not yet time, or whether they were patient, or lazy, or both. He might not have agreed with them, but they seemed to have noticed that he was not yet quite dead.

from "Vulture Country" by Hal Hubbard

They drove around the house several times. It was hiding behind tall trees, encircled by a high wall. They pulled their rented car over a few feet from the locked gate. Maggie took out pencil and pad and began to write while Benjamin switched on his tape recorder and dictated:

"The house is two stories high comma with large balconies running around it period. There is a lot of filigree woodwork comma a good example of the kind of Swiss-chalet type of architecture that was built in this part of Port-au-Prince around the turn of the century period. Some of the trees in the front yard comma beyond the elaborate iron gate and the curving driveway beyond comma are palms, bananas comma. . . ."

He pressed the stop button and turned to his wife. "What are these called?" he asked, pointing.

"Mangoes," she said, "and those over there are breadfruits."

He went on dictating:

". . .mangoes and breadfruits period. In the back of the house comma separated by the pool comma is the guest house period. It sits slightly higher than the main house comma and to the right of it is another structure with a thatched roof where the servants live period. The flowers are everywhere and their tropical smell is heady period. If you asked anyone who lives here they would say Monsieur check spelling Hal period. Hubbard comma for the Haitians comma is too hard to pronounce period paragraph."

"It's good," she said as he put away the tape recorder.

"What did you write?" he asked her.

"The way the neighborhood looks," she said.

They had arrived in Haiti two days earlier and had been busy doing research ever since. They had talked the editors of *The Ladies Home Journal* into an advance against the article they promised to deliver. The piece would be titled, "The Women in Hal Hubbard's Life." Neither of the Horns had any idea if there were any, but the editors at the *Journal* were excited. Maggie and Benjamin were even more excited, because they expected their article would lead them to the first authorized biography of Hal Hubbard. Ever since Hal Hubbard had won the Pulitzer Prize for *Goodbyes* the Horns had been dreaming of winning a Pulitzer Prize for their biography of Hal Hubbard. But their mutual dream did not stop there.

They came to Haiti well prepared. They had come by the total sales figures for each of Hal Hubbard's books, five novels and two collections of short stories, and they saw "further potentials" in each of them. They knew that he had no agent, that all his contractual agreements were being handled by a New York lawyer. The lawyer obviously was not aware of all the money that could be made if Hal Hubbard's writings were milked real well. The movie rights to three of his books were still unsold, but they were more interested in becoming the official representatives and producers of Hal Hubbard's works for television. They also foresaw that if they were in charge of doing the productions they would demand more for Hal Hubbard. Besides the short story, "The Hired Hands," which had been made into a movie poorly received by the reviewers and the public, only *From Zero to Fifty* and *Teresa* were bought by Hollywood, for what the Horns considered inadequate sums. *All of Us* was under option, again for too little money, and they would promise Hal Hubbard, if he placed them in charge, some artistic control. The major writer in America was yet to realize his full potential, and they were well prepared to let him know what that might be.

They were both in their thirties and had pooled their writing talents and made adequate money from the articles they wrote about celebrities. But being a "hot" team was only the beginning. They envisioned themselves as "celebrity managers," and Hal Hubbard was going to become their first client. He might not think he needed them, but they needed him and would make the need convincingly his. They would insist that he needed protection for the quality he possessed and would offer themselves as a buffer against cheap exploitation. They would become his biographers and managers, and it would not cost him a thing. They would take a percentage of the take, and he would remain in artistic control. They knew that he could not resist what they were offering him. And he in turn, like the article for *The Ladies Home Journal,* would become a stepping stone for them to bigger and better things.

They had planned their strategy carefully before setting off from New York. They knew that Hal Hubbard did his drinking at the Olaffson Hotel, and that's where they made their reservations for a month's stay. They would meet him casually. They would not mention that they were in Haiti to do an article about him. His often-quoted dictum: "You can write anything you wish about my work, even misspell my name, but I don't give interviews," made him the Garbo of the literary world. All that, the Horns intended to change. And they could afford to wait. Hal had gone fishing, they found out on arrival, and nobody knew when he would be back, not even his friend Pierre, the bartender at the Olaffson. But Pierre told them that on his return, his first stop would be at his favorite watering hole, "to celebrate his catch." For the last few years, Mr. and Mrs.

Horn's life had seemed to involve more planning than living, more waiting than enjoying. But the rewards they planned would compensate for their foresight and patience.

Benjamin Horn had been born with a unique talent, cultivating people as a gardener cultivates flowers and vegetables, knowing their needs and what he could do to fulfill them. At seventeen, when he was in a Nebraska high school and living with his seven brothers and sisters and a mother recently abandoned by her husband, he read an article in the *Reader's Digest* about public relations and its reigning priest, Mr. Marion Strassberg. He decided that day to do something few young men were willing to do, to apprentice himself to a master. He emptied his mother's sugar bowl of her savings and took a bus to New York City. From the bus station he walked straight into the offices of Mr. Strassberg who, the *Reader's Digest* stated, was "the best public relations man in the world." One of the secretaries tried to stop him, but he went past her, opened the door and confronted Mr. Strassberg, who was standing at the window idly picking his nose.

"I want to work for you for a year without any salary," Benjamin Horn announced.

Mr. Strassberg paused for a moment and looked at the young man from head to toe.

"What will you do for me for a whole year," Mr. Strassberg asked. "Teach me how to dress?"

Benjamin was wearing his oldest brother's only suit, which he had put on when he lit out of house, leaving Nebraska to make his fortune. When they talked about that first meeting years later, Mr. Strassberg liked to recall the way Benjamin looked: "like a prairie dog," he would say, "and you were such a snot. You sure had the hootz that day." "Hootz" was Mr. Strassberg's favorite word, an anglicized substitute for hutzpa. Not only did Benjamin get the job of "leg man," but he was allowed to stay in one of Mr. Strassberg's upstairs servants' rooms on top of his large brownstone. For a whole year, Benjamin worked for no wages. He was fed and clothed and taught the trade of a public relations man by the master himself. He also, totally and uncritically, absorbed Mr. Strassberg's philosophy of life, which was summed up on a silver plaque over his desk:

Know thyself the screwer when screwing and a screwee when being screwed.

His apprenticeship consisted of the latter while hoping for the former. All he knew about people he learned from his employer. Mr. Strassberg's aphorisms were accepted by Benjamin Horn as if they had been filtered through the ages, but they were stated with such good humor that they might have been accepted, by someone less serious, as merely jests. Benjamin accepted everything in perfect seriousness.

"When with an asshole act like a bigger asshole."

"It's a dog-eat-dog world but our job is to seem like cats."

"There are two kinds of people basically, the shitters and those who are shat on."

"Everyone has something sacred up their assholes. Always bow to the sacred."

"The world is revolving all the time, it's called evolution. You want revolution, you got a dream. You want evolution, you got reality." This was evoked when Mr. Strassberg caught Benjamin reading Karl Marx. "Groucho, Chico, and Harpo are the only Marxes you ought to be reading about, and maybe then we'll get one of them for a client. Don't read about dead people on my time."

On the day that Benjamin graduated to a salaried employee, Mr. Strassberg bought him lunch and told him the bottom line secret of his profession:

"You want power over someone, learn his vulnerable spots, his weaknesses, and always attack through them. The name of the game is dominance. Find a need and cater to it. Get your strength from someone's weakness and let them lean against you."

At thirty, Benjamin was ready to leave his guru and strike out on his own. By then he knew that he wanted to be a writer. Mr. Strassberg helped him to get started by assigning to him one of his clients who wanted to have a book ghosted. In the next year he ghosted autobiographies of an actress, a politician, an industrialist, and a book by a self-made millionaire that made the bestseller list. Because he was so busy, he advertised for "an apprentice writer" and from the applicants picked one Maggie Wolny, who had recently graduated from Vassar on a scholarship and came from Polish peasant stock. She was quite willing to learn everything Benjamin was willing to teach her, and she in turn became his apprentice. They married within two months and became equal partners in what they liked to term "our promising future."

On his wedding night, Benjamin confessed to his bride that he had had it being a screwee and was eager and ready to become a screwer. This led to the one and only misunderstanding the couple was to have. Maggie burst into tears, fearing that her husband had found her sexuality demanding. Amidst tearful explanations, for Benjamin too cried that night, it became apparent to the bride that her husband was an ambitious young man, resentful of having had no visible credit for any of his ghosted books, and that he wished to become a writer on his own. Before the second consummation of their marriage, the two decided that they would collaborate, and that their efforts would involve writing about celebrities. Hal Hubbard's name was mentioned between them that night as the one writer they would write about one day. But it would take several years before this project was to materialize.

Long before leaving for Haiti the Horns had hired a secretary, for now they needed someone to transcribe their voluminous interviews with celebrities. Sally Reynolds was not paid very well, but they made her believe that they had plans for her that would include marrying someone famous. Sally possessed the qualities both Benjamin and Maggie considered essential to the wife of a celebrity: she had a thick skin, the tenacity of a terrior, combined with what amounted to organizational genius. She was tall, very thin and rather attractive, and in spite of her height gave off an aura of vulnerability, a need to be protected, which hid well her ability to protect herself. On the day of their departure, they both decided that she would be an ideal wife for Hal Hubbard. Maggie gave Sally a copy of Jane Austen's *Pride and Prejudice,* with the opening sentence underlined: "It is a truth universally acknowledged that a single man in possession of a good fortune must be in need of a wife."

From Haiti, Benjamin sent a postcard to Sally on which he wrote:

How would you like to be the next Mrs. Hal Hubbard? We will be meeting him soon. We found out he's partial to blondes; Maggie suggests you bleach your hair in the meanwhile.

They talked about how advantageous it would be to marry Hal off to Sally, how she would help them if this happened. Also, in anticipation of this match and of their own involvement in Hal Hubbard's life, they made an outline of what they believed were Hal's immediate needs and weaknesses and called it their "working bio."

Fear of poverty: He was once poor (in Paris), and as he grows older, he might feel the need to defend himself from that ever happening again.

Fear of mediocrity: We will present him with an outline of THE PROFIT POTENTIAL on all his works. We will suggest that he designate us as his official QUALITY CONTROLLERS and managers, otherwise his works might be artistically PERVERTED.

Need: HIS NEED FOR PRIVACY need not preclude a campaign to SUSTAIN THE LEGEND CREATED AROUND HIM.

Productivity: While outlining his FUTURE PRODUCTIVITY we will try to make him realize that there is money to be made by writing articles (Benjamin acting as OFFICIAL PHOTOGRAPHER, Maggie as agent).

Past interests: GET HIM INTERESTED IN TRAVEL!!! Africa! Spain! Paris! REVISITED!!!! And ITALY!!! Each has potential for articles (for us too!) and BOOKS!

Incentive to do new stuff: SELL HIM CREATIVITY!!! (A recollection of Paris during the '20s! Italy, how it looked to him during WWI.) Get him excited about remembering how things were and wanting to see how things are now. (How about a piece on the new expatriates!) Insist the two of us come along, as protection, as well as friends.

Immediate PROMO: If bites, while in NYC arrange for press conference, and possibly a PROFILE in *The New Yorker*!!!

Our hold on him! PROMOTE SALLY REYNOLDS TO HIM!!!

They convinced themselves that he was stagnating in Haiti and that his creativity would dry up if he stayed here much longer. They saw his isolation as "counter-productive." "A writer needs exposure," Benjamin said, and Maggie nodded her head in agreement.

"First priority must be travel," they told each other because they already saw themselves in his company.

They talked endlessly, by the pool and in their room and at their meals, and made careful plans how they would, in time, subtly bring up the subject of the biography, which both considered their "ace in the hole." They even consulted all the clippings about Hal Hubbard they had brought with them and discovered in an article about him that he was "ever so slightly paranoid." They talked paranoia and convinced themselves that the way to make Hal trust them was to make him believe that their friendship for him, their admiration, would best qualify them to undertake the job of writing about him. "A friend is ever so much better than a stranger," Maggie said, using the Deborah Kerr accent she was cultivating. She spoke rarely, leaving the vocalizing of plans mostly to her husband, but her supportive attitude, her readiness to agree to all his plans and projects, made him happy that she was an equal partner in everything. They now both felt they should forget the article that had brought them here, unless he opened up; they would, first of all, make themselves extremely useful to him.

"I will be his first buddy," Benjamin volunteered, "and I will find out his weaknesses and make him want to lean on me."

"And I will learn by listening," Maggie said.

The Horns had hired two Haitian boys to hang around the harbor, and they were to let them know, for the princely sum of ten dollars, the minute Hal's boat docked.

Although by then they had read everything written about him and had seen numerous photographs of Hal Hubbard, the Horns were not prepared for the impact of actually seeing him. The man who entered the bar, taller and heavier than they had expected, bearded and wearing a soiled pair of Bermuda shorts and a torn shirt, was indeed "larger than life." From the top of his unruly graying hair to his dirty sneakers, he was a *somebody*. Both, having been used to meeting celebrities, knew that he would have IT. They had once written an article about IT, identifying it as an "Identity Tremor," the very emotional and physical reaction that was evoked in the proximity of someone famous. Hal Hubbard had IT in greater measure than any of the celebrities the Horns had met.

"Take away the kids' beers, Pierre, and set them up with our special rum sours on me," he said to the bartender; then, turning to Benjamin and Maggie, he asked: "You here for the scenery, the voodoo, or me?"

"All three," Benjamin said. The well-prepared indifference they had been going to feign evaporated instantaneously.

There was no one else in the bar, the hotel had only a few guests, and it was three o'clock in the afternoon, siesta hour. They both watched him now as he stretched his arms and moved his shoulders up and down in a circular motion.

"Jesus, I'm stiff," he said, then turned to Benjamin. "You play tennis, by any chance?"

"No, but my wife Maggie does." Benjamin got up and shook hands with Hal and introduced himself and then Maggie. "You learned at Vassar, didn't you?" Benjamin said turning to his wife.

"Yes," said Maggie, swallowing hard. She had not been so visibly flustered since she met John Wayne at Sardi's, the first time she had collaborated on an interview with Benjamin, who was not then her husband.

"Did you bring your racket?" Hal asked her.

"No," she said, "but. . . ."

"Got to get some exercise in the topics or you become a rummy," Hal said and laughed.

They drank their drinks for a while in silence.

"You staying here, at the Olaffson?"

Benjamin nodded his head.

"It can get you broke," Hal said. "You run out of money I got an empty guest house. You can use it. You'll find some tennis rackets there."

Jesus, said Benjamin to himself. God, said Maggie to herself. It would be like taking candy from the baby. Years later, they often remembered how they didn't even have to lie to Hal Hubbard that first day. After the third rum sour, Hal asked Benjamin if someone had sent him out here to interview him, or was this a freelance job. Benjamin hesitated, and before he answered, Hal slapped him on the back and said:

"If we're to get along, you don't bullshit me, and I don't bullshit you. If you got an advance for some article about me, you lay it out on me, and I'll see if it's worth cooperating with."

That's as close as Benjamin Horn ever came to a moment of truth.

Unaccustomed as he was to placing a direct value on honesty, he now placed his future on it.

"*Ladies Home Journal*," he said and Hal slapped his thigh and laughed.

"That a new one on me. What would the ladies at the home journal like to know about me? I can give them Pierre's recipe for the rum sour to sweeten their lives, but maybe Pierre won't want to part with it."

"Look, we don't have to. . . . "

"Who's we?"

"My wife and I write together."

"Oh, I thought. . . . " He seemed lost in some speculation for a moment, then he turned his attention back to Benjamin. "What were you saying?"

"We don't have to bring the article back. We don't work for them, it's not like our jobs are on the line."

"Caught a nice marlin, would they be interested in that?"

"They'd like to know about the women in your life," Maggie said softly, but Benjamin rammed his elbow into her ribs, and she regretted it immediately and promised herself not to speak again unless spoken to.

Hal Hubbard did not seem to have heard.

"Those goddamned sharks! Took one side off the marlin while he was still fighting. They'd eat anything, those bastards!"

"Does the invitation still stand, for the use of the guest house?" Benjamin asked.

"Sure," Hal said, suddenly looking very tired. "It's yours."

They fitted themselves easily into Hal's routine. Hal was working on a long story, "The Vulture Country," and some days the work went well and he would read to the Horns at lunch what he had written that morning. On those good days Hal would play a set of singles with Maggie. She gave him a good game without ever endangering his chances of beating her. They would go, each afternoon, to the Olaffson bar and drink their rum sours, and together they would have dinner at home. On the days when the work went badly, he would drink his lunch and then he'd go out, alone on his boat or sparring with some native boys. The Horns stayed on in their guest house and made sure they did not interfere. Unless they were asked to come along, they were the unseen guests.

On one of the bad days he called to them and asked if they wanted to drive up to Croix des Bouquets with him. They went eagerly, and on the way there learned that a year before, Hal had bought a grain storage shed and converted it into a training camp for local boys. He wanted to own a piece of a heavyweight, but so far there had not been one good enough. He had outfitted the shed with punching bags and had a ring built and would often supervise a group of young Haitians in what he called "the manly art of violence." On that first day he went three rounds with the best of the boys. Benjamin, who knew nothing at all about boxing, thought he did as well as the professionals. On the second visit there, he asked Hal if he could take some pictures and maybe write a story about the place.

"It's sure better than writing about women," was all Hal said.

That day Benjamin sent the check back to *The Ladies Home Journal* with a letter saying that Hal Hubbard believed women to be that part of his private life which was not for publication. Then he and Maggie wrote an article about the gym and sent it, together with photographs of Hal's protéges, to *Look* magazine. It was accepted, and now the Horns knew that they would pay attention to the signals from the quarterback himself.

Some days neither tennis, nor boxing, nor fishing seemed to hold any interest for Hal. On those days they would see him walk aimlessly around his house, lost in his private thoughts. They had devised between them a small deception. They told Hal that Maggie had to have access to the kitchen to cook a special concoction for Benjamin's flaring ulcers, which meant that one or both of them could often be in the main house, observing what Hal did. They were keeping a journal and taking copious notes that they would airmail for transcription to Sally, who kept being advised that it wouldn't be long before she entered the picture.

Going to the Olaffson bar, for "repairs," as Hal used to say, became a ritual. Often, both Benjamin and Maggie wondered why it was that Hal was more outgoing with strangers than he was with them. Whenever there were tourists at the bar, he would appoint himself "the official explainer of Haiti" and would talk to them more than he was willing to talk to the Horns. But at other times, he would pretend to those who recognized him and wanted an autograph that he didn't even know this "Hal Hubbard fellow everybody thinks I am." On those afternoons Benjamin and Maggie, noting that he spoke about himself as if he despised himself, wished to God they had some knowledge of psychiatry to translate this phenomenon. "He's a windbag, I hear," Hal would say. "As far as being a writer, he's had it. There are better writers than him studying in every college nowadays."

They would analyze whatever he said, after writing it all down as best as they could remember, afraid of carrying a tape recorder but wanting to very much. Benjamin thought Hal was putting himself down like that because he was "fading" as a writer, and Maggie thought he was only making fun, that it didn't mean anything. They argued some about it, Benjamin convinced now that they should call their biography *Fall of a Giant*, that they should watch for signs of a mental illness perhaps, and Maggie standing up to him and saying that Hal'd only had a bad day at the typewriter.

On those days when Hal felt like talking about Haiti, he would both make fun of it and love to it.

"You can't understand about this place," he once told a black American couple, "unless you realize that, unlike the American slaves, these people freed themselves. They didn't need some liberal-minded white to do it for them. You should do some reading, about Toussaint l'Ouverture, Pétion, and Christophe, and you should bring back what Haiti is to the other American Negroes. But maybe you shouldn't. Maybe it's better that you don't understand, or even know how it was with those who came here some three hundred years ago. They were different, you see. They were the best of the African crop, the princes of Africa, those who came here. The ones who came to the United States were the peasants."

The black American couple left in a huff. And Hal turned to Benjamin with a smile and said, "They can't take it. This country's too much for them." Later Hal would worry about the incident. But that was later, when everything worried him.

He often made the tourists laugh with stories of Haitian ingenuity that allowed them to survive, happy, against the odds. He would tell of the Haitians' resourcefulness and what he considered their obvious charm. "They're all poets here! Impractical and wonderful. That's why I live among them." One of his favorite stories, which he would repeat and never tire of, had to do with a local chairmaker who was approached by an American store owner. The American was interested in importing the chair the man was selling for a dollar at the marketplace. The American wanted to know how much the chairs would cost him if he were to order a thousand of them. The Haitian chairmaker took a week to figure it out, finally coming up with a figure of three dollars a chair. "How can that be," the American wanted to know. "An order for a thousand chairs should bring the price down, not up." "Ah, but Monsieur forgets," the Haitian explained, spreading his arms in forgiveness of the American's shortsightedness, "you forget that it takes much more time, and work, for me to make a thousand chairs instead of just a few."

Within two weeks, Benjamin and Maggie were accepted by Hal as his "minor league Boswells, in charge of catching errant words of wisdom and processing them." They took over the voluminous mail and coped with all the requests. Letters came from people who wanted nothing more than an autograph, students who needed help with their book reports, professors who were after a personal evaluation, by Hal, of his own work or sometimes theirs, or those working on their doctoral theses who wished to reassure themselves of some facts. There was also a contingent of people who thought Hal could help them financially. Maggie made up a form letter in which she explained that because of the volume of mail he received, Mr. Hubbard was unable to respond personally to each letter.

On his own, Benjamin had written the editors of *Look, Life, The Saturday Evening Post,* and *Esquire* magazines, opening for bids a proposed article, "Paris, Quarter of a Century Later," by Hal Hubbard. When the answers came, *Life* led the bidding. All Benjamin had to do now was to get Hal's acceptance. He hoped the money would be incentive enough. With the alimony Hal was paying Carole, and the child support, Hal often said, "She must be living much better than I do. If I don't watch it, I'll be headed for the poorhouse." When he said it the next time Benjamin saw his opening.

"How would like to revisit Paris?"

The *Life* editor wrote Hal that they would like him to research the article in the company of his three children, a sort of a running remembrance of things as they were. In anger Hal wrote back that he would do the article in the company of the Horns, who "promise to

185·

do a good impersonation of my children, the real things being busy."

Hal discovered that his passport had expired. Benjamin went with him to the American Embassy. A week went by, and the passport did not arrive.

"They have something on me at the State Department," he said one morning at breakfast to Benjamin and Maggie.

"You mean they've got something on you as the unofficial ambassador to Haiti?" Benjamin said.

"Why did you say that? Do you think the ambassador resents me?"

"I was only joking," Benjamin said.

"Why would they deny me my passport?" Hal wanted to know.

"Nobody's denying. . . . "

"Maybe they're never going to give me one," Hal said, and looked worried.

"Now you're joking," said Maggie. But Hal didn't seem to be joking.

"They're holding it against me, my having been an expatriate in Paris and now my living in Haiti." There was an edge of hysteria in his voice. "When I still owned the house at Martha's Vineyard, I was a resident of Massachusetts, but now that I don't own any real estate I could be in danger of losing my citizenship. I didn't vote in the last presidential election. Could that be it?"

Benjamin tried to make light of it.

"*The New York Times* didn't have anything on the front page about you losing your citizenship."

But Hal didn't seem to have heard.

"They might be making a legal case against me," he said. "They might be after confiscating my royalties. We were spreading payments, which is legal, but. . . . " He stopped again, and then, in a lowered voice, leaning against the table and looking searchingly at Benjamin he said, "My tax accountant died suddenly last month." Benjamin waited for him to finish this thought, but Hal seemed now to change his mind. "There are a lot of people in Washington talking about anti-American activities. It's possible that I am considered to be anti-American because I live here. Isn't it possible they'd hold that against me at the Internal Revenue?"

"That's crazy," Maggie said.

The words hung in the air as if they were made of neon signs.

*

He didn't think himself going mad. But he suspected that they might have already written some editor if there would be an interest in Hal Hubbard's lunacies. They had written, without his permission or knowledge, to *Life* about Paris. Getting him to go back there, back to Lee, to that past, might unhinge something. And it was then, having figured out that much, that Hal began to think that the Horns wanted him crazier than he was. They were trying to trick him into craziness.

Like the time they went to dinner at the Olaffson and a new waiter, who knew English far too well, was taking care of them. It was Benjamin who suggested that he might be an IRS agent. But the idea was not implausible. He weighed carefully the cons and pros and thought it was far more likely that Benjamin Horn wished him, Hal Hubbard, to *think* there was a possibility that the waiter was an IRS agent. He hated himself for wasting time on such concerns, interesting as they might be, but the Horns were playing along, even encouraging him. For what reason? If indeed they were writing about him going over the edge, that would be reason enough. Wasn't it Maggie who, at one point, thought that the house might be bugged and Benjamin who suggested they eat on the veranda?

The first time they ate on the veranda, they talked in lowered voices, and Hal suggested that the Paris trip better be postponed. Was it theirs or his idea that he buy a piece of land or a house somewhere in the States? He didn't know. And yet it was important to know.

"Where would you like to live?" Maggie asked.

He hadn't thought of that, and he grew confused, but they looked happy, expectant, waiting for him to answer. And that's when the idea came to him that he didn't want to live anywhere, just establish residence. Maybe, he thought, while they still waited for him to answer, the government was building up a case against him and he was living outside of the States, so he said to them, "I would like to establish a residence in a place where I would vote from, pay my taxes."

"Real estate taxes are important," Benjamin said.

Important for what, he thought. But they must know, and so he decided right then and there it would be safer to agree and said, "I'd like to drive around, maybe as far as Colorado, or New Mexico. I'd like to rent a car in Miami and see where I could pick up a few acres and maybe build a house."

If he hadn't said that, if he had not been so afraid of threats, unseen but felt, ununderstood threats, Sally might never have entered his life. But Sally already knew the Horns. And he had let the Horns in, and by then they, not he, were in charge.

"Could we come along?" Benjamin asked then.

"Sure," he said because for some strange reason he knew that if he didn't let them they would reveal themselves as his enemies. And the time for that was not yet.

"I'd like to have someone join us," Maggie said. "It's a young woman we know by the name of Sally Reynolds."

He asked them who Sally Reynolds was.

"Oh, just a friend. I think you'd like her. She's easy to get along with."

"Two couples traveling together," Benjamin said, "won't arouse suspicions."

The word "suspicions" was used by them deliberately, of that he was sure. But was it important who said what and why and when? The difficulty lay in the fact that without details the Horns had no substance. Not yet, not then. There were nothing but details while they were around him. And what of the substance? Was it then that he began to lose his own substance? Was that what went wrong? The turn, for there had been a definite turn, happened then, during those days of waiting for the passport, waiting to go to Miami and protect himself with American real estate. His craft gave him whatever substance he ever had, and he was not writing, couldn't write, not then, not under the pressure they created with *their* suspicions.

They were next to the last on his list, and he would use the advantage he had with them that he did not have with the others. He had read their manuscript. *Fall of a Giant.* He had to give them credit. They had a good title. It would sell. He himself had always had trouble with titles. Was it an error on Sally's part, Sally who never made errors, to send the unopened manuscript of that book to him in the clinic? It had been addressed to her and inside the package there were two letters. The whole thing could have been engineered carefully. A seeming carelessness got the package to him, unopened, and copies could have gone to her. For what purpose? He had not figured that one out yet, but would in time. There was no rush. He was right on schedule.

"Time for your nap," the nurse said, and cut off the daylight with the flick of her wrists closing the drapes. "A nap a day keeps the doctor away."

"Wasn't that an apple a day?" he tried, but she was gone. No. Apples had to do with the knowledge of evil. From Genesis, where the real decline began. He reached for the letters.

Dearest Sally,

I wouldn't bother you at this point, but the fact that we have so many commitments regarding Hal's writing and career does affect not only him and us, but also you. As you well know we had you on our payroll for a full year while you were living with Hal. You wrote us, after a year, that you didn't feel you were earning that money, and we stopped the checks. Hal had written us that although he would not marry you, he made a new will leaving you as his chief beneficiary, and we were glad for you. The point of all this is that we find it, at this time, exceedingly difficult to pay our bills. Not that you owe us any money, but we do feel you owe us loyalty. Many of the projects and plans we have for Hal date from before we introduced you to him. We had sacrificed much, financially, while being at his beck and call. We had done our best by him under very trying circumstances, and we had exploited his productivity but now we fear he will not be producing much, even if he gets better, for which we pray. We must make a living. We must know what to expect from him, and you must let us know how things are. After all, our own book is all that we have at this point. Please read Benjamin's letter carefully and keep well.

Love, as always,
Maggie

There was another letter, from Benjamin.

Dear Sally,

It is most urgent that we finish this book. Our editors feel that it should end now, with an indication that Hal has no more future as a writer. YOU ARE THE ONLY PERSON WHO KNOWS IF THIS IS SO. Please: 1) read the book in its entirety and make any final corrections of factual things, and comment on anything you wish. 2)

Let us know what you believe Hal's future holds. If you wish, your letter could be published as the last page of the book.

Do you think he will ever write again? I have been going crazy because I really don't know how to end *Fall of a Giant*. If he recovers and writes again we will come out like fools, and of course he will never speak to us again. IS IT AT ALL POSSIBLE FOR ME TO SEE HIM???? I'd give anything for a visit, even a short one, with him. I'd go to a bank (our advance on the book, as you well know, was spent years ago) and borrow the money. PLEASE ARRANGE THIS FOR ME. After all, if it was not for us, you'd never have met Hal.

I know things have been tough for you, but if you wish to have your "side of the story" told, let me know. Our book would be the proper vehicle for this. As you can imagine, his many friends and fans might suspect that you "drove him crazy." We've tried to minimize any such suspicions in the book. I am sure you won't find anything that is unflattering in the manuscript. Old friends have to stick together, what? If you wish to add anything to the book, please feel free to do so, and I know you won't want to be paid for such a labor, but you might think it wise, from the "public relations" standpoint.

If he tried to kill himself, he might try again. I would like to know what you feel about that. As a friend, would you advise us, should we wait for the end, or bow to our publisher's wishes?

Love, Benjamin

It was the first book he had ever read about himself, and it amazed him, while reading it, how detailed it was. A laundry list of his decline and fall. They were not writers, and yet they were the authors of this particular account and as such they would be listed in library indexes. What was that basic difference between authors and writers? For one thing, everyone who gets published becomes an author, but not necessarily a writer. Many writers never get published, and that's what keeps them from becoming authors. But what the hell, he wasn't lecturing, he was just trying to figure out what could have made their book good. It was no good. And the reason it was no good was the same reason a bookkeeper's account of finances was not a good read. It lacked the guts, the blood, the heartbeat. It made him into a public legend, a lifeless, boring old man going slowly crazier and crazier. But even the craziness within they didn't cope with, didn't even take a guess at. What was mainly wrong with their book was what was mainly wrong with their lives. They never risked anything important. They did risk money and time, but nothing else. They lacked a connecting link to the soul.

A rather frightening possibility existed, however, to be totally fair to the Horns. What if, during all the time that they knew him, he, Hal Hubbard, evidenced no soul? What if, in the arrangements they had made for his whoring under their management, he was no better than what they had seen? What if, with the arrival on the scene of his life of one Sally Reynolds, he had abandoned all responsibility and accountability? What if life is not worth living is exactly what they described? What if they were *accurate* in their reporting?

The stench that arose from such speculation was unbearable. And yet it had to be coped with, and the coping would be best done if he, like them, got himself organized. He had to take up the thread with the first article that they had engineered after engineering his meeting with Sally Reynolds.

"Paris, As It Once Was" appeared in *Life* a few months after their trip there, in 1953. The trip had been postponed a few times and, by the time they set off from Haiti, the Horns were frantic. Maggie's course in photography, for she was going to take the photographs, was not paying off in immediate returns. Their joint appearance, before he and Sally came to New York, on a television show, did not help matters. They had represented themselves as Hal Hubbard's "sole agent-managers, television producers" and a dozen other things, and he had laughed at their ability to weave such a net around him. But Sally had not laughed. She had been outraged. The Horns had been stunned at the change in their meek ex-secretary.

It was she who was going to hold their future in her hands. She had bloomed into an efficient, self-assured companion-manageress. And he had laughed at their surprise and embarrassment to discover that they could not approach him directly anymore. By then he had allowed Sally **to** take the reins of his life, and so he could disintegrate rather comfortably.

The article by Hal Hubbard, when it appeared in *Life* magazine, only remotely resembled Hal's private recollections of his life in Paris in the twenties. He had kept Lee out of those memories, and without Lee there was no substance, just details. The Horns, in *Fall of a Giant,* had juxtaposed those differences and saw a definite "schizophrenic pattern developing." What he had fought for all his life, keeping his life apart from his writing, they tried to put together. But, he didn't know, of course, back then, that they had already begun their book about him, that they already had spent the advance they got for it. If he had known, it would have been a short chapter, not the longest one in their book. If he had known about that book, he would not have talked in front of them. But he talked, and he had been petty and vindictive and sometimes extremely cruel about the people he had known. And they had taken it all down. Had he been wired, or had they? Where was that ever-present microphone hidden? But even then, even without knowing, they got nothing from him about Lee. He had said only one thing about her to them, that "she was my only true love and my only true friend." And yet they had written pages about her. And for that crime they were invited to the party.

But there must have been "normal" moments on that visit to Paris. How cleverly they had edited them out. Maybe the editing was done under pressure from the publisher. After all, the whole success of the book had to depend on the progression of his craziness.

After he finished reading that chapter, he had tried to imagine the kind of conversation that might have taken place in the offices of the publisher of *Fall of a Giant,* before the Horns set off for Paris.

"I want you two to be on the lookout for queer stuff. What I want you two to do is throw some kind of a scary light on the guy. The guy's been marked for suicide, see? So you tap things inside his head from time to time. And write it all down, the small crazy things he does and says. And get adjoining rooms and use the keyhole, for Christ sake, so we can get some sexy stuff about him. Can he get it up?"

In Paris, Sally became the Horn's friend again. It was she, not the Horns, who would bring Hal's anger to the surface. She was accident-prone, and each time something would happen to her, Hal would respond with irritation, as if the accident was happening to him, as if he was losing control. Hal would often say to the Horns, "I wouldn't mind living with an efficiency machine if it wasn't breaking down all the time." They had made, or attempted to make light of his irritations with Sally, but always there was that hint of things going downhill:

> Sally's efficiency, with which we were well acquainted, was evident in the records she kept of all our deductible expenses, in keeping us on schedule, in confirming our hotel and restaurant reservations, in getting our clothes back from the cleaners, and in a hundred small ways being helpful. She was unsuccessful in making Hal cut down on his consumption of liquor, which was considerable. Her attempts in that direction angered Hal the most.

Benjamin and Maggie stored Hal's little quirks like squirrels store nuts for the winter. And there were quite a few quirks: his undisguised disgust with homosexuals and "other perverts," as he called anyone who did not seem totally male or female. But it was up to Maggie to be on the lookout for "nonverbal communication." It was she who noticed that Hal was vain about his appearance only in the presence of pretty young girls, brushing his hair back and sitting straight whenever one was around. He often worried about his health, but never verbalized his worries. Preferring to let someone else drive, he indicated mistrust as a passenger put in unsafe hands.

They were looking for his paranoia everywhere and all the time. Reading their book, Hal was surprised to see how well he had been then. His bad temper, his caustic remarks, his impatience with Sally did not add up to anything indicating insanity. He suspected the Horns were tempted to invent unseen threats for him, arouse his suspicions for the intent of their book. But he could not blame them for his future. They were not powerful enough to instigate what happened later. For that job they must have appointed Sally. But this was their ledger entry, not hers.

"Spain Revisited," published in *Look* magazine. This chapter in *Fall of a Giant* contained a little more excitement.

San Sebastian, during the annual car race was loud with people, charged with excitement. Hal was mobbed by fans who recognized him, but the Horns saw him grow progressively more angry. The magazine insisted on having one of their own photographers for this part of the trip, and Hal resented the man, who was now always hanging around him. He claimed he was being "persecuted" by "that damn camera, cocked like some fucking gun at me."

The Horns made the following entry in their book:

> He seems to hold some anger against the past and against the years that have eroded his youth. Often he looks as if he was contemplating something within him, perhaps a ghost, or how things could have been.

The above was to be the best passage they would write, and sensing now their own developing talents as writers, they grew bold. From a Japanese tourist, Benjamin bought for $500 a miniaturized recording device that was not on the American market yet. By putting the microphone under his lapel and the small tape recorder in his pocket, he could get verbatim anything important Hal was saying. He used it the first time on the day the photographer wished him to pause for a picture with Juan Olivar, the son of Manolo Olivar, who was the model for the character of the bullfighter in *From Zero to Fifty*.

"I won't pose with the young punk," Hal said.

"But why?" Benjamin asked. "It would be. . . . "

"I got to hate his father," Hal said.

"But you made him a very heroic character in your novel," Benjamin said.

"I don't want to talk about it."

But two nights later in Pamplona, after a bullfight in which Juan was brilliant, when Sally and Maggie had gone to bed, and Benjamin and Hal were drinking in a café, he went on what Benjamin would call "a recollection binge," in his book. Benjamin was certain that while he talked, continuously and without interruptions, talked more freely than he had ever done before, something was happening inside Hal's brain. The past was becoming unglued, perhaps, and merging, in some strange and dangerous way, with the present.

Tit for tat and all that. While everyone was playing games, so was he. He also had an unfair advantage back then in Spain. He had discovered Benjamin being armed with the recording device. He didn't know then they were writing a book on him. He thought it was part of the spying equipment. And that night he tried something for the hell of it. He tried to dictate. He had never done this. Since he was getting to be rather good at reporting, rather than creating, he reported into the hidden machine while all around them people were eating and drinking and, some, eavesdropping. He was sure that Benjamin would be impressed by his recollections. He would make something of them, for he was going to be coherent and long-winded and talk, not in choppy sentences, but the way Benjamin imagined a lot of writers write. Those who use dictating machines. He had been against machines in a machine age, and he was anxious to take one and see what it would do to him. In *Fall of a Giant* what he said went in intact:

> When I met him in Pamplona I wanted to know everything about Manolo Olivar. I came to the hotel where he was staying with a notebook of questions. But what could he tell me but lies? I was an American, after all, young and in love with the idea of bullfights. How could he tell me that the reason he went into this dirty business was for the money and nothing else? He needed the money to fill his empty stomach and the stomachs of his mother and brothers and sisters. He told me nothing of the fear he felt each time he had to face the animals.
> I had few heroes then. That I chose Manolo Olivar as one was maybe just an accident. But in this peasant boy from Andalusia, I felt the kind of strength that by now had disappeared altogether, the kind of strength that has nothing to do with trappings, such as will. The strength that comes from nature, from the soil, not from books, learning, whatever rewards civilization can bestow on strength that is willed. The strength that comes from the mere capacity to survive.
> Anyway, when I saw him that first time in the ring, disdainful both of the animal and the public, I thought he could teach me what I still did not know about raw physical courage.

He drank down his glass of mazanilla and remained silent for a moment while Benjamin turned off the recorder in his pocket, waited for him to go on, and watched him. His face, which was always expressive of his feelings, was passive. A table of tourists where there had been much laughter and singing was now empty, but the café was still filled with late diners and drinkers. More than half of them were foreigners come to Pamplona for the bullfights and the never-ending celebration of the *fiesta* of San Fermin.

"I don't think Manolo liked me very much for what I was doing," Hal talked again, as if more to himself, as if thinking things out, not looking at Benjamin, making circles with his wine glass in front of him on the table. "What I was doing was trying to romanticize this whole business of fighting bulls. I always called them 'brave bulls,' while he himself preferred to think of them as 'bichos.' I don't think he liked the fact that I was a writer while he himself could neither write nor read. He had not even learned by then how to sign his name, and his manager was stealing him blind. But he was happy. His family no longer went hungry, and there was always a smoked ham hanging somewhere in the hotel closet, and he would go to it, like a starving animal, even when he had his fill of food. What could he tell me, that year in Pamplona? That the scars of hunger were worse than the scars from bull's horns?"

He drank down his glass and filled his own and Benjamin's. And then he laughed, and Benjamin did not know if he was laughing at himself or at his memories.

> I was very impressed with his wounds. When he was being dressed in his *traje de luces,* I made notes about how many gorings he had received, and where, and marveled at the strange design the wounds' trajectories left over his young body. "I still have my *cojones* intact," Manolo said to me. And we both laughed. He was going to give me what I was after, the romance of the *corrida de toros.*
>
> We would meet each day after the fights, in this café. Maybe he knew that if he was going to drink the *manzanilla* we paid for, he would have to listen to us analyze what we had seen. It would appear that we saw more from our seats in the *sombra* than he did from the sand. We talked of "tricks" and told him how proud we were that he, Manolo Olivar, never stooped to them. We didn't know enough to see how often he had to punish the bulls more than he needed, for fear that those heads, when it came time to kill, would not lower enough. We didn't know that his *picadors* drew more blood than they should. Nor that the horns were often shaved, especially on the Miuras, for he dreaded them more than the rest. We respected the way he fought, "cleanly and truly," while he wished he could kill the animals like they used to, years ago, as soon as they came into the ring. He was good at killing maybe only because that meant the end of his own agony. But we didn't know any of this. ✲

A young American couple approached their table and were waiting for him to stop talking. Timidly they now asked for an autograph. Hal looked at them with great weariness and said that they were mistaken. He was not Hal Hubbard. "That one died in Pamplona some time ago." They smiled, not knowing if he were joking, so Hal turned to Benjamin and said, "Tell them the truth." And Benjamin said, "It's true, Hal Hubbard is dead." And the couple waited around for a moment, then apologized and departed. Hal remained silent, and it seemed to Benjamin that some thread that he had held was now gone, or tangled up with other threads. When he spoke again, it was in some other gear, in neutral, he was more detached, as if none of this had anything to do with him, but with some character from one of his novels.

"When he met the American's wife and his friend, Manolo Olivar must have thought them both too innocent for this ambitious young man, this writer. He sensed something bad in him, something the writer himself did not yet know was there, inside him, waiting to hurt the two people he traveled with, his wife and his friend. The peasant boy, who was a bullfighter now, was born with insights. He felt sympathy for the writer's friend and for the writer's wife. Maybe he smelled, in the friend, fear. The friend was filled with it. But fear must smell the same no matter where it comes from, what its causes are. The writer's friend confessed to the bullfighter that he had passed an animal in the fields at night and that the writer had told him that this thoughtless act would cause some *torero's* death. Manolo must have thought that it gave the writer an unfair advantage over his weak friend, so he took the fear away. He himself was sick of fear and did not wish its unnecessary presence on the weak man.

The American writer resented this interference. He grew suddenly more critical of Manolo's performance in the ring on the following day. The writer asked the bullfighter if it was true that most of the *toreros* wore those tight pants because they were all *maricones* at heart. Manolo knew that the writer asked that question because he was a dangerous man when crossed, and he had crossed him by telling his friend that he would not cause anyone's death. Manolo, the peasant's son, knew that the writer would have been happy to fight him, to hit him, that that was what he was after. But he was cunning. He took him where it would hurt the writer more. He took him on his own turf.

197.

"Why are you really interested in bulls?" Manolo asked the writer.
"Because of what they symbolize," the writer said.
"What is that? What do they symbolize?"
"Spanish attitude toward death. The Spaniards have chosen the bullfight to exorcize death. Each time they see a *faena* they see death in the bull, and the killer of death in the bullfighter." The writer was quoting himself. He had just written a piece on the subject.
"Bullshit," Manolo said.
The writer knew himself right but tried to understand the young man and said, "You've grown sick of it, haven't you? Sick of fear."
But the bullfighter interrupted the writer. "I've grown sick of people, of the fear that people give me, not the bulls."
"You take fewer chances with animals," the writer said, sticking a *bandarilla* of words into the bullfighter, who shook it off.
"You're learning more. I was never a fool, not even when I was starting out. If you are to write about what I do for a living, make sure you know who the real enemy is. The public. The public destroys more bullfighters than the animals. The animals only gore or kill, the public murders."

Usually by this time at night, Hal would feel the liquor and his talk would be affected by it. The slurred words, the edge of nastiness, a weariness would come over him, but not that night. He was thinking aloud, trying to remember truth and pain, but Benjamin did not understand this nor did he know that Hal Hubbard was finally willing that night to face certain memories never told anyone. And while Hal Hubbard talked on, Benjamin was thanking God for the tape recorder. He would send the tape to the publisher and suggest he use it as a sales promotion gimmick. And perhaps the publisher would get the opinion of a psychologist as to what it all meant, especially that change of gears to the third person singular.

Hal called to the waiter for a bottle of cognac, and Benjamin went to the men's room then and changed the tape. When Hal began to speak again he kept his eyes on the dirty tablecloth, no longer looking around or at Benjamin.

Instead of enemies that night they parted friends. For they shared a distrust of people. Fifteen years later they met again. The American writer was now covering the Spanish Civil War for a newspaper. He was much different from the young man of before. He had a different wife, which made him different, but that fact was not alone in making him different.

They started as they had before, with Manolo lying to the American because that's what he thought the American was after. The by then Manolo knew this war to be as useless as all other wars. And again, after the lies came the truth. They got drunk together, good and drunk, on the cognac in the silver flask that the American carried with him wherever he went. And being drunk made Manolo stop his lies and tell the American how he really felt.

"It's the second time," the writer said to the bullfighter, "that you take my dreams and step all over them."

"I'm in your debt twice then, for doing you two favors," Manolo said, and both laughed, and laughing together, being warmed by good cognac that the American could afford, made them feel they were *familiares*. And that is when Manolo, the bullfighter who would never fight again because in two weeks he would be dead, leaving behind an only son, that's when Manolo Olivar asked the American what he was after this time in Spain. What did he want to prove with his life.

Hal stopped talking, took a big gulp of his cognac and got up. The story wasn't over, and this both of them knew. Walking to their hotel, Benjamin asked, "What happened, what did you say to him when he asked you what you were trying to prove with your life?"

"What did I say?" Hal looked as if he was trying to remember, but it must have been an act. After a moment he said, "I lied to him, as he had lied to me, but I lied to him for the first time. I said, 'I am in Spain for the same thing I'd be anywhere else, to prove to myself that life is worth living.' That's what I said to Manolo. And he said to me, 'Worth the trouble?' 'Worth the joys,' I said. And Manolo, who was to leave a son behind, who was to grow up to be as good as his old man, he looked at me then, and he took it all away. He said, 'Life is as worthless as *mierda*.'"

That was the end of the story, but Benjamin, wanting to be sure, asked, "Is that what made you hate Manolo Olivar?"

But Hal was through talking for the night. He didn't answer.

Before morning, Benjamin had finished the entry for the day. He ended it with some guesswork:

199.

Hal always felt that Spain was the only country where he could be stripped naked. Spain is his soul's nemesis. It was there that he turned against his friend, Larry Dort.

It was there that he lost his literary innocence. And it was there that he found Manolo Olivar. Although he had the arrogance of youth going for him when he first met Manolo, and the cushion of success when he saw him for the last time, neither was protection enough. Manolo went for the jugular. Hal knew all along that Manolo knew some truth, and the truth, all along, was that life was worthless.

The reason he is so ill at ease with Manolo's son, Juan Olivar, is because by now, that has become his truth.

Having written this down, Benjamin woke up Maggie and made her listen to the tape, and then he read to her the passage. And then he said that he understood the bottom line about Hal Hubbard. "His condition is very clear to me now, he is sick unto death of living."

The remission happened in Italy when Hal began feverishly to work on his new novel *Beginnings*. He gave them a bad time in Italy. He wanted to protect himself from them and used his novel as an armor. But novels as armors don't work. It was more, all of it, like an endurance race. They were all after him to give what they needed for the contracted articles, and he was after what he really was, a novelist.

If the patient thought himself on the road to recovery, the diagnosticians saw it merely as the last attempt of the dying patient to deny the approaching death. When a year later, *Beginnings* came out, Benjamin and Maggie must have been cheered to read that, at the end, the protagonist died.

The novel came out to very bad reviews. It was judged to be "sentimental slush" by *The New York Times Book Review*. The Horns' publisher began to have second thoughts about their book. Benjamin prevailed upon the man with the argument that Hal Hubbard's position in the world of literature was not undermined by his latest novel. He then wrote Hal, inviting himself to Haiti, but Hal wrote back saying that he would like to go to Africa and that Horn should make "profitable arrangements" for a magazine piece.

Benjamin contracted with *Look* magazine for an article to be entitled, "The Last Safari." He insisted that Maggie do the photographs and, because the editors were enthusiastic about this, accepted a much smaller sum. Hal was unhappy about the financial arrangement and complained in the letter that Benjamin was getting inept "at extracting money. After all, I now have to support my mother, my sister, Carole, and my daughter. I am worried about money since *Beginnings* was totally demolished by what we must, lacking a better word, call critics."

Hal kept delaying his departure for Africa, and Benjamin's publisher was expressing pessimism over the book. "It's been years since we signed the contract. Those months in Europe with him don't really amount to anything sensational. Can't you dig out some dirt, sexual preferably, about Hal Hubbard? After all, we were going to have an exposé here." Benjamin became nervous because the publisher was hinting that he wanted his money back and might have to sue him to get it. Hal kept postponing his trip. Then, in spite of all precautions, Maggie became pregnant. When finally Hal decided to go to Africa, she couldn't come with them.

There was a definite change in Hal when he arrived in New York. He was almost taciturn. He seemed to be lost in thought and uninterested in seeing any plays, something Sally wanted to do. Benjamin had arranged for a profile for *The New York Times Book Review,* but Hal made no effort to be interesting in front of the writer. He just kept talking about buying guns and supplies and getting on his way to Nairobi. He paid little attention to Sally. He tended to ignore her, and he ignored Benjamin. He walked out on a party Sally gave at the Plaza Hotel on the eve of their departure, came back way past midnight, and would not say where he had been.

The distance he put between himself and everyone else continued on the long plane trip. But once they set up camp and he was to go after his first lion, he became animated.

Benjamin was there when Sally shot and missed the lion. He did not go into the bush with Hal after the wounded animal. Hal didn't want anyone, not even the hired hunter, to go after the lion. He went alone as they all waited by the jeep. An hour after Hal had disap-

201·

peared, the hunter, taking a handful of gunbearers, went after him. They brought him back unconscious. He had lost much blood, and, in the opinion of the hunter, he could not recover. When this opinion was confirmed by the doctors in the hospital to which he was taken, Benjamin hurriedly flew back to New York. On the plane he finished what he thought would be the last chapter of *Fall of a Giant* with these words:

> A lion's embrace stifled the life that was, for all practical purposes, over some time ago. Hal Hubbard, probably the most important writer of this century, pursued to the end his passion for adventure. Before going into the bush after the wounded lion he told us, "It's a job that best be done by me. I have the least to lose." But was his death an accident of courage, or was it a noble suicide?

Upon arrival in New York Benjamin Horn was interviewed by the press. Yes, he'd witnessed what had happened. It was in the last chapter of his book, which he'd just turned in. While the chapter was being copyedited, the news came from Africa that Hal Hubbard was recovering from his wounds. Benjamin rewrote the chapter, and his publisher once again expressed doubts as to the book ever coming out and his ability to recoup the advance that Benjamin had spent a long time ago.

"It's just a matter of time," Benjamin assured him. "We are going to be the only ones with a book about the decline of Hal Hubbard. He's a very sick man. The book coming out within weeks of his death or breakdown is sure to be a success."

"Are you going back to Africa?" his publisher wanted to know.

"I can't afford it unless you want to send me there."

The publisher declined.

A few months after, Benjamin received a wire from Hal Hubbard.

> WANT TO GO SPAIN DO PIECE ON BULLFIGHT SEASON, FOCUS ON RIVALRY BUILDING BETWEEN JUAN OLIVAR AND EL ANDALUZ. MIGHT BE BOOK IN THIS TOO. MAKE BEST ARRANGEMENTS MAGAZINE. HAL

It took Benjamin two weeks to sell the idea to *The Saturday Evening Post*. With the contract and the check, he flew to Spain. The change in Hal was even more dramatic now. He walked with a cane, talked in shorthand, made pronouncements, and he was never alone. He had gathered a group of aficionados who were traveling with him in a convoy of cars, following Juan Olivar and the new sensation nicknamed El Andaluz. When Hal saw Benjamin, he asked him why he had come.

"To be around you," Benjamin said.

It was clear that Hal did not need him now. He had two dozen people who were around him all the time. It seemed he never wanted to be alone.

Benjamin stayed in Spain only a month. During that time Hal had complained to him several times that he could not "pick up the tab for everyone." Benjamin said he would pay his expenses out of his twenty-five-percent share of the magazine money. But Hal said that that percentage was way out of line. That the most he was entitled to was ten percent, and that money had already been spent.

"I've kept all the receipts," Hal said. "Want to see them?"

He made it unmistakably clear that he did not want Benjamin around, either by ignoring him or saying to whoever was around that he was "sick and tired of freeloaders." Benjamin was clearly being treated like a fired servant.

Benjamin left in May, but not before talking to Sally.

"What's happening with Hal?" he asked her.

"He's trying to prove to everyone that he's a living legend," she said. "And he found the greatest believer in crowds."

On Benjamin's return, the Horns added a chapter about the changes in Hal. Benjamin decided to get a job while waiting for the inevitable to happen. The only chance they had now with *Fall of a Giant* was for Hal to die soon.

In June, Benjamin read in the newspapers that Hal was in New York, on his way to Santa Fe. The bullfight season had been cut short by the serious goring of Juan Olivar. When he called the Plaza Hotel, Hal said that he didn't feel like having lunch. They were leaving for Santa Fe the next day. The article had been mailed directly to the magazine without Benjamin going over it, as had been his habit with the other ones.

Benjamin went to the Plaza that evening and caught a glimpse of Hal as he was getting into the elevator. He looked much older. His face was bloated more than it had been in Spain. His novel, *Round-*

about, had just come out to unanimously rave reviews, and it was generally agreed that he would receive a Nobel Prize that year. But he did not look happy. He looked ill.

In April of 1957, Benjamin was awakened by a phone call from Sally. She told him that Hal had tried to kill himself and was in a private clinic in Albuquerque. She said that the doctors diagnosed him as paranoid-schizophrenic.

They didn't talk long, but Benjamin got the idea while on the phone that his book would have to be rewritten to make Sally look better. He would need her full cooperation. The day the job was done he mailed the manuscript to her.

He waited four weeks for her reaction, and when it did not come, he called her, but her phone had been changed to an unlisted number. Later that night he received a wire:

HAL MUCH BETTER. WANTS TO CELEBRATE HIS BIRTHDAY AUGUST 15 WITH FAMILY AND FRIENDS. HE WANTS YOU AND MAGGIE TO COME. BRING BABY. WE'LL BE HAVING A PARTY IN SANTA FE. LOVE, SALLY.

Dear Abby,
I have a problem. Someone who I believed to be a friend has done me dirt. Actually I think the whole incident is pretty funny. But maybe it isn't. What would you do if someone tried to bury you before you were dead?
Perplexed in Albuquerque

He looked at the letter he wrote on the stationery of the clinic and tried to see if it could be improved without lengthening it. He decided it couldn't, then crumpled it up and threw it toward the wastepaper basket. It made it, and he smiled.

Dear, dear Abby. I truly do have a problem. What do I do with the Horns? They came at me in Haiti, where there is no tradition of bullfighting. Cockfighting, yes, but no animals with horns are raised for the sole purpose of entertaining the crowds. I have been gored by the Horns. In spite of the fact that I tried as best I could, in very strenuous circumstances, to stay awake under the horrendous barrage of their excessively boring presences, I have been gored. In the groin area, which is not the best of areas to get gored by the likes of the Horns. The wound will only be fatal after death, however, which is the reason I write to you, compassionate soul, and not to a lawyer or to the local coroner who will not notice, while examining, that the internal bleeding caused by the Horns precipitated certain events, or lack of events. . . .

He stopped thinking aloud because it was frightening to dictate like this inside his private bathroom while sitting on the pot. He came here to sit and think and began to talk, which was something he often did, failing to bring along a magazine. He would dictate all sorts of letters to all sorts of people, famous, infamous, known, and totally unknown. And each time he dictated one, he got frightened by his sheer insights. The one he wrote to Jacqueline Bouvier Kennedy began with: "Dear Lovely Lady Married to a Candidate for President of United States, I detect a certain lack of warmth between you and the man you married. Could it be that you married him not out of love but because the young man had a future and was endowed by family ties with wealth? You too have money, dear lady, it shows in your face and the way you dress and do your hair. But every man of destiny, and your husband is certainly among those, needs a caring wife. Do you care, Jackie darling, about him? I am not in the habit of asking public questions, your evaluation of how good a man he is to aspire to this high office. I ask you a personal question. How do you love him?"

After he finished dictating that one, while sitting on the toilet, not out of necessity but because this was the best place for dictating, he began to fear that he was the only one in America who knew something about the young Kennedys. Could it be that he was becoming psychic under the barrage of psychological probes? Was there something rotten there, in that marriage? There was something rotten in the marriage of the two Horns. One breathed with the lungs of the other. And they breathed out Sally for him. Of course they were not her parents, they did not conceive her in some incestuous moment of lung-mating, but Maggie and Sally must have come from the same factory. A factory, somewhere, perhaps in New Jersey, which was manufacturing "faithful women." Faithful they were, but what more? The faithfulness thing was for advertising purposes. "We guarantee our product to be faithful." But what else was the product supposed to do? Usurp? Slurp up? Who was making the models and why? Was there a tie-in with the insurance companies? The surviving live-in-mate shall benefit . . . Kennedy, Benjamin

Horn, and Hal Hubbard all seemed to have shopped there. Did Kennedy know it? Horn obviously did. He put in an order the moment he was old enough to know of the existence of the faithful women factory. And they probably sent along an application blank for a friend. And he filled it out for Hal Hubbard. And they shipped Sally to him in Miami. According to Benjamin Horn's specifications. "Another one like mine, taller and blonde this time; this one goes for a friend." Was the trouble now because the factory had a marriage warranty and he did not use it?

The New Jersey manufacturer of the wife-dolls implanted a smile for the lips, a smile that was always there. Jackie had one not unlike Sally's and Maggie's. The public smile. Were they only making them for "public men?" But Benjamin wasn't all that public, how did he rate his?

Dear Manufacturer of Wives who are faithful and carry special burdens, I got one of your models. Will send in specifications of what went wrong, under separate cover. Could it be it doesn't work because you have to marry it? Do you make repairs under the circumstances? Or modifications? What, exactly, is the essential quality of your Sally-Maggie-Jackie model? I don't seem to be quite clear as to what exactly their deeper meaning is all about. Or is this secret information not available to husbands? Request answer on the preceding questions. Perplexed in Albuquerque. They would probably answer by checking off one of the boxes in a form letter of reply. Which box would it be? Your request denied? Your request does not include needed data? Your request does not apply since you did not marry model we sent. We only deal with morally sane people.

He took a shower next, standing under the fine spray with his mouth open, letting the water tickle his tongue. He was sticking it out at himself and his insights. He was just a man who had a silly habit of sitting on the pot when there was nothing better to do. But, golly, gee whiz, he was a fallen giant to somebody.

And that, ladies and gentlemen, would have to do for tonight. Gored in the asshole by the Horns of fate! That, ladies and gents, is what he probably deserved. No less. No more.

Sally Reynolds

> SALLY Reynolds, the daughter of Mr. and Mrs. Horace Reynolds, left this week for the Big City (New York City to you!) to work as a "Gal Friday" to that couple by the name of Horn who do all those delicious pieces on celebrities that you see in your favorite mags. We predict that it will not be long before our Sally snatches a celebrity for a husband!
>
> from The Pompton Lakes News,
Social Notes, Pompton Lakes,
New Jersey, May 23, 1945

Although her home was barely twenty-five miles from New York City, Sally felt she was going to an uncharted continent. Behind her she was leaving the two people who had sheltered her from life. Her attachment to them, and theirs to her, by now had taken the form of willing and gentle slavery. She was leaving them because she had been told by a man she had loved, but who was now dead, that she must "emancipate herself." She had promised him that she would.

Mrs. Horace Reynolds was forty-five and Mr. Reynolds in his

sixtieth year when they found themselves expectant parents. At first Mrs. Reynolds thought she had "a growth of some kind" and wished to be operated on, but her doctor prevailed in his diagnosis that she indeed was pregnant. "I still think it's a growth of some kind," Mrs. Reynolds said to her husband on the day she checked into the maternity ward of the hospital in Pompton Lakes. After the delivery, she greeted Mr. Reynolds with a frown and an admonition, "you will never fool around with me again, and don't you ever talk to me about it."

Mrs. Horace Reynolds, although a domineering woman, had no maternal instincts whatever, and Mr. Reynolds, henpecked for years into submission to his wife's needs, hardly knew what was expected of him in the very unexpected role of a father. As long as the baby was small and slept peacefully, waking only for her bottle and her daily bath, their usual routine was not much interrupted. When she was two, however, the daily bridge session with a couple the Reynolds knew, and who happened to be their only friends, was curtailed to twice a week, and completely abandoned when Sally was four and Mrs. Reynolds reached her menopause.

Mrs. Reynolds, without reading anything on the subject or consulting anyone, believed that her principal duties as a mother were to keep her daughter warmly clothed and well scrubbed and free from all danger of contamination.

As a child, what Sally suspected or knew about life and people she learned neither from books, friends, or by herself, but secondhand from her mother. She knew that all men were animals and that the only safety from them was inside the house. Mr. Horace Reynolds had been totally "declawed," as his wife termed their chaste relationship. He had been banned from the master bedroom and relegated to the living room sofa at night. During the day, Mr. Reynolds, who had retired from his meter-reading job at the gas company, stayed in the basement, where he secretly imbibed sweet wines and was forever repairing something or other. Also secretly he listened to a hidden radio in his private domain. He spent all his time down there, except for meals and whenever he was wanted for whatever chores or errands.

By the time Sally was six she learned to please her mother by simply staying inside the house. She had no one to play with and few toys. But her mother talked to her constantly, instructing her in "the ways of the world." Sally was told that good grades in school would denote a good mind. She learned that wearing a sweater, even in the heat of summer was the best protection against cold germs. She learned that Catholics, Jews, and Negroes were "dangerous, because they propagate as fast as they can and will one day take over the world." She knew that the devil was ever busy and that foiling his attempts at perverting a Christian woman was a full-time job. She accepted the fact that America had been a great country once, before the influx of "riffraff and the coming to power of Democrats, Communists, and other destructive elements who, since the death of Calvin Coolidge, have taken over the land."

When Sally was six, Mrs. Reynolds, unable to find a private Protestant school that she could afford, was forced to enroll her daughter at the nearby public school, where most of the children were Italian and Irish. Ordering her daughter to "never so much as talk or in any way associate with this Catholic trash," Mrs. Reynolds accompanied Sally to school each day and picked her up each afternoon. Together they would walk home, sometimes stopping at a supermarket and twice a week at the cemetery to visit Mrs. Reynolds's family grave. Each Sunday, together with Mr. Reynolds, they would attend church services. Otherwise they stayed home.

Each night before retiring, mother and daughter took turns reading passages from the Bible. Mrs. Reynolds preferred the Old Testament to the New, which she claimed "was poorly translated," especially the passages dealing with Jesus' tolerance of the frailties of human nature, and his concept of love and brotherhood among all men.

Ever since excommunicating her husband from her bed, Mrs. Reynolds had nightly dreams. Each morning, while preparing breakfast, she would tell her daughter about these dreams which varied only slightly. Mrs. Reynolds dreamed into the future, when she would be a widow and bedridden. Sally would be taking care of her, and they would live, the two of them, in "this house, which my parents left to me. It's never been Horace's house." A few times, Mrs. Reynolds dreamed that the gas company, in recognition of Mr. Reynolds's long service as meter-reader, did not charge them for the use of gas. A man from the gas company would bring this welcome news to Sally's mother as she'd stand over her husband's body in a funeral parlor. "He always looks better dead in my dreams than he does alive," Mrs. Reynolds would marvel.

On occasions Mrs. Reynolds's dreams included a fire that burned all the surrounding houses to the ground. Mrs. Reynolds would wait impatiently for this variation on her basic dream. "It will be just as it was when I was growing up," she would tell her daughter. "The nearest house will be a half mile away, and there will be orchards and fields all around instead of all those ugly chicken coops with all them Pope-worshippers inside." Each time she dreamt of the conflagration she would seem at peace with herself.

By the time she was of junior-high-school age, Sally considered her mother "her one and only friend." Sally was extremely polite, neat, respectful, and responsible and did not have to be reminded to keep warm. Although Sally always got straight A's, she was not liked by any of her teachers. The general opinion among the children was that the very tall girl was "a queer one." Over the years Sally got used to overhearing unkind remarks made about her, and developed what she herself considered "a thick skin."

By the age of sixteen, Sally's mind was prim and totally devoid of interesting prospects for the future. Her outward appearance was just as regrettable. She wore the plainest of dresses with white collars and cuffs. She combed her short brown hair severely close to her head. She was one of those unmemorable people one encounters and can't remember anything about except that they are tall and wear glasses. Although some, like Sally, don't wear glasses, the impression lingers on that they do.

If any person could be said not to be on speaking terms with life, it was Sally at the age of sixteen. But life, being brutally bad-mannered and insensitive to anyone's dictates, forced itself on Sally in the person of Mr. Fred Baldwin, the newly appointed Pompton Lakes High School Student Counselor.

Mr. Baldwin was the first person Sally encountered who actually listened to her. Of course he was paid to do so, and was very good at his job. When he was not listening he would counsel. He was probably the first one of very few high school counselors to look to the future and predict that one day there would be jobs in such nascent fields as plastics and computers.

Sally was sent to Mr. Baldwin's office to find out the "direction in her adult life." When she saw him she thought he looked like her father must have looked some thirty years before she was born. That first day she told him that she was at a total loss as to what she should do after graduating, that she had few, if any, interests outside her family, that she was an only child and "not like kids my age." There were long pauses, during which Mr. Baldwin would light his pipe and look at Sally while Sally looked at the top of his desk. She came back several times in the next few weeks to tell him more, although there was not much to tell. He encouraged her to fantasize.

"What would you like to do with your life?" he would ask.

And for the first time, Sally began to imagine that there might be life for her after all. Thinking that she might be best suited to be a secretary, Mr. Baldwin asked her to give him a hand with his files during her free periods.

Mr. Baldwin thought her a curious young girl. He had a theory that American women would evolve into a very different breed, untouched by any civilizing influences from the past. Sally represented that vacuous stage in their development that worried Mr. Baldwin. He decided to take a particular interest in her.

His very proximity during the hour she would spend in his office enchanted her. She would lie in bed at night making lists of things she adored about him: his tweed jacket with leather patches at the elbows; the way he would light and draw on his pipe; the way he leaned back in his chair and rested his head; the way he could listen to the students and then gently counsel them; the way he looked at her, quizzically, as if guessing at her most secret thoughts. That he existed and she knew him seemed a miracle. That he took interest in her and let her work for him made her life exciting.

By her senior year, Sally Reynolds, with Mr. Baldwin's guidance, knew that she would become a secretary. She was taking typing and steno, and he had taught her all about filing. For her eighteenth birthday she asked her mother if they couldn't have Mr. Baldwin home for dinner. Her mother agreed only because this was to be Sally's birthday gift. Her daughter had told her several times that Mr. Baldwin was a wonderful person, and she had misgivings about this man who might lead her daughter astray.

Mr. Baldwin found the evening excruciatingly boring. Mr.

Reynolds tried to promote the idea that the best job for "young whippersnappers" was in meter-reading. Mrs. Reynolds wanted to know if there were many "perverts" among the riffraff in Sally's high school. Mr. Baldwin thought that the atmosphere of bigotry and senility would permanently damage Sally, and the next day he sat her down and explained to her that once she graduated from high school, she must not live at home.

"Where would I go?" she asked helplessly, for she could not visualize the world outside of her home.

"Well, why don't you start with New York City? You could come home weekends. But for God's sake don't live at home. Promise!"

She promised. The next day, Mr. Baldwin was found dead in his bachelor apartment. He had had a massive heart attack.

Sally bore her first tragedy with great stoicism. In her heart she knew herself to be a woman, for she had loved a man. The least she could do for him was to keep her promise. Upon graduating from high school, she went to New York for the first time. The city scared her, but a promise was a promise. The first employment agency advised her to go to a secretarial school; her chances at a better job would be greatly increased if her skills improved. She took bookkeeping as well as typing and steno and graduated at the head of her class. She was commuting home each day, which made the separation from her parents less painful.

At twenty she found the perfect job, with the Horns, as their "girl Friday." The work they were engaged in seemed exceedingly glamorous to her. After a few months of commuting, the Horns talked her into moving to New York City. She rented a room in a hotel for women. She would come home only on weekends. Mrs. Reynolds was devastated by this decision and predicted dire consequences. There was much talk about sin and the ever-busy devil, and how to fight both. Sally promised her mother that if anything should happen to her father she would come home and live with her. This pacified Mrs. Reynolds somewhat since she thought her husband was not long for this world.

Within two months of Sally's move to New York City, both her parents were dead and the house burned to the ground. The firemen guessed that Mr. Reynolds was trying to repair the gas furnace when it exploded.

Sally bore this tragedy as silently as she had borne the death of her beloved Mr. Baldwin. She put the insurance money in a bank, sold the land on which the house stood, and took stock of herself. She was all alone in the world. She was highly efficient at her job, she loved working for the Horns, and they were happy with her. Her job was secure. Nothing attracted her to people her age. If she were ever to marry it would be to an older man. She felt herself quite a bit older than her years, always had. She was a good cook and sewed well. She would make, some day, a good housekeeper to a widower with children. But she was in no hurry to improve her life.

On the day the Horns left for Haiti, leaving her in charge of their apartment, she did what she had wanted to do for a long time. She had her fortune told. The Gypsy said to her that a friend would shortly take her fate in his hands. That evening she dug up from among her few personal papers the clipping from the Pompton Lakes newspaper. When Benjamin wrote to her, asking her how she would like to be the next Mrs. Hal Hubbard, she was not totally surprised. She had believed, without any reservations, what the newspaper had predicted and what the Gypsy fortune teller had told her. To make it all happen, all she needed to do was to bleach her hair.

Becoming a blonde seemed magically to change Sally into an outwardly more assured young woman. For the first time in her life she was going to think of herself as attractive. She would even start wearing heels now. Under the dryer she read two magazine articles that made a profound impression on her. They were both in the same issue of *Cosmopolitan* magazine and seemed to have been written just for her. Actually she thought them miraculously well timed and she would later think that they were responsible, more than anything else, for changing her life.

> Something strange and wonderful happens to women after a war. Those of marriageable age dedicate their energies toward making their marriages work. United, in some primeval sense, to rebuilding the world, they make better wives and mothers. Those post-war marriages are more fruitful and successful than any other. There seems to be a renewed STRENGTH in those women who have lived through a war

213·

and the men who have been through the war make better and more steadfast husbands.

Reading these words, Sally Reynolds, for the first time in her life, felt herself part of a generation of women, not alone in the world. The second article impressed her even more. It was entitled, "What It Takes To Be a Wife of a Famous Man." When she finished reading it, she tore off the page which included these words:

> When it comes to great writers, the wives know that they deal with men whose primary work happens inside their heads. The organization, the imagination, that it takes to create characters and move the novel's plot, leave their novelist husbands almost totally helpless when it comes to everyday coping.
> The successful wife of a novelist must have the following qualities:
> An organizational genius.
> The ability to cope, without seeking his advice, with all the details of living.
> A sunny disposition that would not be overshadowed by his changing moods (which darken often).
> The capacity to deal with all the interruptions that might dam up the creative flow.
> The grace to deal diplomatically with such destructive and time-consuming things as the stream of mail that comes into the house and all the uninvited guests that tend to drop in.
> But, most of all, what a wife of a well-known writer must do is to sublimate her life to his and help him to be free of worries, so that his productivity can continue with fewest interruptions.

In the same article, the author mentioned the most ideal places for writers to work; Santa Fe, New Mexico, headed the list. On her way home from the beauty shop, Sally picked up a book on Santa Fe and, after reading about this "city different," decided that Santa Fe would be their home.

She made a list of what she must do to prepare herself to be Mrs. Hal Hubbard. She would read all his books and all the books and articles written about him. She would keep, on her dresser, a picture of him. She went to the library and cut out one she liked from a magazine. She took home with her several books on hunting and fishing, and after reading them, decided she would have to practice fishing somewhere. This would have to wait, but each day now she went to 42nd Street and practiced shooting in a shooting gallery. She also went to Abercrombie's and bought some hunting and fishing clothes.

She knew, beyond a shadow of a doubt, that she would make Hal Hubbard a good wife. If she had nothing in her background to interest him, she could offer him all her quiet qualities. If he was now eager to settle down to a peaceful and productive existence, she would create for him the perfect atmosphere for this. She would organize his life and be his secretary, his housekeeper, his hostess, and protectress of his privacy. The only thing she was unsure of was whether she could ever go to bed with him. She hoped he was too old for that.

By the time she left for Miami, Sally Reynolds, now twenty-two, was ready for Hal Hubbard. She had trained to become his wife only for three months, but she had trained intensively and well.

Even after Benjamin and Maggie left them in New Orleans, Hal kept her at a distance. He was trying to make her feel free to leave, too. He protested about being able to go on alone, saying that looking for a place to establish his residence might be a bore for her. He guarded from her all his fears of the government being after him for some real or imaginary infraction of his citizenship or crimes as a taxpayer. He kept treating her as a "traveling buddy," and showed no attraction to her as a woman. She was both happy and, to her surprise, disappointed by this. Although she told him that she had money, he insisted on paying all her expenses. She thought that he feared the temptation of having in any way become dependent on her, and she had to make him understand that there was nothing there to fear.

During a picnic, on the second day when they were alone, she cut her finger slicing a melon. At the sight of her blood, all his reserve seemed to vanish. He disinfected the wound, stopped the bleeding, bandaged the finger, and when he looked up at her, there must have been something in her eyes, for he leaned and kissed her and told her she had been very brave. The night before she had been thinking that perhaps because she was so tall, he thought her as strong as a man and as independent. She had to appear less self-possessed, perhaps even helpless in a situation that wouldn't affect his high regard for her work. When he kissed her, she knew that she had been right. He wanted her to be dependent on him. She was glad she had decided to cut herself while slicing the melon.

After that, he began to treat her more like a woman, but neither of them made an aggressive move toward the other. Yet they began to touch; when passing food their fingers would meet, and he started to open the car door for her as they changed places. Each would drive fifty miles, and then change. They would cover only two hundred miles a day that way. Stopping whenever they felt like it, lunching at great length, in the afternoons they would look for a motel in which to spend the night. They always had separate rooms and he made sure, each time, that they did not adjoin.

On the fourth night of their trip, Sally twisted her ankle as she was going up to her room. He carried her and gently lowered her on her bed, asking if the ankle hurt and whether she wanted a doctor to come and look at it. She reached out to him, and he kissed her.

"I must take care of you," he said. They made love that night, and he was very gentle with her and asked how could it be that she had not been with a man before.

"I was waiting for you," she said.

Her mother would not have approved of her living in sin. And neither did she. She had hoped that Hal would tell her he loved her, and that he would propose marriage. But he didn't seem to want to confuse needs with love. She knew that the way he wished to protect her was different from the way she wished to protect him. Her way would be secretive while his was open.

When they arrived in Santa Fe, he said that he hoped they would not have to stay in a hotel for long, and she found a house for rent that same day. She established a routine for him, so he could write. She made a list of what he would want in a house and spent her mornings, while he wrote, looking around. She knew how to keep out of his way and learned to cater to his needs. And he liked her cooking. He began to talk freely to her about "this phase of my life," as he put it. He was exhausted, he said, "by emotional involvements." He needed a rest, to clear his head of problems. If he had to cope with everything, he couldn't write. And writing was everything to him. "Without it I can't live. I need a special climate now, a climate of calm."

She created that climate for him in their rented house. She made it a refuge.

Within two months she found "a perfect house." Huddled between two foothills of the Sangre de Cristo, it was the last one on the Old Santa Fe Trail, with views toward the southwest, the Manzanos, the Ortiz, and the towering Sandia. The day she brought him there and saw, as they walked around it, that he was pleased and happy, she felt like a bride when he said, "It will be our home."

She furnished it with primitive New Mexican furniture which she tracked down, looking for it as far away as Taos, and she bought a bearskin for their bed, and when they moved there she made love to him wordlessly, the way he wanted. She began to be helpful to him in a hundred little ways, quietly guessing at all the needs of this man who had not spoken to her of love or marriage. She could wait.

She made a list of all her inherited qualities that would help her be a good wife to this strong and yet vulnerable man. She had, from her father, the gift of being merely a presence, the ability to be unintrusive, and not hurt when ignored or mistreated. And she had her mother's qualities of perseverance, strength, and patience. Caution would guide her tendency to be domineering and willful. She would, she decided beyond and above everything else, endure.

She continued her training. She knew that one day he would ask her to go hunting with him and her days of practice at the gallery on 42nd Street seemed not enough. When she read, in the Santa Fe newspaper, an article about a champion target shooter, she called him and hired him to give her lessons. She advertised for someone to teach her how to fish and found an oldtimer who told her all he knew about it and went fishing with her. She bought books by Conrad and Kipling and others who wrote about raw, physical courage.

But most of all she saw to Hal's comfort and peace of mind. She stocked the house with his favorite wines, brandies, and wrote to the Olaffson Hotel bartender for Hal's favorite rum sour recipe. She took over the job of answering Hal's correspondence. She found out the birthdays of his family and friends and marked them down on her calendar and had cards and presents ready for him in time to send, needing only his signature.

*

They had lived in their house for three months before Hal talked to her of how he felt about this "business of living in sin." He told her how difficult, he felt, it would be for her to commit her life to his. "I'm a bastard," he said. "I drink too much and get depressed when the writing goes bad, and I hit out and hate everything and everyone around. All I could offer you is a used-up body and a mind that might crack. I'm no bargain, Sally. I'm sorry you didn't come into my life years ago. I might not be in the bad shape I'm in now. You're good for me. And I'd want you for a mate, but the ship is a leaky one and it's heading for bad weather and rocks."

"I've got a compass," she said. "It will keep us on course."

One night he brought out a bottle of champagne, and, while they drank in front of the fire, he told her for the first time that he loved her. He wanted her to believe it, and she did. And then he said, "Would you marry me, in spite of everything that is in store for us, and without promises from me?" And she said yes, yes, yes! She thought he would kiss her then and hold her to him, but he kept staring into the fire, and when he spoke, he said, "Let's pretend we're married. Do it with a bang, give a party, as if it was to celebrate our marriage. I need to let them know we're residents here. Let's invite the press and anyone else who'd come to our wedding if there was one."

"Why do we have to pretend? Why can't we get married?"

He kept looking into the fire. "What I want to do," he said, "is make out a will and leave half of whatever might be left to you. My three kids can make their own way, but there would be enough for them too. I want to set you up for life, so you won't have to worry. I want you to stay with me, be my buffer zone. But I think it's best to make people believe that we don't live in sin. I want to legitimize your condition."

Sally realized that if official marriage was what her mother and father had had, the secret nonmarriage-marriage that Hal had offered might turn out better. She asked when he wanted the party and whom she should invite and what the invitations should say.

"Why don't you have them printed to say that Mr. and Mrs. Hal Hubbard request the pleasure of your company."

The next morning she had the invitations printed and sent one of them to Maggie and Benjamin Horn. A few months later Benjamin requested information as to when and where they got married. She wrote back saying please, please, it was a secret, it really didn't happen, but they didn't want anyone else to know that they were not married. She realized as she wrote that letter that she would never be Hal's widow and wondered why the thought of surviving him had entered her head.

During the party, she saw, for the first time, how good he was with a crowd. She had thought him to prefer being alone, a solitary man, but he was marvelous with people. She had made all the arrangements, and they came, over a hundred of them, from the press and from the writers and artists who lived in Santa Fe, and the house was flooded with them.

He didn't sleep with her that night. He stayed up until daylight streamed into the large living room where she had gone to sleep, amidst the noise, in the corner of the couch. She had expected to remember that night as the most romantic night of her life, because she decided that she would try to delude herself that they were married, but all there was to remember was the fact that they had a good party, and five years later, in Spain, when it seemed that he wanted a party every night, a crowd around all the time, when she was not enough, maybe never had been, when the hunger to be surrounded by people seemed to her a disease of Hal's, she remembered that night.

They stayed in Santa Fe another few months, but they were not good months for Hal. He had been working steadily. He was half through with his novel *Hurricane Season* when he began to complain that what he had done was no good, "a travesty of what I could do." She suggested he needed a rest and arranged for the old fisherman to talk Hal into taking a few days for fishing. While they were gone she retyped the manuscript and made an extra carbon and locked it in a trunk. She had by now established several files for his papers and kept scraps that he discarded, and pages that she found in the wastepaper basket. While she was working on this Benjamin called her and proposed what he called "a deal." She was going to talk Hal into going to Europe to do the article he owed *Life* magazine. Benjamin, in exchange, would keep their fake marriage a secret.

Before Hal returned from his fishing trip she wired Benjamin, saying that they would be in New York next week, that this was a good time for them to go to France. When Hal came back, she greeted him with the announcement that they should no longer postpone the trip. "Your writing, you say, isn't going well, and *Life* magazine can't wait forever, after all, they did give you a considerable advance. This is a good time to make the trip. I wired Benjamin that we are coming."

As she spoke, she noticed the change in his eyes. She knew that he was angry and expected him to shout. He only said, very quietly and slowly, "It's one thing to be helpful, but no lady should feel free to take the pants off her man."

He got up then and left the room and did not come down for dinner. She cried for the first time, not knowing what she should do. Finally, late that night, he came downstairs and saw her huddled by the fireplace, shaking with fear, her eyes red, and he hugged her and said he was sorry.

"I was not mad at you, I was mad at myself for not having destroyed what I had written of that damn book. You retyped it, you shouldn't have bothered. I burned it all."

"Oh, no! It was a wonderful book."

"It was no good, a writer knows better than a typist when it comes to writing. But if you want to go to France, we shall go. I wanted to go to Haiti first. You haven't seen our homestead there."

She promised him she would never meddle, never do anything that concerned his career without consulting him, ever again. And she told him she would much rather go to Haiti than to France. Then she sent Benjamin a wire which read: NEVER THREATEN OR TRY TO BLACKMAIL AGAIN IF YOU KNOW WHAT'S GOOD FOR YOU. SALLY.

She had taken French lessons in Santa Fe and began to study Creole the day they arrived in Port-au-Prince. The house looked run down, the carpets were worn, the furniture needed recovering, the drapes were faded. She got busy changing things around. He had hoped that she would want to go on the boat for a long fishing trip, but she was busy building a nest. So he went alone and spent four days away, and she thought that she had lost him.

It was then that she promised herself never to leave him, to stay by his side even if he didn't want her there. She had been deaf to what the children had said to her in school, she would become deaf to anything unkind he might say. She would not take another chance at losing him. She needed that resolution in the next seven months. Hal wrote letters to old friends suggesting they visit, even inviting strangers for dinner. She treated them all with cool composure. No amount of people would crack the shell she was building around her relationship.

Her efficiency was unfailing, her good humor constant. Hal would often compliment her, calling her a "good soldier" when he would bring a group of tourists back from the Olaffson bar. But often, when he was in a black mood or had drunk too much, he would call her a "goddamn machine," and she would have to turn her eyes away from his face which seemed to mock her. Once he told her that she was nothing more than his "keeper," that she thought him an animal, and if he was one, he was a wild animal and had hatred for his keeper. But he had been very drunk that night, and she didn't think he meant what he had said.

She was well aware now of his importance as a writer, and tried to husband his energies, to deflect, whenever she could, the invasions on his time. In subtle ways, unknown to him, she would try to give him space from people. She would censor his mail, not allowing some letter to reach him. She felt that he had a debt to his talent and that he could not go on for weeks without writing. Once, when he sat on the veranda complaining that he could not write, she said that perhaps he lacked discipline.

"What the hell do you know about my craft?" he asked.

"Doesn't it require discipline, doesn't everything?" she asked.

"Is that what keeps you going?"

"I think women have more discipline than men," she replied.

"What else do women have?"

"Patience and more kindness than men. But maybe I'm generalizing."

"What else?"

"Gentleness."

"How about strength? Are women stronger than men?"

"Maybe we tend to survive better, and if that's strength, maybe we are stronger."

The following morning Hal came down to breakfast wearing one of Sally's scarves around his neck.

"For good luck," he said.

"With what?" she asked.

"The writing."

That evening he showed her the pages he had worked on all that day. He was very pleased with them. She read them and thought them very good.

"If a scarf brings you such luck, you should always wear something of mine," she said.

"You wouldn't mind?"

"I'd be flattered," she replied.

He worked well, and later than was his habit each day now. He would usually come down before lunch for a drink, and when he was still upstairs at one Sally went up and, without knocking, entered his study.

He was sitting at his desk writing and did not hear her come in. He was wearing one of her robes. She left the room quietly. A few days later he called down to her and when she came up to his study he was sitting at his desk, wearing a dress of hers.

"Ever since we've had that talk about the sex difference I've been dressing in your clothes." He stood up and turned around for her, and then walked in imitation of a model in front of her. "Do I look terribly silly?"

"No," she said.

"I feel silly and degraded." He sat down again. "But you know something? I've been writing better than ever." He handed her a chapter and she read it.

"It's better than anything you've done since we've met," she told him.

He had removed her dress, and for the first time since she had known him, cried in her arms.

By 1953 when they finally left for Paris, she had become used to her role in Hal's life. He needed her more than he knew, but at the same time he resented her more than ever. In bed he would be gentle and kind and loving, but outside of their bedroom he used her to hit out at his angers and his frustrations. The first time Maggie saw Hal "demean" her, as she later said, Sally defended Hal.

"He doesn't mean to hurt me, and I'm not hurt," she explained. "You know what kids say, sticks and stones might break my bones, but words will never hurt me, or whatever."

"Don't you have any pride, any self-respect?" Benjamin asked her.

She only smiled and said it was not a matter of pride or self-respect, it was a matter of love and devotion and understanding. She had learned from her father how to be tough and take abuse. Besides, by then she knew that they needed each other and nothing else mattered, and that their mutual needs might not be someone else's idea of love.

She had become more accident prone, but thought of it as "a protective device." Her body, and not her mind, was taking the beating. In New Mexico and Haiti, whenever she hurt herself he would become solicitous. But in Europe that changed. When she cut herself, spilled something on herself, or slipped in Hal's presence, he would take her clumsiness as a personal affront. She consoled herself with the thought that perhaps they had grown so close that he felt it was he who was losing control of his body, not her.

In Paris, in their bedroom once, as if confessing something that had been in his mind for some time, he said that with Lee, it had been wonderful, in bed and out.

"I'm glad," Sally said, happy that he had been happy in his youth, as she had not.

"She was the only one I ever loved," he said. "She was the only one who didn't turn on me, who didn't feast on my soul, who didn't want to destroy me."

Sally was sure he didn't mean to insult her. She asked, "Do you think I want to do those things to you?"

He looked in her direction, but not at her, as if she were transparent.

In Spain, when he could not write, when he was raging against his inability to put the words down on paper, she suggested, gingerly, he put on some of her clothes. "It seemed to work in Haiti," she said.

"If I can't write with my balls I won't write at all," Hal said, snapping the pencil he was holding in half.

"What's important for you is to write. If that helps, why don't you do it?" She handed him her scarf. "Nobody will know," she said, and left the room so she would not see him tying it about his neck.

That day he never left his hotel room, and did ten pages that pleased him and delighted the Horns. She sensed by then how helpless he must have felt as a child, without the power to stop his father from pulling the trigger. Did he feel stronger when he was dressed as a woman, and from that strength derive something that enabled him to write well? It didn't matter! Anything that produced results was, in her eyes, legitimate. Perhaps they had suffered similar wounds? Whenever she wore slacks, didn't she feel more at ease? It was a healthy way of exorcising whatever might have gone wrong in their childhood. She had thought that he understood this, as she understood it. But one night, while still in Pamplona, he raged at her, saying that she wanted him dead by making a mockery "of what I do for a living." She was making him into "an abomination," he yelled, and accused her of wanting to turn him into some kind of freak, "just because I will never marry you." He swore he would never wear any of her clothing again.

They had a suite in Pamplona, and he took to sleeping on the couch in the living room. It was there, in Pamplona, that she fantasized for the first time what it would be like for her after he died. Because she was practical and well organized, so was this fantasy. She thought that she would sell the house in Haiti and live in Santa Fe. And she would devote her life, after his death, to publishing his letters, and some old stories and poems that she had found in the files in Haiti. She would edit whatever was left of his words and provide scholars with insights that only she had into this man.

When they came back to Haiti they slept in different rooms. There was to be no war, only an armed truce. He used his hatred to write *Beginnings,* the book that she would consider his revenge. He worked on it all day, every day, and she would only see him at dinner, and he was finished within three months from the time he started. When it was clear to her that they would never marry, she told him one night that she wanted a child, but he said, "My books will be our children. We will make them together, see them grow together, and let go of them together." Although she asked him to see the novel he was working on, he only showed her the dedication. It read, "To Sally, who keeps secrets well."

He did not trust her not to look at his work and had gotten into the habit of locking the door to his study and being there when the maid cleaned up. This keeping her away from what were to have been their "children," more than anything else, made her angry with him. Had she been able to visualize a life without him, while he lived with someone else, she would have left him then.

One afternoon he came downstairs with an envelope in his hands. "It's finished," he said, his eyes as bright as she had ever seen them.

"It's awfully thin," she said, looking at the envelope. "Is it a short story, or an article?"

"Good things come in small packages. It's a novel, and it's the best one I've ever done."

"Could I read it?" she asked, knowing the answer. "You once said your books would be our children."

He smiled and said, "That was before."

She waited for him to say "before" what, but he was walking to the door.

"What is it called?" she asked.

"*Roundabout*," he said.

She waited until the door closed behind him and then said, "It's not a good title."

He stayed away all that night and came back in the morning to get his fishing gear.

"Can I come with you?" she asked.

"A man's boat is his castle," he said, "and this man doesn't want visitors."

When he was away, the proofs of *Beginnings* came in the mail. She read it and cried. The female character was a woman who was systematically destroying the man she loved.

He didn't wish her to come to Africa, hoped she wouldn't want to go. He asked her why she insisted on coming along. "I want to be with you. Besides, I've always dreamed of shooting big game. Please, let me come," she begged. The article he was going to do for *Look* was to be called "The Last Safari." And maybe that is why he said, "We will be together to the end."

It seemed impossible to her that she missed killing the lion intentionally. She knew that Hal would go after it, into the bush, alone. He had said, the night before, that if one of them wounded the animal he didn't want anyone else to go after it. Maybe he too thought it would be a good and right death for him.

Something deep inside of him changed when he survived the

wounds. He seemed to know that she had wished, had almost caused, his death. He no longer hated her. He was now afraid of her.

He would not allow her to be alone with him. He hired a nurse to be in his hospital room during the day and another one who stayed there at night. And when his son came, he kept him around. He had told her very little about his children. She had not even known that Carl was a priest and lived in Africa now. All the dark fears put there by her mother, fears of the Catholics, seemed to rush at her whenever Carl looked at her. She thought that Hal might tell Carl that she wanted his father dead. She imagined things they said about her, for the young man looked at her in a strange way. She found herself chattering, saying silly things whenever she was around him. Something weird was happening to her, and there was no one to talk things over with.

While Benjamin was still there, she had a chance to speak to him about how bad things were between Hal and her. He thought their "marriage" was going fine, mistaking their mutual politeness for an improvement. And so she said nothing to him. Maybe it was Africa that made her feel so insecure, so close to wildness. She had strange, frightening dreams at night, and a feeling of dread during the long days.

She knew he was not well enough to go to Spain again. After two weeks of traveling with him and the crowd he surrounded himself with, she decided that she needed time to think, to be away from him. She said she would rent a house in Cordova and stay there.

When he came to visit her he was not alone. He had in tow a dark-haired, petite woman, who couldn't have been more than twenty-two or three. When she walked across the room to meet Sally, her hand outstretched, her hips undulated as if she was dancing.

"My name's Brenda," she said. "You must be Sally."

"I must be," said Sally, observing that Brenda wore no brassiere.

At dinner, when Hal drank too much, Sally wanted somehow to caution him, for she knew how alcohol might thwart his performance. It was no surprise to her when, after dinner, Hal took Brenda for a long walk and did not return for hours. Sally would wait. And survive.

When Juan Olivar was gored and the season for Hal was over, the article for *Life* done, he wanted to go back, not to Haiti, because it would be too hot there in the summer, but to Santa Fe. When he told Sally this they were alone in a room for the first time since the accident. There was no malice nor fear in his eyes. She thought that maybe he too wanted to erase everything bad that had happened between them and start off again.

He must have seen the hopes in her eyes. "Santa Fe might be a good place to work in again," he said.

"Yes," she said. "Will you go back to *Hurricane Season*? It was a good book."

"If it was good, how come I burned it?"

"I've kept a copy," she said. "When you read it again maybe you'll like it."

There were two wings in the house, one was hers and one his now. They would meet for meals. Hal didn't talk much, but she knew he was working his way out of "the mess" that *Hurricane Season* was in. While he worked upstairs, she would read downstairs, or walk in the hills, or drive around. She no longer thought of his books as their children. She would have them all, his orphans, one day.

They were alone except for the help, Maria and Luis, who lived in the little house in the back. They entertained rarely nowadays and no guest came except his editor who stayed only two days. One evening, sitting across from each other, at the long table, she smiled at him and said, "You could dictate to me, if that would make it easier. I really would like to help, if you let me."

"How will you kill me?" he asked.

She tried to make a joke of it.

"With a poisonous mushroom," she said.

"When?"

"Maybe tomorrow."

"Lunch or dinner?" he asked.

"Breakfast."

Then she laughed because this game was silly and walked around the table and put her hand on his shoulder. "What's the matter?"

He turned his head and looked up at her. "Don't you still wish me dead?"

"Listen," she said to him. "I hit the lion. I didn't kill because I'm not perfect, do you understand?"

"You wanted that lion to kill me."

"You could have sent the hunter. You could have sent nobody and let it die!" She hadn't wanted to cry, but she did now because she had broken the code. Wounded animals were not left to die, not even if you had to sacrifice your life to put them out of their misery.

"You didn't have to go into the bush after it," she said through the tears, knowing it wasn't true.

He pushed his chair away and stood up.

For a moment she thought that now that the air had cleared about what happened in Africa, he would put his arms around her again. Instead, he turned and went up the stairs, with each heavy step shattering the silence of the room.

She took a room in an Albuquerque hotel to be near him, but for the first week he didn't want to see her. The doctors thought it would be best if she waited.

"He'll be fine after a few treatments," the doctors said.

"What kind of treatments?"

"He's suffering from acute paranoia, and he's also schizophrenic."

"What kind of treatments?"

"Shock treatments."

She had seen the movie *The Snake Pit* and shuddered with the memories. "What will the treatments do to him?" They explained that they would have an effect on his memory, and at first she thought he would not survive the treatments, that they would affect his ability to write, and she wanted to tell them that he could not be subjected to them. But then she began to think that maybe, with the past gone, they might have a future together.

The first time she saw him at the clinic, he lay with his eyes closed, and she cried in silence at the change in him. He seemed half his size under the blankets, his face ash pale. His beard had been shaved. He looked like an old man, and he was not sixty yet. She held his hand and did not talk, and he said nothing to her.

The following day he was sitting up in his chair by the window and spoke to her.

"This must be the ugliest city in the world," and she laughed and came and sat down at his feet, but he kept looking out of the window, at the treeless street that seemed to stretch over miles of gas station neon signs. "It's all greed out there," he said.

She saw him four more times before he told her that she should go back to Santa Fe, that he would be all right, that he just needed time. He seemed sedated, but the doctors told her that was the effect of the treatments. The last time she saw him, before she returned to Santa Fe, he held her to him and said that he needed to know she was not angry with him.

"Of course not," she said.

"I'm sorry for having been such a bastard," he said.

"I was just as bad," she said. "I want you to get well, and be your old self again. I need you well."

"Will I ever write again?" he asked her. In the hush of the room, it seemed like the most important question in the world.

"Yes, of course," she said, her throat dry. "You will write even better now."

But he had closed his eyes.

"Go back and wait for me in Santa Fe," he said.

She left after talking to the doctors, who told her that they would not release him until he would not try to harm himself again.

"He seems so fine now," she said.

"Not yet," they said. "But it won't be long before we send him home to you."

The next day she found out that Hal had received the Nobel Prize. She had the phone changed to an unlisted number because she didn't want to lie to anyone about where he was and what had happened. And she didn't want anyone to call her Mrs. Hubbard.

When the letter from him came a few days later, asking her to arrange his birthday party, she felt uneasy. She hid the guns in the basement and promised herself that she would watch him. She didn't want him to die, not any more. Not now.

The good Doctor Konski had just had a haircut. His shorn neck reddened when he introduced the young man:

"This is Doctor Turk from Santa Fe."

"How do you do?" said Hal. Dr. Robinson, the future biographer of Hal Hubbard's madness, as usual, was silently sitting in the corner, pad in hand.

"Would you mind if I sat in on your session?" Dr. Turk said with a slight British accent.

"Make yourself at home," Hal said. He had trouble suppressing a smile, after a cliché like that. Was he working, per chance, on the pathology of insanity among contemporary writers?

"Would you like to talk about it today?" asked Dr. Konski. The "it," Hal knew, was the day of his attempted suicide.

"The strange thing about that day," Hal said, having rehearsed what he would say "is that I don't remember a thing about it. Not a blessed thing," he said and smiled, and then turned his head slightly and smiled the exact same smile at Dr. Turk. "What did Sally tell you about it?"

"Your wife thought that the breakdown was precipitated by your depression over your writing, which wasn't going well," Dr. Konski said.

Hal was after something else.

"Yes, that I remember. Being depressed over the writing. But that was the day before. What did I do on the following day?"

"Apparently you went out for a long walk and then came back even more depressed. Your wife was in the kitchen preparing a drink when she heard the gun cabinet open...."

So, she didn't tell! She merely lied.

"Oh, yes," he said now, tapping his forehead for emphasis, as if tapping in an errant memory that had come unhinged. "Your saying that about Sally fixing a drink brings it all back!" He waited and Dr. Konski waited and so did Dr. Turk who might, just possibly, not be a doctor at all.

"What do you remember?" Dr. Konski finally asked, for he had been waiting for this singular revelation of what had brought Hal Hubbard the Nobel and Pulitzer Prize winner to the gun cabinet.

"Actually what I saw was a large rat, and I was going to kill it."

"Did you say anything about the rat to your wife?" Dr. Konski asked.

"Did she mention it to you perhaps?" he said, all eagerness now.

"No, I don't think so."

"I guess I identified with the rat and aimed at the wrong thing."

The three of them waited now. What was there to say? As a climactic session, this was nothing to write home about. Dr. Turk coughed discreetly and then asked the question that he must have prepared for the occasion.

"Dr. Konski filled me in on some particulars, and since my specialty is the study of repeating patterns and justifiable paranoia, I wonder if you had been thinking about your father's suicide before...."

"Haven't thought about it for years, actually," Hal said, affecting ever so slightly a British accent. "But that's a good point. Did you know that not only my father but my grandfather shot themselves with the gun I reached for that day?"

"Yes, I did," said Dr. Turk.

Again there was silence. Uneasy. And now he had to do the commercial because something might go wrong if he didn't.

"I have to confess something," Hal said, reaching for a cigarette and lighting it before continuing. "Until yesterday I didn't know for sure whether or not it would be painful for me to talk about, or rather to try to remember, that day. But this morning, when I woke up and felt so fine, I thought to myself, what the hell? I might as well get it over with. But frankly my state of mind then, and my state of mind now, are so totally different that I couldn't even guess at what would make me wish to shoot myself. All I want is to put all that behind me and get back to some writing."

He had said all this so easily, so perfectly, so . . . confidently, that he gave himself a smile of self-congratulation.

"Your wife told me," Dr. Konski said, tapping his pencil silently against the pad he held in his hand, "that you struggled so much she and your houseboy had trouble holding you down. Do you remember the struggle?"

"Well . . ." he leaned back and blew a ring into the air in front, it was fairly perfect. "I think I remember shouting something about not wanting to hurt anyone but myself. I must have given up on the rat...."

"The rat might have appeared to you symbolic."

"Of what?" Hal asked, sounding interested.

"Possibly of your own state of mind, the inability to escape some difficulty that loomed larger than your ability to cope with it."

"Possibly," Hal said, and put out his cigarette. He reached for the glass of water that was always there for the patient to drink from. "Identifying myself with a rat probably did happen that day, actually. But I couldn't state that as a fact since I don't really remember what went through my sick mind."

Bite your tongue, he said to himself, wishing madly now to give them a commercial, how the good doctors at the clinic took in a demented man and how well he got under their care! Dr. Turk with his repeating patterns and justifiable paranoia specialty might not swallow it all. Dr. Konski might. Hal had tried a few days ago to get in that kind of a commercial, but was interrupted by Dr. Konski who thought that the thanks were premature. "Wait until next week," he had said.

"Do you think," Dr. Konski was now asking, "that you might wish to hurt yourself again?"

"Not now," Hal said. "I've had time to sort things out. My fears of not being able to write as well as I used to will have to be coped with when they recur. I haven't been writing for so long now that I don't know if I can or cannot write as well as I did once. I'm not going to jump the gun...." He laughed pleasantly. "I mean, I won't guess at this. I shall take it easy, and do my best, and try to be pleased at having a chance again at writing."

He coughed now himself, hoping he would not end up puking. It was a miserable speech, unworthy of his talents as a writer, but it sounded sincere. The good doctors bought it. He could see that. They were disappointed that he did not choose to make it more literary, perhaps worthy of quoting at dinner to their wives, but he had expressed what each reformed looney must wish to express: hope and repentance, and not wishing to do "it" again.

The rest of the session was taken up by a sort of a mild inquisition, and he did well—he hoped. He didn't give them anything immortal or memorable, but he did give them the impression that all he wanted was to get the hell out of there.

As he was finally getting up to leave, Dr. Robinson stopped him.

"Writers have special insights," Dr. Robinson said. "As a writer, could you sum up for us?"

"I'll be happy to," Hal said, having anticipated that sort of question from Dr. Robinson. He would talk slowly for his benefit. "Even before you analyzed me as a schizophrenic, I knew myself to be one because I am a writer. Writers do lead two lives. The actual one, which might be termed personal reality, and the life of whatever book we're writing. But the two lives flow in and out of each other as we write, in perfect harmony when we write well, and somewhat at odds with each other when the work is not going well. Same mind, not deranged but creative, moves in and out of two orbits, so to speak." He stopped and looked at Dr. Robinson, who was busy taking every word down. "I hope I'm making this fairly clear. I mean, the creative mind is slightly different from the noncreative mind, wouldn't you agree?" The three doctors nodded their heads, but not very enthusiastically.

"I am at a disadvantage here, of course," he continued with a slight smile, "knowing shit from Freud. But, take it from me, I know the difference between being sane and creative, and insane and noncreative. During the past several years I became, through luck perhaps, surrounded by realists. And some kind of disturbance took place in my life because of the influx of so much reality."

He had to tell it straight, without showing too much effort at concealing what actually seemed funny to him now.

"My creative life fell into the hands of a couple called Horn. They were in the same profession, making their living at writing, but you might say they were at opposite ends of the writing periscope. I took the long view, and they were at the close-up lens."

He was going too far afield with this. He should give them something more simple. He took a drink of water, lit a cigarette, and sat deeper in his chair.

"Anyway, when these people invaded my usual turf, which previously had been inhabited by dreamers, I tried to become a realist like them. I met Sally, who, like them, was a superlative realist. And problems arose. Realists are very nice people, but they don't trade dreams. Actually, trying too hard to look at life as apart from my art, I began to have difficulties with both. My work, and living."

That was reasonable and very close to the truth. It did sound rather dull, explained this way. But what the hell, he was not here to entertain. And he was cleaning his cobwebs. Fair enough.

"It all conspired rather nicely, this last decade of my life. We have

Eisenhower in the White House, and the country became one big pool of stagnant realism." He laughed easily, hoping that they were not Republicans and would not take offense. "But I needed daily dreaming, you see, being a writer. It had been my diet too long, and I have thrived on it. So I didn't do too well on the bread and butter of realism, and I guess you might say that the necessity to live at arm's length from reality finally got me in trouble. I wished to escape back."

"By killing yourself?" Dr. Turk asked.

"Well, you might say that death is the greatest escape."

He waited for Dr. Turk to say something. "I guess you're saying artists must function on different levels. . . ." Dr. Turk seemed to have trouble accepting this.

"Yes, we are strange ducks," Hal said, smiling easily.

"How will you cope with what you understand about yourself now?" Dr. Turk asked.

"Well. . . ." He put the cigarette down and rubbed his hands together in what he felt would seem an optimistic gesture of a reconstructed realist-dreamer. "I will try to make Sally understand that dreaming is part of my trade. I suppose I'll let her attend to that part of our life that has to do with hard reality and I'll excuse myself from too close a proximity, remaining an artist at all times. I think that's the best way to go. Don't you?" He stood up, this being as far as he intended to go. Leaving everything on such a practical level was a stroke.

"I have the clearest picture yet of what might have gone wrong," Dr. Konski said to Dr. Turk.

"I believe this was a very productive session," Hal said and reached his hand to Dr. Turk. "I'm sorry it was so dull for you." And then he winked toward Dr. Robinson and left.

Walking back to his room he kept the middle fingers of both hands raised inside his pockets. That session, for a change, had been close to being a pleasure.

Hal Hubbard

THE ledger was complete now except for one more entry. Himself.

There existed a possibility that he had not been shooting at the real enemy. If what he had been doing for the past month was dancing around the inevitable, like in a bullfight, the slowing down of the enemy with the *picadors,* using *bandarillas,* working the cape, it was now time for the last phase, the *faena* to begin.

Perhaps, like Hemingway, he had confused the last stage with physical courage. It was a bitch of an occupation. The bullfighter, each time he went to work, had to end something. The end was the whole point of starting.

The dedication, as the bullfighter takes the muleta in hand, begins the end. It doesn't happen suddenly, the ending. There is more fancy preliminary work with the muleta, which is harder to manage than the cape, being less than half the size. It is with that smaller target for the bull that the bullfighter is judged. The tricks become fewer now, and if they exist, they become more visible. The work has to be closer, and it becomes more dangerous. Then the bullfighter exchanges the light wooden sword for the real thing.

The beauty of the kill, which cannot be avoided, lies in the fact that it has to be done without fancy tricks at all. And perhaps that is why they call it the moment of truth.

The sword's target, the opening between the bull's shoulders, is very small. It cannot be aimed at unless the bullfighter positions himself directly in front of the bull, and it cannot be reached unless the bull's head is down. That toss of the head, Hal knew, at the moment of going in for the kill, was what scared bullfighters shitless. Because the toss, then, results in a chest wound that usually leaves the bullfighter dead.

It is at the kill that the truly brave get separated from the ones who fake it. There are two ways of faking it; turning the moment of truth into a half-truth. Or a lie.

A bullfighter who turns it into a lie goes in avoiding the horns, plunging the sword partway into the bull's lungs so that it bleeds to death slowly to the accompaniment of the *aficionados*' derisive whistling. The tourists applaud the other kind, whose *picadors* provide an animal half-dead, with no strength to toss upward its horned head.

He had decided to dedicate his moment of truth to Lee, and having so decided he could not cheat. He would have to be prepared for all the risks in an honest job of ending.

He had been a better writer than a man. While writing, he understood more. Self-destruction did not come easy to him. He fought against his father's last message—that life was not worth living—by fishing the marlin out of the high seas, by challenging wild animals to combat, by good drink and good food, by the exhilaration of finding the perfect words for a story, and by his love for a good woman. Lee had been perfect for him. Yet he had let Carole lead him away from Lee as if he were a foolish schoolboy without a will of his own.

He had tried—till the vessels in his head nearly burst with the effort—to keep his writing free of the cant he saw everywhere, but after Lee the writing began to atrophy.

He'd loved life, but less and less, until he didn't love it at all. He had to go back to the day he saw his redemption and couldn't reach it.

He had not written a single word down for over a week. Before then he had sweated over one paragraph for a month. He was writing about love. He didn't believe what he wanted to say. What he believed was that it was possible to make sacrifices for one you loved. He wrote about that, but it wasn't enough. He had to confront the reality of his hero's love, but on paper it seemed a fraud.

When he was trapped, like a rat in a maze, he no longer knew how to solve this writing problem because now it had to do with his life problem. He decided to talk to Sally about it. He came down, early in the morning, and he told her what he knew so far.

"I know you love me. I don't know how to love you back."

"I know that too."

"I think I've lost my ability to feel love. I must know this for sure."

"Love is not all that it's cracked up to be," Sally said. "I've read somewhere that its chief characteristic is that it is perishable."

"So is life," he said.

They talked a long time, truthfully for once, but he could not let go of the idea that he was talking oranges and she apples, or the other way around. He could not convince her that he had a problem that he had to solve and therefore realized that, in the end, she would be of no help to him. That's when he asked her if she would leave him. They compromised. She said she would go to Haiti, and he could stay in Santa Fe. "If you're alone for a while," she said, "maybe you'll find yourself." They made love, or rather had sex, something they had not done in quite a while. Immediately afterward, she began to make lists of all the things she would have to do.

Early the next morning, while she packed, he went outside. He felt suddenly very fine, as if washed and renewed, and began walking down the empty road. The sky to the east was red and there was the great stillness which he used to love when walking had been a habit. After he reached the Plaza he took a turn and walked behind two small children holding hands. He helped them cross the street and, as he did so, realized he could love those two small kids, strangers to him. He recognized the feeling.

He followed the children inside their day care center and a young woman greeted them with good-morning hugs. She had long hair that fell around the children's shoulders as she bent over them, and the feeling he recognized now encompassed her. And then she saw him and smiled and asked if she could help him, and he said yes and asked her if he could stay. She told him her name was Judy and was welcome to stay as long as he wished. He sat down among the children, who were in a circle on the floor, and listened to them make up stories. When they had all taken turns he had to take his.

"There was once a kingdom," he began, and the feeling of loving them all was there, was part of him, the room, the teacher, the children, "and in this kingdom there was an enchanted princess. She was enchanted because, in her presence, adults turned into children. The magic inside of her made everyone happy and very wise. One day, into the princess's enchanted kingdom, where everyone was a child, came an old man. But at the sight of the princess, he did not turn into a child."

"Why not?"

"What was wrong with him?"

"The old man had to stay an old man to protect the children and the princess because there were dragons around now and the old man was the only one who knew how to fight dragons."

"The princess didn't know?"

"No."

"The children didn't know?"

"No."

"Just the old man?"

"Yes."

"More."

"The old man had gained a lot of experience over many years of fighting dragons, and that's why he came to the kingdom of the enchanted princess. So that everyone inside that kingdom would be safe."

"The end?"

"The end."

They laughed and clapped their hands and told him it was the best story they had ever heard, and someone asked if he would stay with them and be their old man fighting dragons for them. He thought about it. They pleaded with him. Finally, he said he would.

They took a trip to the city dump, and everything he saw and everything he heard that morning had meaning, made sense, and he was very happy knowing that there was something inside of him that was unwasted still. They shared their lunches with him, and Judy, their teacher, was not unlike Peggy, for she too had a gift of laughter. He asked her if he could come back again, and she said anytime, the kids would love it. Most of them had no fathers, she explained, a few had it very rough at home.

He complimented her on her way with kids.

"No," she said, "I am just a good hugger. I found a way of making a living doing what I know best."

By the time he left, he was sure it was not too late for him. He had tried going back, to the time of Lee. Over the years he would dial her number and hang up before she answered because he never knew what they would say to each other. It always seemed too late for him and her. He needed to go back further, to what he missed before Lee.

He hurried home now, running some of the way, and before taking off his jacket, before Sally could ask him where he had been, he sat her down and told her everything. He would convert part of the house to be used by the school. He would find a merry-go-round for the back yard, with carved horses and maybe an old organ. He would send for the catalogue from Schwarz and order toys. He would join them at story time and would tell his share of them. It wouldn't matter if he wrote or didn't write, but he was sure it would be no trouble, writing, now that he knew that he was starting with the hugs.

It all spilled out in almost one breath of hope. He himself would now be needed in equal measure as he was needing. Sally did not interrupt and when he was finished, tired from the excitement of telling her so much of what the future had in store for him, he asked what she thought.

"It all sounds wonderful, dear," she said. "But you're not in any condition for it now. I will stay and take care of you."

She went to prepare the afternoon drinks and before she came back with them he was standing by the gun cabinet. His condition was terminal. Sally, who loved him, but whom he could not love, knew the truth. And now he knew it, too.

He had ignored the others who were there, at the clinic with him, until the last day. He looked at them now. The other casualties. They were not unlike him. Only details of their lives were different, but they were scared and wounded and what had gone wrong with them was what had gone wrong with him: they had believed some original lie, tried to make it a half-truth, and it was too late to go all the way back to it. They all had tried, in their different ways, eventually to make the lie the truth, and that job brought them all here.

Help would not come from the doctors, he knew now. Maybe, as he had once suspected, they were all unhugged ones. He had asked Judy, during that day, why everyone at her school was hugging each other, and she told him hugging was the start of loving, she was teaching them that, to be good huggers because they were so young and would not be ashamed to learn that there was more to come. He wished he could now, before leaving, say something to the others about hugging. He even thought that he might ask a nurse to introduce him, as the writer who wanted to say a few words. He had given a few commencement speeches in his time, but he had not given a speech about hugging. But for that, too, it was too late now. Who among them would not be ashamed of such a simple remedy? We have gone so far afield, he thought, unto sophistication.

He looked at each of them, the two dozen or so mostly middle-aged and old people, well-to-do, for the poor were not in private clinics, and he knew that he could never write about them. He always wrote about the strong, not the weak.

He had often thought in the past that Sally was wasting her talents on him. She, too, had bought a lie, but he did not know what it was. She bought a kind of lie that wouldn't have hurt much had she become a camp director, for she had a genius for organizing people, planning for them, arranging everything in the most efficient way. She had always tried to erase herself in his favor.

She had chartered a plane, which was now carrying them to Santa Fe. Later it would bring the guests from the Albuquerque airport. She had come at eight in the morning, looking timid and not quite as tall as he remembered. She made a great show of gladness over the way he looked, and he gave her a bearhug when she presented him with his birthday gift, a gold watch on which she had inscribed: "Peace and happiness I wish you, Sally." He accepted the watch because he thought someone somewhere should have given him one.

She clung to him but did not know how to hug him, maybe not having learned as a child, and it was still there, in her eyes, in the sharpness of her gestures, in her voice, that fear of him that had been there since she realized that he could indeed be dangerous to himself. "You've turned against yourself," the good doctor had explained when he asked what his opinion was about the incident of his attempted suicide. She watched now for signs that this turning had been cured.

Besides the pilot, there were two men on the plane. She didn't explain who they were, and he would not worry about them. She talked too much and too excitedly, trying to hide her uncertainty of him. She had hired some horses, hoping that somebody would want to go out for a ride. Around five a mariachi band would come to play. And they would have fireworks, she got hold of some wonderful fireworks for the evening. Did he remember the lousy fireworks they had in Haiti and how much the Haitian kids loved them, well, she had ordered another case of the better ones to take to Haiti in the winter. They would go to Haiti for the winter, wouldn't they?

He smiled at her and she went on with the laundry list of all she had done and was planning to do. She had invited only the people he wanted, but she'd asked some friends for drinks after dinner, if he didn't want them to come she could call them all and cancel.

"That's fine," he said and smiled at her and held on to her hand to make her feel more secure. Could he guess who had been most excited about coming?

"Benjamin."

Yes, Benjamin, and they laughed together over that. They were bringing their child; they had named the boy Hal.

"I wonder after whom?" he asked and again they laughed easily together. What would he think of asking Yolanda to come and visit them in Haiti this winter? Wonderful, he said. She wanted to ask him something but didn't know how to ask, she confessed.

"Go ahead and ask," he said.

"Why didn't you invite Lee?"

"I don't know," he said. "I should have," he added, afraid that she might have done it.

"Maybe next birthday," she said.

"Yes," he said.

She chatted on, continuously, even in the car she kept it up, and he continued to smile and continued to hold on to her hand. It was too late now for her to go after the truth. Neither of them was guilty, just irresponsible. And he nodded his head and listened hard and finally earned a look without fear from her.

"I can't believe how well you are."

"I feel fine, just fine and mellow," he said. And then, like a good schoolboy, he said, "I'm truly sorry about all the trouble I've caused you."

"Oh, that's all behind us now," she said and squeezed his hand.

Maria and Luis were at the gate of the house, their smiles infected by their fears. Or maybe by the fact that their Spanish minds were unable to grasp all the things they'd seen in this house, unable to understand the reason for him, the famous, rich Anglo writer, having gone bad in the head. Their own minds, when they tended to crack, went quietly or very loudly; his cracked somewhere in the middle of that range. The Spanish were more graceful, perhaps, in escaping the truth or accepting lies.

Everything looked just the same except that the gun cabinet was gone. Where did she hide the guns, he wondered, and then he saw the lock on the basement door, a lock that had not been there before, and he knew the guns were down there. There was a window on the north side of the house, and he could climb through it and get the gun. He had thought often of how he would do it. Hiding it inside the pants legs, he would take the shoe off as the cake was brought in. He would blow the candles out at the same time he'd blow out his brains. His wish would be to fall back; not into the cake.

She handed him a glass of champagne, and her toast was for many years of happiness and good writing, and he took her face in his hands and placed it against his shoulder. And he was grateful she was not talking for a moment and that he heard her heart beating loudly. She held on to him, and he gave her points for that, for holding on when he no longer needed to. Then they clicked the glasses, and she said, "To you." And he said, "To us," and gave himself points.

They went to the kitchen, and he sat in the sun by the window, while she scrambled eggs for them and fried some ham and made espresso, keeping up a steady stream of talk, and he did his best to answer, to chat back, while he marveled at himself at the same time.

He didn't want to see any of them!

He didn't need to see any of them!

He would not see any of them!

Three stated facts that came easily, suddenly brightening up the day.

After they ate their breakfast, she asked him what he was going to wear and whether he would shave. He tried too hard to find answers for her. It was only a little after nine-thirty, and he knew how hard it would be for her to keep an eye on him for the next few hours, before they would all arrive. He wanted to make it easy for her and said that he'd like to take a walk behind the house, into the Sangre de Cristo foothills.

"Can I come?" she asked.

"Sure," he said, "unless you have things to do."

"I have a lot to do."

"Then I'd better take a short walk alone," he said.

"Are you sure?"

Again the look of fear came back, he had thought it was gone for good. Sure of what?

"I won't be long, I'll walk a while. I need to stretch my legs. I feel stiff. The exercise will do me good. I'll sit down in the sun when I get tired. I missed the views. It will do me good, and I'll be out of yours and Maria's way."

Was he talking too much? He said it all to her, in a casual, calm voice, and the offer was too tempting, his being out of the house, away from the basement and the guns, and she looked grateful and not at all worried or concerned. But she wanted to be sure that he was walking where he said he would walk, not toward town, that teacher and those kids. She was watching him from the kitchen window, and he waved at her, and she smiled and waved back, as if she were not spying, just seeing her man off for a short walk.

When he looked back again, halfway up the hill, he saw that she had stationed Luis in the yard. He pretended to be repairing a pigeon cage, but he knew Luis was there to keep an eye on him. He sat down and looked toward the town, partially hidden in the hollow of the hills, and said good-bye to the kids and to the young woman who took care of them during the day. Then he turned his face toward the Jemez in the west and thought back to the time when they had first come here, he and Sally, and bathed in the hot springs and made love by moonlight in the steaming waters sacred to the Indians. And then he looked toward the Cerillos and the Ortiz mountains, which he liked better than the Sangre de Cristos.

He got up and began to walk toward the crest of the hill and remembered what Sally had said when she found the house: "It's not in the shadow of Monte Sol, and it's a good thing because they say there is an Indian curse attached to it. Whoever lives in its shadow goes mad." And he walked into the shadow of Monte Sol. From there, from its shadow, he looked down on the house. He could see Luis still in the yard and he waved to him. He could see the winding driveway and, right below, the stretch of Old Santa Fe Trail, houseless, to the left. He started to count the arroyos he could see from where he was now.

And then, suddenly, something shifted inside his brain. It was as if a whole mass of gray cells had separated itself and made a turn, and with that shifting, something opened up to allow a very precise command: *run!* He didn't bother going to the crest of the hill, but began running down the side. And he kept running directly ahead, not seen anymore from the house, and the land here seemed as uncharted as his brain. He was on some new territory, and he felt the excitement and newness within and without.

Running, he saw something else run. A rabbit, one of those long-eared, ugly creatures that abound in those parts. It seemed to be suffering some strange curvature of the spine, and it limped badly. It must have been caught, but had managed to escape a dog; the rabbit's right rear leg was just barely hanging on, the skin torn off to the bone, the leg bent and stiff, hitting the ground as he hopped on his three remaining legs. Going somewhere to die. And that's when it came to him, the final solution, as overwhelmingly true and right as the decision that he did not need for them to see him die.

He began to run faster now, down and then up a ridge, and then he turned to his left, toward the endless chains of mountains ahead. He had a head start. She would not start worrying for an hour at least. He looked at his birthday watch; 9:50. He had over two hours before they'd all arrive, and she wouldn't do anything until they all came.

Then they would talk and someone would say that they ought to call the police, Benjamin, perhaps. But they would wait an hour more, perhaps two, because of all the embarrassment that calling the police would cause. Sally would get on the phone and call Dr. Konski before doing anything else.

He was out of breath, his chest heaving, a sharp pain of exhaustion spreading to his legs, and he stopped to rest. He would have to remember to breathe more regularly. What could he cover in four, five hours? Ten, fifteen miles? Or more?

The ponderosas and the aspens were about that far away. They grew thick and would afford him cover from the helicopters. They would send the helicopters after him, and maybe dogs as well. After all he had freed himself so they'd try to catch him. He laughed suddenly because now he felt he was one with all the wounded animals in the world. He would not be like the lion, he would not seek cover somewhere in the brush and wait, ready to make his last attack on those pursuing him. He would keep going, like the wounded deer, until he dropped. The truth was he had been trying to lead his life as if he were a lion, though he had always had more in common with a frightened deer. But the crucial difference was that he was, after all, a man.

The piñons smelled good. In the fall they would be picked clean of their nuts, whole families spreading like human locusts into the hills until all the cones were empty, every sweet nut shaken out. But very few would go this far, they kept near the roads. There were no roads here, not even trails; maybe some hikers from St. John's college went this far, but maybe nobody had been here in a long time, not since the Indians roamed free in those hills or maybe not since the Spaniards who looked for gold.

He was running better now, keeping an even pace and breathing more regularly. You get used to everything; the body takes over without the help of the brain after a while. A long-distance runner doesn't think. He just runs. He was never much for track, except maybe he was. Someone had once written that he was "a long-distance runner of a writer." Who wrote that? It didn't matter, but he would like to have remembered the name.

It felt good running. One with the animals. It didn't matter any more who had wounded whom, he must have done as much wounding as anyone. But dying was a private business. Always was. Always will be. The end of the line, where everyone gets off except the conductor.

He stopped when he saw his first deer. He was upwind of it, and the doe turned her head and for a moment they both looked at each other. If he had a gun, would he shoot? He had shot a fair share, but he wouldn't shoot this one. Maybe that's why people hunted, each other, as well as the animals. Alike, but not the same. They had much in common. A need to kill was there in both. And fear, that was common to both. But the motives were different.

There was an absence of fear in him now. When he laughed he scared the deer. He took off in the same direction. Somewhere behind them the rabbit was dying, still running on its three good legs, dragging the useless one behind. Or maybe he had bitten it off by now.

He became aware of the great silence. There was not a sound except for his feet pounding the ground and his heart pounding inside his chest. He stopped and listened and heard a stream somewhere ahead. It would taste good to drink. When he reached it, he knelt down and took the cold water in his hands and brought it to his lips and drank, not deeply, just enough to find pleasure, and then he let the water go between his fingers, liking the way it sparkled before hitting the ground. Then he reached for some more and splashed his face. Life was good. He had no quarrels with it now. No quarrels but a few regrets. The main one was Lee. At ten he should have been old enough to have known how his father had felt and helped him change his mind. But on the whole, perhaps he did no more nor less than anyone given the advantage of freedom to screw up. It was time to go. There were miles yet to run. And when death came it would be a private business, between him and God.

When he felt the first tightening, a vise-like grip, surprising in its pain, he was wondering why he had not thought about God for so long, not since that day on the boat with Carl. The pain took the memory away. He kept on for a while, moving slowly now, holding on to that center of pain that was his heart, pressing his hand against it as it struggled on. He was now among the ponderosas and the aspens and the air was cold and thin, and the last thing he was aware of was making a bet with God that he would not make it to the top of the next rise. He almost lost.